Also by A.L. Hatcher

The Blood Eagle: A Tess Dane Thriller (book 1)

River of Lies

A Tess Dane Thriller

A. L. Hatcher

A L Hatcher Author

ISBN: 979-8-9889438-2-2

ePUB ISBN: 979-8-9889438-3-9

Library of Congress Control Number: 2024906682

Book Cover by C. Rothe

Edited by She Wrights Words, LLC

Dedication:

To Mom and Dad, for always being there for me
and going along with all of my crazy dreams. I couldn't
have done this without you.

Prologue

Thursday, July 7th, 8:42 a.m.

"9-1-1, what is your emergency?" the female dispatcher inquired as she answered the call. She was met with silence. After a second, she repeated herself, "9-1-1, what is your emergency?" Another short pause and then the operator heard something. Someone was breathing, their breath coming out in short, stunted wheezes.

"Hello? 9-1-1, do you need assistance?" the dispatcher asked a third time, although she was already sending police to the caller's location—a house in a quiet Ohio suburb just outside of Crawley. They rarely got calls out to that neighborhood.

The heavy breathing continued on the other end of the line. The dispatcher couldn't tell if the caller was male or female, but based on their breathing, she could tell they were distressed.

Suddenly, she heard a slight moan. Someone crying? The caller remained quiet, saying nothing. The dispatcher looked at the timestamp on the call. They were forty-three seconds in at this point.

"Hello? What is going on?" the dispatcher asked urgently. "Are you okay?"

"Hello?" came a male voice, strained and broken. A sob came through the dispatcher's headphones.

"Yes, sir. I'm here. What is your emergency? Are you in need of police assistance or an ambulance?"

"I don't know." A pause followed by a sob. "I don't know. But I—I can't find my wife."

"When was the last time you saw her, sir?" the dispatcher asked as she quietly typed out the information to law enforcement that were responding.

"She was here last night, next to me in bed. But when I just got home ... she's gone."

"What makes you think she's missing, sir?"

"I just got back from the gym and found the door from the garage to the house open. When I came inside, it looked like ...."

"Yes?"

"Like there was a struggle. There is blood on the kitchen floor." The man began sobbing.

"Okay, sir. Help is on the way. Please go outside and wait in the front yard until the police get there."

"Just hurry. My wife is missing!" and then the line went dead.

Chapter One

(THREE DAYS EARLIER)
Monday, July 4th, 7:31 p.m.

"Good grief, what a way to end Independence Day," Deputy Miles said as he and his partner, Deputy Scafferty, slid back into their cruiser and called in to dispatch.

"Yeah, this is unit three-two-four. Be advised that the complainant was drunk, and the situation has been de-escalated. Both parties have left the premises."

"10-4," the Swain County Sheriff's Department dispatcher said. Miles and Scafferty took their time writing up the report for their latest call: two individuals at a Fourth of July cookout who'd gotten into a fight over one being knocked into the swimming pool. Even after answering the call, Miles was still unsure who had done the initial shoving as both individuals were dripping wet and spitting mad when he and Scafferty had gotten on scene. Other party goers, in various states of intoxication, all seemed to have a different story as to who shoved who first—and the whole thing was an epic pain in the ass. Miles just wanted to be done with it all and get home to his own family.

"Let's call it a night. We were off thirty minutes ago," Scafferty said, taking a sip of his lukewarm soda. The cruiser's warm interior had reduced the icy drink to nothing more than tepid watered-down soda, but it was wet, and he was thirsty.

"For real," Miles agreed, pulling the cruiser out onto the highway and heading back toward the station. They'd only gone about a mile when their radio blared to life.

As reports of a possible domestic assault came flooding over the speaker, Miles and Scafferty gave a collective sigh. They were only two blocks away from the address. Mumbling under his breath, Miles radioed in, letting dispatch know they were en route.

Moments later, as they pulled down Clover Hill Lane, they could see a man standing at the end of his driveway flagging them down. Miles pulled to a stop, and the man approached the vehicle.

"Are you the one that called in a domestic situation?" Miles asked as he stepped out of the vehicle.

"Yes, sir. My name is Newton. Harold Newton," the older man nodded, stepping backwards to give Miles more space. He shoved his glasses up his nose and patted down his balding head as he watched both officers approach him.

"What seems to be the problem?"

"It's the new neighbors," Newton said, pointing over his shoulder to the house next door. "They were just yelling and carrying on. I was out on my deck cleaning up after a barbecue, and I heard them screaming at each other. Then it sounded like something was breaking, like glass."

"Okay, Mr. Newton," Miles acknowledged as Scafferty came and stood next to him. "Have you heard things like this before?"

"Sometimes, but never this bad."

"How well do you know the neighbors? What are their names?" Scafferty asked. Newton looked at Scafferty and shrugged.

"I don't know them that well. They've only lived there for a couple of months. His name is Neil something. Slater ... Slaydon, maybe? I can't remember the wife's name. All I know is that she's pregnant."

Miles and Scafferty exchanged a look and then gazed back at the property behind Newton. The house in question looked well-maintained. A two storied Colonial in a cookie-cutter neighborhood, where all the houses looked similar, just sided in a different color. This one, in particular, was white, with black shutters and a dark red door. Peonies, in various shades of pink, grew along the driveway, and potted ferns hung from the front porch. At the moment, the house and its occupants seemed quiet.

"How long ago did you hear the screaming and yelling?" Miles asked, adjusting his duty belt around his waist.

"Just as I called you guys. Maybe ... five minutes?" Newton shrugged, looking back and forth between the two deputies.

"Okay, sir. We will take it from here then," Miles said as he and Scafferty slowly made their way up the driveway.

Out of the corner of his eyes, Scafferty could see Newton standing at the edge of his yard watching them. Miles knocked on the door and waited for the homeowners to answer. After what seemed like a lengthy wait, the front door finally opened.

"Officers. How can I help you?" greeted the man who'd opened the door. He was in his late twenties, early thirties with dark brown hair and bright blue eyes. Miles supposed most women would find him attractive, as he kind of resembled the "McDreamy" character on the Grey's Anatomy TV series. (At least that's who Miles's mother was always going on about, "McDreamy this, McDreamy that".)

"Hello, we are with the Swain County Sheriff's Office. Are you the homeowner?" Miles asked, noticing the man's slightly nervous demeanor. A light sheen of sweat had broken out on the man's forehead, and even in the July heat, it seemed off.

"Yes, Neil Slaydon," the man answered with a smile that didn't quite meet his eyes. A look of slight confusion crossed his face. "What seems to be the problem?"

"We've received a call about a possible domestic disturbance. Someone heard some shouting and fighting coming from this residence. We've just come to do a welfare check. Make sure everyone is okay and there isn't a problem," Miles explained.

"Oh, sure, sure," Neil shrugged, suddenly acting a little fidgety. As though he'd rather be anywhere but there. "Everything is fine. Just had the TV up too loud, I guess. My bad."

Miles wasn't buying it. He kept his gaze on Neil for a few seconds and then asked, "May we come in, take a look around? Who else is here with you?"

"Just my wife. She's laying down at the moment."

"And her name is ...?"

"Jessica," Neil supplied quickly but said nothing more. The three men stood there for a second, quietly sizing each other up.

"May we speak with Jessica?" Miles asked as Scafferty tried to sneak a peek past Neil. Noticing the gesture, Slaydon pulled the door tighter against him in an effort to keep out prying eyes.

"Well, as I said, she's laying down at the moment. Pregnant," Neil stated, as though that cleared up any and all confusion.

"I can understand she's pregnant, sir, but we've received a call that there was screaming and glass breaking heard from this residence," Miles insisted, even as Neil was looking over at Harold Newton's front yard and scowling.

"I just told you. I was watching TV, and the sound must have been too loud. I'll turn it down," Neil said, unconsciously shifting from one foot to the other. He muttered something that sounded like "geesh", but Miles couldn't say for sure.

"If your wife is laying down resting then why is your television so loud?" Scafferty pointed out. Neil shot him a slight glare.

"Look, nothing was happening. My wife is sleeping. The neighbor is nosy. And this," Neil gestured between the three of them, "is stupid, an epic waste of time."

"Let us speak with your wife, or we will have to get a warrant," Scafferty said, getting fed up with the man's attitude.

"A warrant?" Neil said incredulously. "Based on what? That I like to watch Marvel movies on surround sound?"

"No, sir," Miles said. "Based on the fact that your wife is now standing behind you and has a swollen, bloodied lip."

Moments later, the two deputies sat on a couch opposite Mr. and Mrs. Neil Slaydon. The couple looked distraught and disheveled, nervously glancing at each other when they thought the deputies weren't looking.

The living room was sparsely furnished, and Miles wondered if they were minimalists or rather, they just hadn't unpacked everything yet. The deputies sat on a gray couch in front of the picture window, and the couple sat on a matching love seat. Between the two couches sat a small coffee table strewn with a couple of used paper plates and a pizza box, the contents of which looked dried out and congealed. As for decorations, there were none. No pictures, no trinkets, no knickknacks. Even the rug on the hardwood floor was boring.

"So, Mrs. Slaydon, can you tell us how you came to get that swollen lip?" Miles said, nodding toward her. He watched as the woman sat at the edge of her seat, as though she meant to bolt at any second. Neil reached over and gave her a reassuring pat on the back, but Miles noticed that his hand remained there, out of view.

Jessica Slaydon laughed nervously as her hands gently rubbed at her rounded abdomen. With a quick glance at her husband, she turned to Miles.

"I'm an idiot, that's all," Jessica mumbled, looking down at the floor. The fact that she refused to make eye contact with either Scafferty or himself was not lost on Miles. "I can't see my own feet these days. I was emptying the dishwasher and tripped—hit my face on an open cabinet door."

Miles nodded and grunted as though he believed her story. He didn't.

"How far along are you?" he asked, gesturing toward her pregnant belly. Jessica looked down at her protruding stomach, her long blond hair falling in waves down around her shoulders, obscuring her pretty face.

"Almost thirty-four weeks."

"First kid?"

"Yes," Jessica nodded as her husband shook his head no. Miles's brow knit together in confusion.

"First time to make it this far along," Neil explained, seeming to notice the discrepancy in their answers.

Scafferty nodded in understanding. He knew the feeling all too well as he and his wife had struggled at first to have a family of their own. Now they had two teenage sons.

"Can you tell us why there was yelling and screaming here this evening?" Miles asked, looking back at Jessica directly.

"I already—" Neil began but silenced when Miles raised his hand.

"Let your wife answer."

"We were watching a movie," Jessica said, looking pointedly at Miles. "I guess it was too loud."

Miles noticed that Neil's hand hadn't moved from his wife's back the entire time they'd been talking. Was he threatening her somehow to silence her? Or was he truly consoling her? Miles couldn't be sure, but something seemed off about the whole situation.

"Could I use the restroom?" Scafferty asked, glancing down the hallway. Looking slightly annoyed, Neil stood and asked him to follow him down the hallway.

Once alone, Miles looked back at Jessica Slaydon. She seemed more nervous now that her husband had left the room.

"Is there anything you'd like to tell me, Jessica?" he asked her quietly. She glanced at him quickly and then back to the floor.

"No, sir."

"Did you really hit your face on a cabinet door?"

"That's what I said."

"It is what you said, but is that really what happened? Or is that what you were told to say?"

Her quick intake of breath was all Miles needed to know to confirm his suspicions.

"Ma'am, I know you didn't fall into the cabinet door. If you just tell me what—"

He was interrupted by Neil coming back into the room, eyeing the two of them suspiciously.

"Did I miss anything important?" he asked his wife pointedly. She shook her head, eyes on the floor.

"This is a nice place you have here," Miles commented, changing the subject. "Have you lived here long?"

"A couple of months," Neil offered, choosing to remain standing next to the couch.

"You guys from around here?"

"Columbus," came Neil's curt answer. He remained looking annoyed at the whole situation, like he couldn't wait for the police to leave.

"That's not so far away. Family still there?" Miles asked, although he knew it would be easy to find out on his own. "It'd be nice to have a support system in place for when the baby gets here."

Neil gave a noncommittal grunt while his wife just sat there staring at the floor. An awkward silence filled the room for a moment.

"Mind if I ask how you got that scar?" Miles asked gently, nodding toward a deep jagged scar roughly an inch long that cut through Jessica's left eyebrow. Upon questioning, she absently reached up and touched the pink line.

"I was in a car accident when I was younger," she said simply, sadness darkening her blue gray eyes. Miles nodded, his mouth pursed in a tight line. Due to the color of the scar, he felt that Jessica was telling the truth, at least in the fact that it happened when she was younger. The scar appeared completely healed and the color had faded with time.

He decided to abandon that line of inquiry and bring it back to more current events, but then Scafferty came back from the bathroom and looked around at the three people in the living room.

"What did I miss?" he asked conversationally.

"Deputy Miles was just wrapping up his questions," Neil Slaydon stated, bringing the questioning to an abrupt halt. Miles took the hint and stood, straightening his duty belt about his waist.

"Well, I guess we should be leaving then. Just wanted to make sure everything looked to be on the up and up," he said as he slowly made his way toward the front door.

"Everything is fine here, officers. No need to worry," Neil confirmed, wrapping his arm around Jessica's shoulders.

But worry they did, all the way down the Slaydon's driveway and back to the Swain County Sheriff's Department. Both deputies had an uneasy feeling about what was going on in the Slaydon household. Something just wasn't right.

Chapter Two

Tuesday, July 5th, 7:55 a.m.

"I'm telling you, Dane, it wasn't normal. Something was weird about the whole thing," Miles exclaimed the next morning before the daily briefing began.

"You think he's beating her?" Detective Tess Dane asked, leaning forward in her seat to see Miles better. Scafferty, sitting in between them, just sat quietly drinking his coffee, listening to the exchange.

"Kinda what I was thinking," Miles admitted, "They both seemed so nervous, and he didn't seem to want her to talk to us when he wasn't around—like she was going to share their secrets or something."

"Definitely something to keep an eye on," Tess agreed. "Hopefully they aren't the new Powalskis."

Miles grimaced. Everyone in Swain County seemed to know that name. Tara and Jimmy Powalski had been a constant drain of energy and resources. From the minute they moved to the county from southern Ohio, they were constantly on police radar: domestic disturbances, noise complaints, disturbing the peace, etc. It was only after Jimmy was arrested on a drug charge and Tara moved back south with the couple's four children in tow that the sheriff's department finally got to rid themselves of all the Powalski drama.

"The Slaydons seem a little classier, but yeah, I get what you're saying," Miles nodded before taking a swig of his morning brew.

Just then, Sheriff Malone, the interim sheriff, walked into the conference room to begin the morning meeting. Since being nominated for the vacated sheriff's position by the county commissioner a few months ago, Malone had been serving as sheriff over Swain County. The officers under his command had all worked with him previously, and he had earned their respect. Malone would remain in the sheriff's position until the next election, as per law, and if he wanted to continue working in such a capacity, he could campaign to be voted in. Tess liked working with Malone as sheriff and secretly hoped he ran for office when the time came.

"Good morning, officers," Malone greeted the room. The voices hushed, all ears on the tall, lanky sheriff standing at the front of the room. "Yesterday was a doozy with the Fourth of July. Let's hope today is calmer," he paused to knock on the wooden table in front of him. "As you know, we are getting closer to apprehending the

Bates brothers over on Quaker Hollow Road. Just waiting on the official lab tests to come through and then we can get them on the drug charges. Miles, Scafferty, if you guys can follow up on that today in between calls that would be great. Once we have the lab results, we'll get the arrest warrant and get them picked up." He turned to Tess. "How are things going with the break-in down at Piedmont's?" he asked, indicating the small discount store on Rte. 68 just outside of Crawley.

"Well, sir," Tess stated, "We were able to collect some fingerprints on the cash register and will be going through surveillance video and interviewing staff members today." Tess then turned to address the other officers. "For all of you who haven't heard yet, Piedmont's Pay Less was broken into last night around 11 p.m. I'm guessing that the perp chose that time because most of Crawley and Camden Town were down on the Square watching the fireworks. The front door was shattered...from the inside. This causes me to think it is an inside job, most likely a disgruntled employee. The manager, Jim Hobart, was kind enough to give us the security footage."

"Hopefully we can make an arrest later today on that, Detective Dane. If you need anything today, please let me know and I can assign someone to help out," Malone offered.

"Thank you, sir."

The meeting wrapped up a few minutes later, each deputy and detective tasked with something to work on in between their normal call outs. Tess said goodbye to her coworkers and made her way to her office where she would hopefully find an email from Jim Hobart with the store's security camera footage.

She liked being a detective. In the immediate months following the death of Sheriff Burrows and the closing of the Torture Killer Case, Tess had found herself on paid administrative leave which meant meeting after meeting with BCI, the Bureau of Criminal Investigation, as they worked through the evidence and statements. Tess had been remanded to attend therapy sessions once a week as she worked through the emotional and psychological repercussions of killing another human being. Once she'd been cleared of any wrongdoing, she'd been given her badge and gun back and was once again on patrol. But because of her keen eye for detail and her ability to think outside the box, she'd been encouraged to study for and take the detective's exam. She'd passed with flying colors and when Detective Malone had been recommissioned as the new sheriff, Tess was given his old office. She'd only been a detective for two months, but she was already settling into the job.

As she sat at her desk, she turned on her computer for the morning. While she waited for it to boot up, she checked her phone for any personal emails or texts.

Noticing one from Denny, her old patrol partner—turned boyfriend, she grinned.

"Hey Tess! How would you like to join me and Natalie for some cutthroat mini golf tonight? She seems to think she can beat us both, lol," his text read. Tess laughed to herself, just imagining nine year old Natalie taunting her dad and Tess to beat her at putt-putt.

"Would love to see you two. What time?" she tapped out her response.

His was immediate. "Great! How about six? Can we pick you up? Come hungry. It's coney dog night."

Tess laughed at that, knowing full well that Denny knew Tess didn't eat hot dogs in any form. "Har har. Yes, six works if you want to pick me up. I'll get a slice of pizza there. :)" She hit 'send' and then put her phone away to go through her work emails. With a sigh of relief, she opened the one from Jim Hobart, time stamped 1:32 a.m., containing the security footage from Piedmont's Pay Less. Part of her hoped that Hobart hadn't watched it already because she was afraid he'd confront whoever the perp was.

Clicking on the link in the email, she watched as the interior of the discount store filled her screen. The cash register and front door were in full view, though slightly grainy.

Tess watched as the last few customers of the day went through the line, paying for their purchases. The time stamp read 9:55 p.m. The store, Tess knew, closed at ten. At 10 p.m. sharp, Tess watched as Mr. Hobart himself locked the front door and then went behind the counter to count the till. While he was doing that, a teenage girl could be seen sweeping the floor with a large broom while a teen boy followed with a mop. Seeing nothing untoward, Tess fast forwarded the video by ten minutes. The mopping seemed to be done and as the two teens unlocked the front door to leave for the night, Hobart walked over to the door and locked it back again. With a wave at the kids through the glass, he turned and headed back to the register, grabbed the money box with the day's profits and began walking toward the back of the store. A few minutes later, the lights in the store went off as Hobart presumably went out the back entrance. When Tess had initially questioned him the previous night, he'd told her that he always left through the rear entrance because he parked back there, and the security alarm panel was right inside the door. Everything that Tess saw on the video matched up with what Hobart had told her.

Hitting fast forward once again, she skimmed closer to the 11:00 p.m. mark, and there it was. At 10:57 p.m. a dark figure could be seen creeping toward the front door … from the back of the store. The person, average height and slightly heavy build, wore dark pants and a sweatshirt with the hood pulled up over their face. The suspect could be seen approaching the cash register and within moments, had it open and was removing the cash from inside. After pocketing the money, the person headed for the door, grabbed a large can of condensed soup from a shelf near the front of the store. As Tess watched, the person threw the soup can directly at the old glass door and it shattered. The intruder then picked up the soup can, haphazardly replaced it on the shelf and then ran away through the hole they'd just made.

Tess ran the video back to capture the best angle of the suspect. She printed the screenshot off and then headed to Piedmont's Pay Less. She had a can of soup to fingerprint.

Chapter Three

The summer sun beat down on Tess as she pulled her car, an older model Jeep Wrangler, into a parking spot at Piedmont's and quickly made her way over the cracked asphalt. The shattered half of the front door had been covered in clear plastic and yellow caution tape from the events of the night before. A handwritten note taped to the plastic told people to use the other door.

The brass bell over the door dinged as Tess stepped into the air-conditioned interior of the discount store. Taking off her aviator sunglasses and hooking them on her white button-down dress shirt, she made her way over to the cans of soup.

She grinned to herself when she noticed that all the cans were lined up neatly, labels facing out, except one that had a huge dent in the side. *This is like taking candy from a baby,* Tess mused to herself. Sliding a glove onto her hand, she carefully picked up the can of soup and placed it in a paper evidence bag she'd taken from her back pocket. Writing down the contents of the bag, she placed a piece of red evidence tape onto the folded top to seal it.

Feeling eyes on her, Tess glanced up to find Hobart standing behind the counter, watching her intently.

"Did you find anything yet? Or are you just stealing soup?" he asked through squinted eyes.

"I found what was used to break the window," Tess said, holding the evidence bag up for the man to see. "A large family-sized can of soup. Tomato bisque."

"So obviously you found something on the video," Hobart said, lowering his voice as he came closer to Tess. He looked over his shoulder toward the back of the store. "Did you see who did it?" he whispered. Tess glanced over his shoulder to see if anyone was around to hear but the store seemed empty.

"I'd like to question your staff, especially those working last night."

"You think it was an inside job?" Hobart asked, a look of surprise and suspicion darkening his face.

"The person was definitely already inside the building. I can't tell if it was a staff member or perhaps a customer who'd been hiding somewhere. All I do know is that they were average height and wore dark clothes. They used the soup can to break the window. Unfortunately, they didn't think about how the glass would shatter, which shows me which side the impact came from. Are all of the staff accounted for?"

"It's only Kara, Millie, Liam and myself. I just hire teenagers usually. They don't cost as much for payroll." Realizing what he'd just said, he cast a sheepish look over at Tess and shrugged. She gave him a look that told him she wasn't impressed with his business model.

"As long as you are paying them at least minimum wage, I can't do anything about that," Tess chastised, "But really, skimming their wages just because they are young is a little pathetic. Would you be surprised if one of them revolted and staged a robbery?"

"Well, when you put it that way ... I guess not," Hobart sighed. "Look, Detective Dane, I don't want you thinking I'm a prick or anything, but it's hard these days to keep the doors open. With all the overhead, the income is barely making ends meet. Everybody wants to shop at the big box store outside Crawley, or they just order online." He sighed then, casting a sorrowful glance at the stained, worn floor.

"I can appreciate that. Times are hard for all of us," Tess empathized. "Regardless, I do need to speak with all of your staff."

Hobart nodded and then disappeared down an aisle lined with seasonal items. Moments later, he appeared again, this time followed by a young girl in her mid to late-teens. The girl's large blue eyes looked concerned as she waited for the adults to lead the way.

"You guys can use my office to talk," he motioned for Tess and the girl to follow him.

Passing through the swinging gray doors marked "Employees Only", Tess glanced around at her surroundings. They were in a store's back storage room, stacks of boxes and supplies littering the floor. From this vantage point, Tess could see another door, armed with an alarm and assumed that was the rear outside door for the store, most likely leading to the back parking lot.

Following Hobart and the teenage girl, Tess wound her way around a stack of cat litter boxes and came to a halt at the doorway of a small office.

Hobart puffed up his chest, as though proud of his small space and ushered them inside. Tess nodded and stepped into the tiny, messy room and instantly wanted to leave.

There was an oversized desk shoved awkwardly into the corner, piled high with stacks of papers and old fast-food wrappers. Seeming to suddenly notice the mess through outsider's eyes, Hobart quickly grabbed some of the trash and balled it up in his hands before throwing it into an overfilled trash can near his feet.

The room smelled moldy with a slight hint of sweaty feet, so Tess took smaller breaths to avoid being uncomfortable. The girl to Tess's left seemed to be doing the same.

"Here, have a seat. Have a seat," Hobart picked up a stack of random papers that had been discarded on a rusted metal folding chair opposite the desk. "I'll leave you two ladies to it. Come find me out in the store if you need anything." Tess nodded at him in acknowledgement as the older man quickly made his exit.

Turning to the young girl standing nervously beside her, she gestured to the vacant chair, "Hi, I'm Detective Dane. You can call me Tess if you'd like. Go ahead and have a seat. I'll sit over here." She carefully picked her way around the overflowing trash can and a cardboard box filled with various office supplies.

Carefully sitting in the green leather chair behind the desk, the springs inside squeaking loudly in protest, Tess looked up at the girl sitting across from her. The internal springs caused the chair to feel lumpy, and Tess shifted slightly to find a more comfortable position. Inwardly she wanted to be done with this room as quickly as possible.

"What's your name?" she asked gently, watching as the girl ran her fingers through her long blond ponytail.

Glancing up at Tess before quickly looking away, the girl mumbled, "Millie Townsend. Do I need to have my mom here?"

"You can call her if you would like. I'll just be asking some vague questions about the event from the Fourth of July. It's not an official interview. I'm just looking for information ... not accusing anyone of anything. If we need to do an official interview later, down at the station to record things and get your official statement, then yes, we will have your mom there. Sound good?"

The girl nodded and seemed to relax a bit as she sat up taller in her chair. Tess gave her a kind smile and then glanced around the room again.

"Let's make this quick, Millie. This room smells like feet, and I want out of here." This seemed to relax the girl even further, and she grinned back at Tess.

"It always smells like that in here." She made a gagging face, and Tess laughed.

"How old are you, Millie?"

"I'll be sixteen in October."

"Nice. Then you'll be eligible for your driver's license. How long have you worked here?"

"I started here last September, so ..." she counted off her fingers, "almost eleven months?"

"And how do you like it?" Tess asked, writing down some notes to herself.

"It's okay, I guess," Millie shrugged. "I only work a few hours a week, mostly after school or on the weekends. More now that it's summer. I'm saving up for a car."

"I'm sure you heard about the break-in last night. Do you have any ideas about what happened?" Tess watched the girl closely, looking for any indication that she was trying to be deceptive.

"Yeah, I heard about it. I didn't work that night though. I was out watching fireworks with my family. Liam and Mr. Hobart worked last night I think. Maybe Kara? Let me check." Tess watched as the girl pulled her cell phone out and tapped away at an app. After a slight pause, Millie nodded.

"Yep, Kara, Liam and Mr. Hobart." She turned the phone so that Tess could see the screen. It appeared to be an app that kept employees apprised of their schedule. Millie was right. Tess made note that Liam and Kara were scheduled until 10:00 p.m. on July fourth along with Mr. Hobart.

"Did you notice anything out of the ordinary recently that stands out to you? Any weird behavior from either customers or fellow employees?"

"All the employees seemed normal the past few days. There were less customers here toward the end of the shift last night. I guess it's because they were going to the fireworks."

"How do you know that if you didn't work?" Tess asked, watching the girl closely. She shifted in her seat, and the springs made another god-awful sound that made Tess cringe. Millie didn't seem to notice.

"Liam told me," she shrugged, still playing with her ponytail. "He sent me a few texts complaining about how boring it was last night and how he just wanted to go home." She flipped her phone around again and shoved it across the desk toward Tess.

Tess leaned forward and picked up the phone, the glittery pink case feeling smooth in her hand. Quickly scanning the texts, she noticed something that stood out to her.

"It says there was an especially rude customer that evening. Do you know anything else about that?"

"I don't know," Millie commented with a bored sigh. "Liam just said the guy was pushy and seemed to be in a hurry. Very rude."

"Okay. And can you tell me when Liam and Kara work again?"

Millie took her phone back and tapped it a few times. Looking up at Tess, she shrugged. "Looks like he should be working the closing shift tonight. Comes in at 4:00. Kara's off until tomorrow."

Tess glanced at her watch. It was just past one now. "Okay, Millie. Thank you for your time. I'll chat with Liam when he gets here."

Millie stood and mumbled a goodbye as she exited the small, cramped room. Tess was quick to follow and made a mental note of speaking with Liam anywhere but that stinky room.

Chapter Four

Tuesday, July 5th, 4:07 p.m.

Comfortably situated in a metal folding chair in the storeroom next to the tower of kitty litter boxes, Tess checked her watch. Liam was late for his shift. Pursing her lips and absently scrolling through her phone, she mentally decided to give him another ten minutes before tracking him down herself.

Just as she was finishing a level of Candy Crush, the door to the storeroom opened and a tall, lanky teenage boy scuffled in. With earbuds shoved in his ears, and his gaze down at his phone, there was absolutely no urgency to his step.

Tess watched the boy silently as he walked across the room, unaware of her presence. He pulled the earbuds out and shoved them in his hoodie pocket before donning a green Piedmont's Pay Less apron. A plastic name tag with 'Liam' hastily written on a piece of white tape covering it was clipped to the front. Given how much of a miser Mr.

Hobart was, Tess wouldn't be surprised if she picked off the tape and found yet another employee's name under it.

"You're late," Tess said simply, quietly relishing watching the boy panic as he turned around looking for the source of the voice. His eyes narrowed when he saw her.

"Who are you?" he asked, shoving his cellphone into his back pocket and clocking in. The old green metal time clock hanging on the wall next to the office door made a loud clunking sound as it punched Liam's yellow time sheet. The boy absently shoved his time slip back into a vacant spot among the other staff's sheets while he looked Tess up and down suspiciously.

"I'm surprised Millie didn't tell you I'd be here. You were late for your shift, and I don't like to be kept waiting."

Recognition dawning on his face, he spoke up. "You're the cop, right?" he asked, walking toward Tess and watching her closely.

"Yes, I'm Detective Tess Dane with the Swain County Sheriff's Office. I'm here to ask some general questions about the break-in last night. Not accusing anyone, just asking questions, okay?"

The boy nodded. Tess gestured toward another folding chair that she had set up beforehand in an effort to avoid the small confines of the office.

With a sigh, Liam slid into the seat, crossing his arms over his chest and yawning as though he were dying of boredom. He sat there silently, his chin on his chest, eyes closed.

"How old are you, Liam?"

"Eighteen," the boy mumbled, as he fiddled around with his apron strings.

"I hear you worked yesterday evening, is that correct?" Tess asked, pulling up the notes app on her phone.

"Yep."

"Did anything happen out of the ordinary the past few days?"

"Nope."

"Have you seen anyone acting suspiciously around here?"

"Nope."

"Did you know that an average person can fart up to forty times a day?" Tess asked deadpan. She got the desired effect, because Liam suddenly looked at her and then busted up laughing.

"Well shit, Detective ... I wasn't expecting that one." Liam grinned, his moody teenage persona falling away.

"Look, kid, I know you don't want to be sitting here talking with me. I get that. But it sure beats working the floor with ol' Mr. Hobart, right?" Tess smirked. Liam laughed again and nodded.

"Yeah, anything is better than that," Liam agreed, "and no, nothing stands out in my mind the past few days but ... well ... I did see some mail on Hobart's desk."

"What kind of mail?"

"Well, I was looking for extra packing tape—we had some boxes of seasonal stuff to move around—so I glanced in his office." Liam paused then, looking over at Tess nervously before continuing. "I didn't snoop, I swear. I just looked at the desk for tape, but I didn't see any. What I did see were two envelopes. They had red letters across the front that said 'Final Notice' and 'Overdue', but I didn't stick around to see who they were from. They looked pretty legit though."

"Okay. And have you heard Mr. Hobart mention anything about financial difficulties with the store recently?" Tess asked, remembering that Hobart had already mentioned that things at the store were getting difficult. But how difficult? Enough for him to stage a robbery of his own store for the insurance money? It wouldn't be the first time someone had pulled a stunt like that.

"No," Liam answered as Tess tapped out some more notes to herself, specifically to follow up on her request to run financials on the store and Mr. Hobart. It was then that she noticed a note from her conversation with Millie.

"Liam, Millie said there was a particularly rude customer last night. Do you remember anything about that?"

"Oh, you mean Mr. Pushy Pants?" Liam scoffed. "The jerk came in a little before close, maybe around ... I don't know … nine? He just started grabbing random shit: trash bags, bathroom cleaner, I don't even remember. What I do remember was that I was helping check out a customer, and this guy gets in the back of the line. The lady I was helping wanted to use coupons and of course that took me a while to scan and explain to her that some were expired. The lady was nice but disappointed, and Mr. Pushy Pants just started huffing, shifting around, messing with his phone. I worked my way through the customers and at one point, Pushy even started muttering under his breath. I'm pretty sure he said "fucking slow" and "ridiculous", but whatever. When I finally got to him, he all but threw his stuff on the counter and muttered for me to hurry up. He was just rude … and gross."

"Gross?"

"Yeah," Liam said, making a face. "He was sweaty, but then again he was ticked off so maybe he was worked up or he was one of those people that over sweats. I had a friend in first grade whose dad was an over sweater. It's a real thing."

"Hyperhidrosis," Tess said absently, as she tapped away taking notes.

"That's it!" Liam exclaimed, "See? I told you it was real." He leaned back in his chair, a pleased expression on his face.

"Okay, well, thank you, Liam, for taking the time to talk to me. I don't have any further questions for you right now but if you can think of anything else that you think may prove helpful, please call me," Tess handed him a business card, and watched as he shoved it in his pocket and headed toward the storefront.

Chapter Five

After interviewing Liam, Tess left to head home to change for her date with Denny and his daughter, Natalie. Just thinking about getting to see Denny again made Tess feel like she had butterflies in her stomach.

Since closing the Torture Killer case, Tess hadn't gotten to see Denny nearly as much as she wanted. He'd had to rush off to another crime scene down near Cincinnati, and she'd gone back to patrol work as she studied for the detective's exam.

Ever since their kiss on the front porch of her house right after Denny was discharged from the hospital with a bullet wound in his lower abdomen, Tess had only seen him a handful of times. Although he made every effort to call or text her daily, it wasn't the same, and it made Tess frustrated.

Anticipation of seeing the two of them had her smiling but in the back of her mind, her brain was working the Piedmont case in overdrive.

Had Liam seen evidence of potential financial collapse of Piedmont's Pay Less or had he misinterpreted what he'd seen? If it were true, did Hobart really stage a break-in just for the insurance money and to save face in town? And what about the pushy customer at the end of the day? Was that important at all? Or was the timing just a coincidence?

As Tess fed Otter his dinner and grabbed a quick shower, she kept turning the facts over in her mind. Even as she was wrapped in a towel and headed for her bedroom, she checked her email on her phone to see if there were any updates about her request for the financial records of Mr. Hobart and Piedmont's Pay Less. That would be one way to clear up a lot of the suspicion surrounding the break-in. So far, there was nothing in her inbox.

While she put the final touches on her make-up and then buckled her strappy leather sandals, Tess's phone buzzed on the bedside table. Standing up, she smoothed out her yellow tank top and denim shorts. As she picked her phone up, a frown formed on her face.

"Sorry to cancel, but I just got called in. Have to get to Cleveland for a case. Dropping Natalie at my sister's on the way. Reschedule ASAP?" Denny's text read.

With a wave of despondency, Tess plopped down on the edge of her bed, staring at her phone. She'd really been looking forward to seeing Denny.

The last time they'd made plans to get together, poor Natalie had come down with strep throat and they'd had to cancel. And now this ....

"I'm disappointed but I understand. Text me when you can. Hope to see you soon," Tess responded and then hit 'send'. She puffed out a frustrated sigh which caused Otter to cock his head to the side as he watched her.

"It looks like it's just you and me tonight, Otter," she said, sliding her phone into her back pocket and patting the dog's black head. His tail wagged at the affection and he nudged her with his nose.

"You wanna go to the dog park?" Tess asked, squatting down to ruffle his ears. The dog's deep brown eyes watched her every move as she stood back up and headed for his leash. When Otter realized that they were, indeed, going for a walk to the dog park, he started barking excitedly and dancing at the door as Tess clipped on his lead.

"C'mon, silly boy, let's go."

Chapter Six

Wednesday, July 6th, 2:45 p.m.

Tess had just finished interviewing Kara at Piedmont's Pay Less. She was happy that she'd once again diverted the meeting from the cramped office to the kitty litter holding area as she had the afternoon before.

Kara Bishop, with her bubbly personality and mass of unruly red curls, had provided no new information. Though entertaining, Kara basically repeated everything Liam had, except for the information about the past due notices. She hadn't seen anything weird or noticed anyone suspicious. Tess didn't know how the girl would in the first place as she talked incessantly and had the attention span of a gnat.

The only thing remotely interesting that Kara had to say was that she too had been forced to deal with Mr. Pushy Pants when he bumped into her in the hardware aisle. He'd been carrying a pack of replacement saw blades and some bottled water when he pushed by her, causing her to drop multiple boxes of nails. He was, according to Kara, a "complete jerk".

Now, as Tess walked down the hallway toward her office, she pondered over what she'd learned from interviewing the employees at the discount store. They all seemed to like the job, considering they were teenagers and probably had other things they'd rather be doing. And none of them seemed to overly dislike Mr. Hobart.

Tess was still waiting for the financial reports to come back and she had her fingers crossed that the fingerprint she collected from the can of tomato bisque would come back with a match with someone already in the system. If not, she'd have to dig deeper and get warrants and parents involved.

With a sigh, she rounded the corner to her office and came to an abrupt halt. Sitting on her desk was a huge bouquet of red roses, their scent filling the room. A grin slowly crossed her face as she reached for the white note sticking out amidst the leaves and petals. *"Sorry about last night. I'll make it up to you. Denny"*

Leaning in to smell the roses, Tess knew she had a dopey smile on her face and didn't even care. Just getting texts or emails from him made her happy and although she'd rather actually get to see him in real life, she understood about the demands of his job. But just because she understood, didn't mean she liked it.

Sending him a quick text to thank him for the flowers, she sat down behind her desk and quickly checked her work emails. Still no financials. Suppressing a sigh, she decided to go check out the store's surveillance tape one more time. Maybe she had missed something?

Knocking on the doorway to the audiovisual room, she waited for Deputy Cooper to notice her. He sat in a folding chair, thick headphones cupped over his ears, watching a grainy surveillance video from a different case. Tess watched him for a second while he fiddled around with knobs and buttons, then wrote something down on the notebook in front of him.

Noticing her out of the corner of her eye, he smiled while pressing the 'STOP' button, and yanked off the headphones, leaving them to dangle around his neck.

"Hey, Dane!" he greeted, "What can I help you with today?" Everyone at the station knew he was the master of manipulation when it came to discerning grainy, pixelated surveillance videos or isolating voices or sounds on audio recordings.

Tess sighed in relief that he was there and available to help and not out on a call somewhere. Stepping into the small, warm room heated by all of the audiovisual equipment, she sat down in the empty seat next to him and glanced up at the various monitors and machinery humming around them.

"Well, you know that break-in down at Piedmont's I've been working?"

Cooper nodded for her to continue as he wrote himself a note. Tess waited a moment for him to finish before continuing.

"I've watched the video on my office computer and didn't see anything but I'm wondering if there is anything else that I might be missing," Tess admitted, "I'm starting to think that the store owner staged the break-in for the insurance money but I'm waiting on the financial report to come through. I'm pretty sure that Piedmont's is in financial distress. The owner said as much offhandedly, and the idea was seconded by an employee."

"Hmmm ... Sounds like a good excuse to stage a burglary. Let's see what you have." Deputy Cooper said, moving out of Tess's way so she could pull up the surveillance video from the Fourth of July.

Cooper leaned in to watch the video closely, stopping and starting a few times to enhance different frames. Tess watched the same scene she'd seen last time: Mr. Hobart counting out the cash register and putting the deposit into the zippered pouch for the bank, Kara and Liam mopping the floor. Around 10:00 p.m. Hobart locks the doors behind the kids as they leave and then takes the money pouch and exits off screen toward the back of the store.

Deputy Cooper rewound the video and then slowed it down to when Hobart was loading the bank pouch. Cooper then pressed a few buttons, enlarging the viewing screen, and proceeded to slowly click through the frames.

"I think you may be right, Dane," he commented, "You seeing what I'm seeing?"

"Yes, I think I do," Tess smiled excitedly, "Go back." Cooper hit the rewind button.

Suddenly there was a knock at the door causing Tess and Cooper to look up to see who the newcomer was. Sheriff Malone stood there, holding two pizza boxes.

"Hey, somebody from dispatch ordered pizza for us. Aren't we lucky?" Malone grinned. "Leave some of the sausage for me though. I have to make a quick phone call but I'll put this in the conference room. Help yourself."

Tess and Cooper thanked him and then turned back to the video, which was still rewinding. "Crap! Sorry ...." Cooper mumbled, hitting the STOP button.

"Wait, pull that up again," Tess exclaimed, pointing to a man walking down the main aisle toward the register with his hands full. "That must be Mr. Pushy Pants that the kids were telling me about." When Cooper looked confused, Tess grinned, "Apparently the guy was like 'a total jerk,' or at least that's what store employees said."

Cooper laughed lightly as he hit PLAY and the two of them watched the grumpy man wait in line impatiently, constantly shifting from one foot to the other. He was tall, thin, and wore black pants with white stripes up the sides, black sneakers, and a dark hoodie, which was weird since it was July. Sure enough though, just like Liam had said, the man approached the register and abruptly dumped his purchase on the counter, his body language appearing distressed or rushed. He looked to be saying something but since the video had no sound, Tess couldn't tell what he said. When Liam handed the man his receipt, the man snatched it and stomped out, nearly bumping into another customer that was entering the store.

"Good grief," Cooper said, shaking his head, fast forwarding the video back to Mr. Hobart and the cash register. "Want me to isolate this time frame?"

"Yes, please," Tess said, getting her mind back on to the task at hand. "I think I'm going to invite Mr. Hobart down here for a little chit chat."

Chapter Seven

Wednesday, July 6th, 6:32 p.m.

"Thanks for coming down here, Mr. Hobart," Tess smiled as she took a seat opposite the store owner. Under the guise of asking a few more questions to clarify some things about the break-in, Tess had asked Hobart to meet her at the end of the day. For one, he would be a little distracted as the evening hours at the store were his most busy, and secondly, because Tess had just received the financial reports for Mr. Hobart himself and Piedmont's Pay Less as a business and boy did she have some questions.

"Sure thing, Detective," Hobart smiled, smoothing out his green button down shirt sporting the Piedmont's logo. "You catch the guy who did this to my store yet?"

"Oh, we are very close to making an arrest," Tess assured him with a smile that didn't quite meet her eyes. He didn't seem to notice. "We just had a few more questions. You know, to clarify some stuff."

"Sure thing," Hobart nodded again, beginning to sound like a broken record. Tess noticed small beads of sweat already forming on his balding head, his eyes darting around the room but never fully on her.

"The first question I had is about this bank statement from Crawley National Bank," Tess started, holding up a few printed documents. "Per their records, it looks as though the mortgage for Piedmont's is nearly ... three ... no four months in arrears?"

"Well ... no, now that is wrong," Hobart asserted defensively. "I paid them, and they just didn't enter it into their books."

"Four times in a row?" Tess raised a dark, well-groomed eyebrow at him skeptically. The sweat droplets on his head were getting more numerous, she noticed.

When he said nothing, she pressed on, "And how about the foreclosure letter that was sent to you on May 30th, and then again on June 28th? I'm guessing if we wait a few more weeks, we'll have a trio of letters to pick through."

She was rewarded with a scowl but decided to ignore it, choosing instead to sit quietly for a moment, watching him. As the silence stretched on for just a couple of seconds, Hobart appeared completely unnerved, and Tess, though enjoying herself, decided not to be too cruel. She leaned into the table, looking Hobart in the eye.

"You see, Mr. Hobart. This is what I think happened," she paused for a moment to add, "Please correct me if I get it wrong." Tess leaned back in her chair, staring him down, his beady eyes still not willing to completely meet hers.

"I think that you've been skimming money off of your own business for months, if not years, and now, in a final hurrah, you've staged a break-in to get the insurance money."

This finally rewarded her with a look from him, and not a nice one.

"I think that you've been claiming only a fraction of the profits of the store and depositing them into the business bank account but making much larger deposits into your personal account. You know, the one at Erie One Credit Union up in Sandusky? Side note .... Did you really think we wouldn't check all this? Tsk tsk, Mr. Hobart."

"You're just making this up. You don't have any proof of any of this," the older man snapped, crossing his pudgy arms across his slightly barrel chest.

Tess picked up the stack of paperwork and emails she'd printed out and shook them lightly for effect.

"It's all here, every transaction." Tess was only lightly bluffing. They had the preliminary financials, but Hobart didn't need to know that. "Looks to me like Piedmont's is bleeding money and that money just happens to be draining into your own bank account. Sure, your personal account here at Crawley isn't very suspicious but then you just had to get one at Erie One." She shrugged, slapping the papers back down on the table and causing him to jump.

"Well, I still don't hear any proof about the night of the break-in. That thief got away with over a thousand dollars!"

"You mean *you* got away with over a thousand dollars," Tess paused for effect, then stood and walked to the door of the room and knocked. In response, Deputy Cooper walked in carrying a laptop and set it on the table near Mr. Hobart so that he could see the screen.

"I watched the surveillance video that you gave me," she told Hobart, "and at first, I didn't see anything untoward. But then I got to thinking. Something was off. So, I asked my coworker here to take a look, and Mr. Hobart! Your sleight of hand was on point!" Tess smirked. Hobart's scowl deepened and he nervously scratched at his chin. Tess could tell that he knew they had him.

"At first, it looked like you were taking the deposit out of the cash drawer and putting it into the bag, but," she nodded to Cooper, "if we enlarge the screen, we can see here that you are only placing the top bill of each denomination into the bag and then quickly, carefully, moving the bag in such a way that it would hide what you're really doing, which is putting the rest of the money back into the cash register." She paused while Deputy Cooper pressed PLAY and Mr. Hobart watched himself skim the cash drawer and leave most of the money inside it.

"Now, according to staff who open the register in the morning, there is typically no money left there overnight. They said that they have to wait for you to get it out of the safe in the back. So, why, of all nights, would you decide to leave money, especially most of it, in the register all night if you hadn't planned for it to be stolen? I think you purposely left the till full so that it could be 'stolen' by you, and you could claim the insurance benefits on it before skipping town. We found out about the plane ticket to Puerto Rico, too, FYI." Tess added out of the corner of her mouth in a conspiratorial tone.

Hobart seethed, staring up at Tess but remained silent except for the quickened breaths he sucked in.

"And remember that time you applied for the custodial job with the school district and had to be fingerprinted? Just so happens that your prints match the ones I lifted off of that can of tomato bisque. Now, before you get all up in arms and say, 'But it's my store! Of course my prints would be on it!' I want you to know that, sure there were other partial prints on the can. But yours? Yours were right on top, nicely overlaying the others, ripe for the taking. And besides, what run-of-the-mill thief would waste the time to stop and replace an item they used to smash a window? Seconds count, Mr. Hobart. A professional crook would have gotten out of there as quickly as possible. It was your passion for always having a neat store and providing an enjoyable shopping experience that caught you up this time I'm afraid." Tess did very little to hide the snark in her voice.

Hobart's face turned a disturbing shade of red and the beads of sweat once covering his head had now turned into rivulets. "Enough!" he roared, hitting the table with his meaty fist. "Enough! It wasn't supposed to happen like this." Then he leaned forward and, resting his forehead on the edge of the table, began to sob.

Chapter Eight

Thursday, July 7th, 9:01 a.m.

Tess moaned as she rolled over to answer her phone. She'd been deep asleep until the phone had rudely started ringing as not one, but two calls and multiple texts came through, and woke her up. It had been a late night, and she hadn't gotten to bed until after three.

She'd been busy arresting two men she'd been investigating for the past month or so. Lyle Hanson and Patrick Borden had been smuggling drugs into Crawley and selling them to highschoolers. Not on her watch. Tess had been busy, totally immersing herself into the case until she got tugged away to deal with Jim Hobart at the Piedmont's Pay Less.

Last night, shortly after booking Hobart for the break-in at Piedmont's, Tess had received a call about the whereabouts of Hanson and Borden. She'd had undercover officers watching their every move, arrest warrants at the ready, but the criminal duo had been elusive for the past couple of days. Tess, though distracted with Hobart, had been waiting for some movement with the drug case.

With the closure of both the Hobart and Hanson/Borden cases, Tess had fallen into bed and had planned to stay there all day to catch up on some sleep.

Apparently, her phone had other plans.

Now, as the phone started trilling yet again, she grabbed it and groggily hit the green button.

"Dane," she slurred unsteadily. Disoriented, Tess rolled over onto her back, bumping into Otter's recumbent form beside her. The dog just sighed and refused to move.

"About time you answered," Malone chastised gently. At the sound of his voice, Tess woke up instantly and sat up, getting a side-eyed look from Otter.

"Sorry," Tess apologized, "It *is* my day off though so ...."

"I know, and I hate to do this, but we just got a call," Malone sighed, "Guy named Neil Slaydon says his wife is missing. Apparently she's pregnant so this needs special attention. All hands on deck kind of thing if you get me."

"Yeah, I get you," Tess ran her fingers through her long dark hair and stifled a yawn. "Missing pregnant lady. We're up against a ticking clock." Another sigh as she swung her legs out of bed and stood up, quietly padding toward the kitchen to make some coffee and let Otter out. "Let me get dressed and take care of the dog. Text me the information. I'm on it."

"Thanks, Tess," Malone sounded grateful. "I owe you. With Greene out on family leave, and Bender and Potanski on vacation, we are just shorthanded."

"It's fine, Malone," Tess yawned, pouring coffee grounds into the coffeemaker and pressing the power button. "I'm just the best detective you have, and you know it," she grinned.

His low chuckle came through the phone, "You're not wrong about that. Even if everyone were on duty today, I'd still want you on this case. A missing pregnant woman could be very bad indeed."

"Yes. I'll stay in touch," Tess agreed before disconnecting the call. With a sigh just thinking about the long day ahead of her, she let Otter back inside and filled his food bowl before heading back to her closet to get dressed.

Chapter Nine

Thursday, July 7th, 9:32 a.m.

Tess made her way up the Slaydon's driveway, the scent of peonies surrounding her. Brushing past the pink petaled blossoms that lined the walk, Tess nodded a greeting at Deputy Miles, who stood just inside of the open doorway.

"Hey, Miles," Tess greeted him with a warm smile despite the grim nature of their visit to Neil Slaydon's residence. She paused as she got close to Miles and asked quietly, "Is this the house you were telling me about the other day?" Deputy Miles just nodded with a sigh. Tess closed her eyes with a sigh for a second, her mouth in a grim line, as she thought about the various scenarios playing through her mind.

"What do we have so far?" she asked her coworker. Miles gave her a slight shrug as he stepped out onto the porch to greet her.

"The husband is inside, in the living room. I have Deputy Kennedy in there with him now. He appears very distraught and agitated," Miles offered, causing Tess to nod in approval. Deputy Kennedy, the Liaison Officer, would be needed there today if the wife was indeed missing. Tess still hoped in the back of her mind that it was just a misunderstanding and Mrs. Slaydon was at the grocery and had simply forgotten to call.

"Any signs of a struggle? Dispatch stated the husband said there was blood?"

"There are a few things that seem out of place. I'd rather you look at the scene first and then we can discuss. Don't want to taint your opinion," Miles commented with a slight grin. "The husband gave us the go ahead to look around in the kitchen."

"Sounds like a good idea, Miles," Tess nodded as she stepped into the Slaydon home. "You really should take your detective exam."

"I know, I know," he muttered under his breath. "I've been so busy taking care of my mom."

"I get it. Been there, done that," Tess murmured sympathetically as she knew Deputy Miles had been a mere two weeks from taking his detective exam when his mother had a stroke causing him to become her main caregiver. His career aspirations were temporarily on the backburner but when he was ready, Tess would be there to support him in any way she could.

As Tess took in her surroundings, she slowly followed Miles past the living room where she noticed a man, in his early thirties, sitting on a gray couch, his eyes swollen and red. He caught Tess's gaze as she made her down the hallway behind Miles and she nodded a greeting. She'd talk to him shortly but wanted to get a handle on the situation first.

At the end of a short hallway, Tess found herself standing in the doorway to the home's kitchen. Remaining still, she let her eyes wander around the scene in front of her.

The kitchen appeared to have been remodeled, but not recently, perhaps within the last five years or so: gray granite countertops, white cabinets, stainless steel appliances. A few plates and cups sat drying in the dish rack and a bowl of fruit, overripe and starting to attract fruit flies, sat on the island next to a small pile of mail. On the refrigerator hung a compact white board with a few grocery items written on it. Apparently the Slaydons needed milk and bread.

On the floor, there appeared to be the remains of a broken vase, the fresh, red carnations it had once held now scattered in a puddle of water.

Next to the fridge was a door, most likely leading to the garage. Hanging on the wall near the door on a small decorative coat hook, was a woman's purse and a blue dog leash.

To the right of the garage door sat a dark cherry kitchen table with four chairs. One of the chairs laid on its side as though it had been knocked over in a struggle.

The fact that the kitchen was entirely spotless was not lost on Tess. In fact, the entire part of the house she'd already seen appeared to be almost clinically clean. And where was the blood that Mr. Slaydon had mentioned when he'd called 911? Glancing around from her vantage point near the doorway, Tess saw no blood.

Miles handed her a pair of blue shoe covers and some gloves to don before she walked into the kitchen on the off chance this really was a crime scene and not just some wife who'd decided to walk away from her husband.

Her black booties fully encased in the shoe covers, Tess entered the kitchen and, starting to her left, slowly and methodically began looking for any clues about what had transpired there.

Stopping at the pile of mail on the island, she picked it up in her gloved hands and flipped through it. Two pieces of junk mail from local retailers, a gas bill, and a flier asking, "Where will YOU spend eternity?" made up the stack—none of which looked very suspicious to Tess.

She noticed how the stainless-steel fridge was just that—stainless. Not a single fingerprint marred its surface in any way. A quick glance at the stove and dishwasher confirmed that they, too, were spotless. Even the toaster on the countertop was pristine.

Either the Slaydons were extremely clean and neat or the kitchen had been recently wiped down. Tess made a mental note and continued looking around.

Pausing at the kitchen sink, Tess glanced around, looking for a trash can. Finding none, she opened the sink cabinet to look. Bingo.

Pulling it out, Tess made quick work of mentally cataloging the contents. It was easy enough because the trash bag appeared to have been emptied recently except for one item.

Reaching in, she pulled it out and unfolded it. The cellophane wrapper for fresh flowers had been balled up and discarded, along with the receipt for them. Tess noted the date of purchase—just that morning.

Tess mulled the find over in her head as she stood and laid the flower wrapper and receipt on the counter. Pulling out her phone, she took a quick photo.

As Deputy Miles came to the doorway of the kitchen, Tess slid her phone back into her pocket and continued looking around.

"What's that?" Miles thrust his chin in the direction of the trash now laying on the kitchen counter.

"Possibly nothing," Tess answered, not looking up at him. "Could be everything. Please bag and tag them, just in case."

"Sure thing," Miles agreed as he went to get some gloves and evidence bags, leaving Tess alone to resume her search.

Where was the blood Neil Slaydon had reported? Had he cleaned it up already? Surely not.

Tess completed her lap of the kitchen and came to a stop in front of the flipped over dining chair. She paused, turning her head in various angles. Something wasn't right.

The chair, laying on its side, was halfway under the table. If it had been knocked over during a struggle, wouldn't it have fallen straight down?

Tess squatted down, reaching out and touching the thin loosely woven rug that was spread under the kitchen table. Just as she thought it would, it wrinkled up when she pushed it.

The rug wasn't wrinkled up when she'd first approached it. The knocked over chair had most likely been staged, but why? Had it fallen over in an actual struggle, the rug would have been shoved up and wrinkled as the chair slid under the table.

Tess took some more photos on her phone and, as Miles returned and began bagging up the trash, she asked him to call in the crime scene team to photograph the kitchen and test for blood. Tess's Spidey sense was going off. Something wasn't right.

Finding nothing else of question in the kitchen, Tess made her way back toward the living room to speak to Neil Slaydon about his missing wife.

Chapter Ten

Thursday, July 7th, 10:25 a.m.

"I'm Detective Tess Dane with the Swain County Sheriff's Department," Tess said, nodding to the husband of the missing woman. His hands were filled with balled up tissues and laying on his lap. He made no move to shake her hand and she didn't offer.

"Neil Slaydon," the man mumbled, sounding hoarse and broken. Though obviously distraught, Tess could tell he was handsome: dark wavy hair, skin that looked kissed by the sun. Even though he was sitting, slouched over, on the couch, he appeared to be tall and athletically built as though he spent a fair amount of time working out.

"Thank you for letting us look in your kitchen. After we finish talking here, do we have your permission to search the rest of your house and property if necessary to look for signs of your wife's whereabouts?" Tess inquired, hoping that a search warrant wouldn't be needed and that Jessica Slaydon would be found quickly.

Neil nodded, "Sure, anything you need to do to find Jessica." Tess inwardly sighed and slipped a glance at Miles hovering in the doorway. Miles nodded at Tess, his mouth in a grime line, as he turned to step outside of the home. He'd already called in the crime scene techs to process the kitchen and any other areas of interest and would direct them where to go once they arrived.

"So when was the last time you saw your wife, Mr. Slaydon?" Tess asked as she sat opposite the distraught husband. His eyes were bloodshot, his eyelids puffy. From crying for his missing wife? Or from lack of sleep from disposing of her body? Tess couldn't know for sure and it was too early to speculate. He looked vaguely familiar to Tess but she was sure she'd never met him before. Some people just have one of those faces.

"She was here last night. I got home yesterday evening and found her packing an overnight bag. She said she was going to visit her family in Cleveland. The problem is that she hasn't returned any of my calls or texts and when I checked with her parents, they said they hadn't seen her. Her car is still in the garage," Neil Slaydon said, his face a mix of emotions.

"Is that normal for her?" Tess asked, making some notes to herself. "Her not answering you?"

"No," Neil sighed, his shoulders slumping. "Normally she's the one that does all the texting. She can be chatty," he added, as though it were a character flaw.

"Does she usually make plans to go off on random trips without discussing it with you first?"

He shook his head, running his hands down over his face and leaning back on the couch.

"I have a report here claiming that you told dispatch that Jessica was here last night, beside you in bed, and when you got home from the gym this morning she was missing. Didn't you see her before you left for the gym?" Tess stated, her eyes roaming over the man in front of her. Her eyebrows knitted together in skepticism as she was keenly aware that he wasn't being entirely truthful. But why? And which story was the closest to the truth? "Which is it, Mr. Slaydon? Which series of events is the truth? Did she go see her family yesterday or was she here all night with you? And if she was here last night, then how did you not see her in bed this morning?"

Neil Slaydon just sat there, head in his hands for a moment, perhaps knowing he was caught out, or perhaps just overrun with emotion. Regardless, Tess knew that his story could be verified easily enough by calling Jessica's family.

Tess leaned back in her seat, adjusted her long legs, and waited for his reply. Finally, the man sighed and looked up at her.

"She was supposed to leave last night but then decided to leave this morning. She didn't say why. When I left for the gym this morning, I thought she was next to me. It was early and dark; the curtains were drawn. I didn't want to wake her, so I bumped around in the dark getting ready. I ... I assumed she was in the bed under the blankets," his voice hitched, and tears threatened again. "She's always cold and has to have all the blankets on her."

"Did you all have a disagreement? A fight of some sort?" Tess inquired, watching him carefully. His jaw twitched slightly and had Tess not been watching him so intently she may have missed it entirely.

"We got annoyed with each other," Neil said, finally looking at Tess fully. "I mean, all couples get on each other's nerves at some point or another." He absently picked at the seam of his black gym pants.

"Being annoyed and fighting are two separate things," Tess pointed out.

"True," Neil agreed. "She's been hormonal and dramatic recently. I think we just needed some space. So, yes, we got angry at each other, but it was more just a couple of snarky comments and huffs at each other. Nothing crazy."

"So, no yelling? Throwing things?"

"No. We don't yell at each other."

"Then how do you explain the call we received over Fourth of July weekend? The one from the neighbor saying he heard arguing and glass breaking from his yard?"

"From nosey Harold Newton?" Neil said, his voice full of disdain. "The man's half deaf and he's always gossiping over his fence with neighbors. He's worse than a woman."

Tess noticed that Neil Slaydon didn't seem to care for 'chatty' or nosey women. He also didn't seem to like anyone, for that matter. Unable to discern quite yet if it was due to grief, or simply his personality, Tess pressed on.

"Yes, *that* Mr. Newton," Tess said, looking pointedly at Slaydon. "What about the fighting he reported?"

"There wasn't any fighting. God, why won't you guys listen to me? I was watching a movie!" he snapped, exacerbated. With a sigh he flopped backwards on the couch like a petulant teenage boy that had suddenly lost his video game privileges.

"Sir, when my officers arrived here that night, they reported that your wife had a bloodied lip. One does not get a bloody lip from watching movies with the volume on high," Tess said, not disguising her annoyance at his immature outburst.

"She tripped over the dishwasher. She already told you that. She hit her face and even dropped a glass on the floor," Neil moaned, sounding annoyed and sighing heavily. "Look, I'm not trying to be an ass but my wife is missing. And in theory, my child is missing also. You should be out there looking for them. Not pestering me on how loudly I like to watch films."

"Well, Mr. Slaydon, you have to see things from our point of view as well. We've received reports of a domestic disturbance." She held her hands up to silence him when he opened his mouth to interrupt her. "We have reports of your wife having a bloody lip. And now, here we are, searching your house for clues about your wife's whereabouts. Can you honestly sit there and not see why we must ask these questions? It doesn't seem shady to you?"

Neil just looked at her, his gaze somewhere between a glare and a look of defeat.

"We weren't fighting," he stated emphatically. "You can say what you want, but we weren't fighting. I loved my wife."

Tess didn't know if he even realized his slip up, referring to his wife in the past tense. "Loved" his wife ... interesting. Tess schooled her expression, making a note to revisit the topic.

"Mr. Slaydon, is there any chance that your wife might have been having an affair? Perhaps run off with a lover?" Tess inquired, watching the missing woman's husband closely.

He shook his head. "Doubtful. We weren't the type of couple to .... abide by the confines of our marriage vows."

"Meaning what, exactly?"

"Meaning we had an agreement. An open marriage kind of thing. You know, don't ask, don't tell?" Neil explained, looking uncomfortable. Tess mulled the information over in her mind.

"And Jessica was okay with this?"

"Of course. It was her idea. I went along with it because I didn't want her to just cheat on me. If she was into having threesomes or whatever, I'd rather be involved than not," Neil shrugged. Tess wasn't sure she fully believed him and made a note to ask Jessica's friends and family for their perspective. For the time being, she decided to change course.

"Where is the dog?" Tess asked, "I noticed a leash by the garage door."

"Max? He passed away two weeks ago. Cancer," sighed Neil, "He was Jessica's dog mostly. We've been so devastated that we haven't gotten around to putting his things away."

"I'm sorry to hear that," Tess empathized. "It's never easy losing a pet."

"No, it isn't," Neil replied, staring glumly at the coffee table in front of him. Tess decided to change the subject back to the night of July fourth.

"So, after the deputies left on the night of the fourth, did you and Jessica go anywhere? Do anything? See anyone?"

"No," Neil stated, "we stayed here all night. After the cops came, it kind of dampened the mood for our evening. If I remember correctly, I finished the movie—made sure to turn it down, of course—and I think she just read all evening. Just like any other night really."

"When you called 911, you mentioned there was blood somewhere? Can you tell me exactly what happened this morning when you got home? What did you see, hear—that type of thing."

"I got home around eight from the gym. Parked the truck in the garage like normal and when I got out to come inside the house, I noticed the door to the house was open a little. At first, I didn't think too much about it. Jessica is always coming and going from the garage and forgetting to shut the door. Anyway, when I came into the kitchen, I saw the vase shattered on the floor and the chair knocked over. There was blood on the floor."

"I didn't see any blood when I was just in there," Tess commented. "You didn't happen to clean it up, did you Mr. Slaydon? Your kitchen appears to be rather spotless."

He sighed. "There was blood on the floor. Not a lot but enough that it caught my attention. I wiped it up without thinking. I– I'm a little OCD when it comes to cleanliness."

"That's fine and all, but Mr. Slaydon, why would you clean up possible evidence when your wife was missing?"

"I didn't know she was missing at the time. I wasn't even thinking like that. There was a mess and I cleaned it up."

Since when was a drip of blood 'a mess'? Tess wondered, somewhat alarmed.

Tess looked at him skeptically. "So why did you clean up the blood but not the flower vase? There is water everywhere. That didn't catch your eye?"

"I didn't see it at first. She bought herself the flowers for Fourth of July, and said they made the house more cheerful. I didn't notice they'd fallen over until I walked around the island."

"So then where was the blood?"

"On the floor in front of the sink. It was just a little bit really." He held up his hands and formed a circle with his fingers. "Like this," he added, indicating the three inch or so circle.

"Okay, so you wipe up the blood, ignore the vase and the tipped over chair. Then what happened?"

"I started to panic, and I ran through the house calling for Jessica. I couldn't find her. She wasn't anywhere to be found. Her purse is here, but not her. She wouldn't leave without it. Somebody took her."

"Why would somebody want to kidnap your wife, Mr. Slaydon?"

"I don't know. Maybe they ...." he looked up at Tess, panic etched in his face. "Maybe they were trying to steal the baby!" He began to breathe faster, almost panting. "I've heard of that happening before. Oh my God ... Oh my God ...."

"Mr. Slaydon, I need you to take a deep breath," Tess said, hopping up and crossing over to where Neil sat, rocking back and forth, lost in his thoughts.

Fearing he was going to hyperventilate, Tess nodded to Deputy Kennedy, the liaison officer, who'd been standing by witnessing the conversation quietly.

Kennedy nodded and stepped from the room to radio in for a medic.

Tess squatted down in front of Slaydon. "Just breathe Mr. Slaydon. Help is on the way."

Neil Slaydon was too upset to calm down though and as Tess watched, the man began sobbing uncontrollably and his panting breaths only increased. Falling to the floor to lie in a fetal position, his face turned a strange purple color. Concerned, Tess called for Miles, who was still outside on the porch.

When Miles materialized, he immediately came and helped Tess pull Neil Slaydon back up onto the couch. Neil took in great gulps of air as he tried to calm himself.

Trying to console the broken man crying in front of her, Tess made shushing sounds as though calming a small child after a nightmare.

They would have to question Neil Slaydon further once he was in a better mental state. Tess sighed to herself as Neil made quiet weeping sounds next to her. Eventually she could hear the distant sounds of the ambulance as they approached.

Within moments, two EMTs entered the home and began assessing Neil Slaydon. Given his current state of emotional turmoil and the unhealthy pallor of his skin, Tess was relieved when they loaded him up to take him to the hospital for observation.

"Well, that was rough," Miles commented as the ambulance pulled away from the curb. "Guess we will have to finish with him later."

"Agree," Tess said, as she surveyed the room around her. Nothing out of the ordinary stood out to her. Just a plain, simple living room, devoid of any knick knacks or color. Still curious, Tess decided to continue her walk-through of the house, looking for anything obvious that would give a hint to Jessica Slaydon's whereabouts.

She'd need an actual reason to go digging through the entirety of the Slaydon's possessions. But there were extenuating circumstances at play–Jessica was pregnant, making her situation all the more dire. Knowing she was covered by the plain-view exception for the search warrant, and the fact that Neil had told her she could search, Tess made a quick pass through of the house.

The upstairs, equally drab and boring as the downstairs decor, was all spotless and wrinkle free. The bed was made with military precision, the carpeting spotless. Nothing out of place.

Tess stood in the doorway of the master bedroom for a moment, casting a glance around her, looking for anything untoward. She saw nothing that stood out at her. Not even a suitcase or overnight bag. Neil had suggested that Jessica was planning on visiting her family for a few days. Unless she was going to pack the morning she left, Tess was curious as to where Jessica's bags were. But hadn't Neil told her he'd caught Jessica packing a bag? Making a mental note to check vehicles, Tess walked over and opened the closet door. Flipping on the light, she took in the stark differences on either side. One half of the closet was nice, orderly, and even color coded. Everything was hung with care or folded perfectly. It was obviously Neil's share of the space. Even his vast array of shoes was neatly lined up on short shelves under his hanging clothes.

Jessica's half of the closet was a totally different scenario. There were various shoes and clothes piled in heaps all over the floor, making it difficult to navigate. Clothes were shoved on shelves and falling off of hangers. A couple of cardboard boxes sat shoved against the back wall with "Jess's Winter Clothes" scrawled on the side in sloppy black Sharpie marker.

Tess made a face to herself at the mess. What an interesting couple, she mused. The Slaydon's appeared to be complete opposites—he was very organized, she very chaotic. Unsure if that meant anything at all or was just an observation, Tess made a mental note before moving on.

She made her way to the bathroom and flipped on the light. Again, she was surprised by how spotless the house was. White bath towels were rolled up and laid neatly on a shelf over the toilet like in a hotel room. The marble countertop gleamed in the overhead vanity light—the chrome faucet spotless.

To her right, Tess took in the clawfoot bathtub, the interior bright white, the outside painted a dark blue. Across the top of the bathtub sat a chrome tray holding a small bar of soap and a sea sponge loofah. The shower curtain, white of course, was bunched up at the end of the tub. The interior of the tub was dry to the touch, the porcelain cool on Tess's skin.

Nothing seemed out of place, so with a sigh, Tess flipped off the light and exited the bathroom. Making her way down the hall, she quickly looked into the remaining rooms: two more bedrooms and another bathroom.

The first bedroom appeared to be used as an office. A large wooden desk dominated the small room, a laptop laying closed on top. Various boxes from the recent move sat stacked in the corner and along the walls. Labels like "Jess's books" and "Xmas decor" were scrawled across them.

Without a search warrant, Tess wasn't allowed to take the laptop and her annoyance flared. Where was Jessica Slaydon? She'd put in a request for one as soon as she could. She also still needed to find Jessica's phone.

Pulling open a flap of one of the boxes marked books, she glanced inside at the contents. It was filled with romance novels, and pretty spicy ones if the covers indicated anything. Stifling a grin, Tess closed the flaps back before heading to the desk.

Opening a couple of drawers, she found nothing exciting: some pens, paper clips, a broken pencil, old student loan paperwork, copies of receipts and mortgage paperwork. The desk itself was pretty empty. Perhaps because it wasn't unpacked yet from the move? Or had someone cleared it out on purpose?

Tess stood there for a moment, her mind whirling as she mulled over everything she'd seen so far. Walking over to the office door she looked back at the room's interior once more, still deep in thought.

Nothing out of the ordinary stood out to her upstairs, though something about the kitchen seemed staged, but by whom? Had Jessica staged the scene in an effort to escape her life? But why? Because she wanted a new start? Or because she was trying to escape Neil? Was he the loving husband he portrayed or something darker all together?

With a frustrated grunt, Tess pushed off the door frame of the office and went to check out the last bedroom. The nursery.

The walls appeared to have been recently painted a light butter yellow, the scent of fresh paint still permeating the small room. A white crib sat flush with the wall, a small jungle animal mobile dangling overhead. A matching changing table sat to the left of the crib and to the right, a wooden glider chair with light gray cushions.

The closet door was shut and stacked next to it were two boxes of diapers. Tess thought it was strange that the diapers were stacked out in the open and not in the closet as nothing else in the room was out of place. Even the knitted afghan was folded nicely and draped over the edge of the crib.

She opened the closet door and found it mostly empty, except for some random baby clothes hanging from tiny white hangers. On the floor sat gift bags full of blankets and toys. *Baby shower gifts?* Tess wondered as she closed the door back.

Standing there for a moment, surveying the room, thinking about the couple who had decorated it, preparing for their new arrival, Tess began wondering. Who were the Slaydons? Were they a loving couple, bent on caring for eachother and the life they had created? Or were they merely going through the motions, like so many others, by trying to get through life and being just happy enough that they weren't completely miserable? Two ships passing in the night while living different, solitary lives during the day?

Heading back downstairs, Tess decided to check out the garage. As she made her way through the kitchen, she noticed the purse hanging by the door again. Assuming it was Jessica's, Tess took it down and carried it over to the kitchen island. The top was unzipped so Tess poked around inside before dumping it out and looking through the contents: chapstick, nail file, coupons for a local grocery store, half a bottle of Tylenol, two lint-covered hard candies, a wallet, and $1.42 in loose change.

Opening the wallet, Tess flipped through the contents found there: an Ohio driver's license for Jessica Elizabeth Slaydon, a well-worn library card, one debit card, two gift cards to local box stores, and a crisp twenty-dollar bill. Two wrinkled receipts had been shoved in the zippered change section along with another quarter and two pennies.

Unfolding the receipts, Tess scanned them both. One was from Target for $72.12 dated June 28th, and the other was from Barnes and Noble Bookstore for $29.32 dated July 2nd. Nothing exciting shouted out to Tess, but she took photographs of the contents anyway just in case. Then, shoving the contents back into the purse, she hung it back up by the door to the garage.

Pondering over the fact that Jessica Slaydon was missing and hadn't taken her purse with her bothered Tess. And where was Jessica's cell phone? Did the missing woman have it with her? Was it somewhere in the house? Had someone taken it?

Moving out to the garage, Tess was once again taken back by the cleanliness of the area. Everything was stored in containers, labeled properly and lined up on shelves along the back of the two-car garage. Along the far wall hung a weed-eater, shovel, and rake. From large rubber-covered hooks attached to the ceiling beams hung two adult-sized bicycles–one red, the other green.

To Tess's left, along the interior garage wall, was a small chest freezer and a sturdy plastic shelving unit holding Cosco-sized pantry and snack items along with some various beverages.

Lifting the lid to the freezer, Tess found some frozen vegetables, packs of ground beef, and three pizzas. Otherwise, the freezer was empty.

Turning to the center of the garage, Tess looked over the two parked vehicles taking up the majority of the space. The first, most likely Neil's, was a black Chevy pickup, newer model, windows rolled up. The second car had to be Jessica's as evidenced by the seat covers sporting a large pink 'J' on them. The car, a dark red Honda Civic, had multiple prisms and beaded necklaces hanging from the rearview mirror.

Stepping up to the driver's side door, Tess tried the handle. It was unlocked much to her relief. Opening the door resulted in an empty fast food cup rolling out and landing loudly on the cool concrete floor, causing Tess to jump a little at the sudden sound.

Unfortunately, the cup wasn't the only piece of trash in the vehicle. The front passenger side floor well was full of various fast food bags, junk mail, a pair of flip-flops, and a Hello Kitty tank top. The back seat was just as messy but in the center of the seat was a brand-new looking baby seat, all ready to go for the big day.

Flipping through the detritus and finding nothing untoward, Tess popped the trunk and went to open it. A baby stroller, the kind that folds up for easy transport, sat in her way so, moving it aside, she made her way to the trunk.

With a deep breath, Tess opened the trunk in one swift movement.

It was empty except for a pair of jumper cables, an ice scraper for frosty winter windshields, and a red OSU hooded sweatshirt.

She'd have the crime scene technicians perform a deeper search of both vehicles but for now, she'd finish her search with a cursory glance at Neil's truck before moving on.

Looking over the bed of the truck, Tess noticed immediately that the truck, like the house, was pristine. Not a fingerprint, smudge, or mud droplet, could be found on or around the exterior of the vehicle and the bed was immaculate.

Trying the doors, Tess sighed when she found they were locked. Cupping her face with her hands, she pressed her face close to the window glass and peered in. Just like the outside, the inside was showroom-drive-off-the-lot clean. Had Neil just had his truck detailed in an effort to rid it of evidence? Or was he just that clean?

Suddenly, one of the crime scene technicians came up to the doorway leading back into the kitchen.

"Sorry to interrupt, Detective Dane," the woman said, "but there is something I think you should see."

Following the crime scene tech into the dining room, Tess came to a halt in the doorway from the kitchen and looked where the technician was pointing.

"There," the woman pointed, indicating a brownish red drop of congealed blood on the edge of a picture frame hanging on the wall near the kitchen table. "Blood spatter. It tested positive for blood."

"Can you tell how old it is?" Tess asked, leaning in to inspect the sample more.

"Not that old," the CSI said. "The drop was a decent size. Mostly dried out but not too cracked and crumbly. Preliminary tests show that it is indeed human blood. We'll send it to the lab for further DNA analysis."

Tess nodded grimly. This finding didn't bode well for Jessica Slaydon. Sure, the blood could be from anyone, for a plethora of different reasons, but the facts remained. There was a missing woman who'd recently called that house a home, who'd hung that picture on the wall with care, and until the source of the blood was determined, no one was above suspicion.

For some unknown reason, Tess did not trust Neil Slaydon. He was hiding something and she meant to find out exactly what it was.

Chapter Eleven

Thursday, July 7th, 2:15 p.m.

While the crime scene technicians finished processing the Slaydon's home, Tess and Miles decided to divide and conquer the neighborhood canvas and then meet back at the station to debrief. Miles went left out of the Slaydon's driveway while Tess made her way over to Harold Newton's home.

As the sun glared down on her, Tess gazed up at the Newton home, so much like the Slaydon home next door. Cookie cutter neighborhoods had never been Tess's dream place to live, but this neighborhood seemed quiet and peaceful, despite there being a lot of police activity and people searching for a missing pregnant woman.

Taking in the well-manicured lawn and the freshly painted front door, Tess swiftly walked up the front sidewalk, mindful of the curtain flutter in the living room window. Someone was watching her approach.

Ringing the doorbell, Tess jumped slightly when the door was flung open almost immediately.

"Officer," the man inside greeted, extending his hand to Tess. She shook it to be polite before discreetly wiping her hand off on her pant leg. Typically not one for enjoying a handshake, Tess cringed inwardly at Mr. Newton's sweaty, limp wristed one.

"Detective Tess Dane with the Swain County Sheriff's office," she introduced herself, eyeing the bespectacled man. "Are you Harold Newton?"

"The one and only!" he exclaimed, sounding rather proud of himself. "I figured you'd be by to talk to me, on account that the neighbor woman is missing."

"And how do you know that?" Tess asked, "It's only just now been reported."

Mr. Newton blushed slightly. "On the scanner," he said, embarrassed for being caught snooping.

Tess rolled her eyes inwardly, annoyed that the random public had police scanners. Even worse when the media did and showed up, adding to the fray. Tess glanced over her shoulder, just to check for news crews. They were good ... for now.

"So, you like to keep up on the latest news in the neighborhood?" Tess said, lightly camouflaging the fact that she basically called him a busy body. He didn't seem to be bothered by her evaluation of him and he nodded proudly.

"Yes, ma'am," he rocked back and forth on his feet, chest out. "Those who don't stay in the know are those that get the wool pulled over their eyes." Not totally disagreeing with him, but not wanting to get off track, Tess ignored his comment.

"When was the last time you saw Neil and Jessica Slaydon?"

"I just saw him get carried away on a stretcher–is he going to be okay?" Newton asked, straining to see over Tess's tall shoulders.

"He's fine," Tess commented distractedly, trying to pull Harold Newton back to the conversation at hand. "And Mrs. Slaydon?"

"I haven't seen her since ...." he paused, thinking. "Fourth of July. Before I called in about them fighting."

"And she seemed well? Did you speak with her?"

"Sure did. In fact, she and the dog, Max, were out on their back deck, messing with the grill," Newton said thoughtfully. "I was drinking my coffee and reading on my deck. She seemed okay. I remember she smiled and waved at me, said something about it looking like it was going to be a pretty day."

"So, just small talk then? Nothing out of the ordinary?"

"No, not really. They just moved in a few months ago and they kind of stay to themselves. I tried being neighborly, and took one of my wife's pecan pies over there, but they didn't seem to be receptive."

"Did they take the pie?" Tess asked curiously.

"Mr. Slaydon wasn't going to at first, but then Mrs. Slaydon smiled and took it. She was nice but quiet. He on the other hand ...." Harold Newton scratched his balding head and then shoved his glasses back up his nose.

"Was Neil Slaydon rude or threatening to you? Or just not very outgoing?"

"Not friendly, borderline rude. He didn't seem dangerous or threatening. More like ... like everyone was annoying him and he didn't want to be bothered."

"Gotcha, okay." Tess nodded. She made some notes to herself before moving the conversation along.

"Have you seen or heard anyone or anything out of the ordinary in the past few weeks?"

Harold Newton leaned up against the door frame, looking over Tess's shoulders again. "I heard arguing from time to time—but nothing over the top, nothing like on the Fourth of July."

"So, nobody new milling around?" Tess asked, flipping back through her notes. The older man shook his head.

"Nobody I've noticed," Newton shrugged, "but I've been working a lot the past couple of days. I retire at the end of the month so I'm trying to train my replacement. Over forty years with the business and I'm stuck training a kid to replace me." He shook his head in dismay.

"You mentioned you saw Max recently?" Tess changed the subject, suddenly remembering something the man had mentioned a few moments before.

"Oh, Max! Their dog!" Harold Newton exclaimed fondly. "He's such a good boy. Big sucker! A Newfoundland mix!" The older man gave a hearty laugh, "He'll slobber on you but he means no harm,"

"He sounds perfect. When was the last time you saw him?" Tess asked, concern filling her voice, considering Mr. Newton had just claimed to have seen the dog three days ago. "I noticed a leash inside but didn't see a dog—or any animal for that matter." Tess was suddenly worried about the well-being of a family pet caught up in this mess.

"Oh, he's always around. Let me think ...." he squinted his eyes, deep in thought. "Yesterday? No. Maybe two days ago?"

"Thanks, Mr. Newton." Tess nodded. "If you remember anything else you think may be useful, please give me a call." She handed him her business card and said goodbye. As she made her way to the next house, her mind was spinning. Where was the dog? Was he with Jessica? Or somewhere else entirely?

Later that afternoon, Tess found herself sitting at an empty conference table waiting on Deputies Miles and Scafferty to join her with Sheriff Malone and present what they'd all learned about the missing pregnant woman, Jessica Slaydon.

Flipping through her notes, Tess eyed the photo she'd been given by Neil of his wife, Jessica. The woman was stunning to say the least. Her long, pale blond hair hung down her back and her smile had a movie star quality to it. Perfectly straight, white teeth–either good genetics or lots of dental care–complimented her face. Her blue eyes sparkled mischievously under well-shaped brows. The only blemish, if you cared to call it that, seemed to be a scar that cut a jagged path through her left eyebrow.

"Learn anything important?" Malone asked as he slid into an empty seat across from Tess and studied the photo in her hands.

"Neil Slaydon is a liar," Tess commented, as she set the photo down and continued leafing through her notes.

"Care to explain?"

Just then, Miles and Scafferty entered the room, mumbling apologies for being late, even though they weren't really, and sat down.

"Tess here was just about to tell us why she thinks Neil Slaydon is a liar," Malone said, scooting his chair to make more leg room for himself.

"He is," Scafferty agreed. Miles nodded in agreement and muttered under his breath.

"Where to begin ...." Tess sighed, sitting up straight to stretch her spine. "The first thing I knew for sure was a lie were the flowers in the kitchen. Neil claimed that Jessica bought them on the 4th of July to 'brighten up the house'. I found a receipt and wrapper from said flowers in their kitchen trash that was dated just this morning. It was almost like he put the flowers in the vase to make it look as though Jessica did it this morning but then slipped up and said she did it three days ago. As in she's possibly actually been 'missing' for three days. I'm not exactly sure at this point."

The men nodded and murmured their agreements that it sounded suspicious.

"We did get the callout there on the fourth," Scafferty offered, tapping his fingertips on the tabletop in thought. "That's the domestic we were telling you about, Dane."

"I read your report," Tess nodded. "Sounds like Neil Slaydon was just as much of a peach today as he was then. I don't know if he did anything to his wife yet or not, but I can say this. He's difficult to deal with but we can't arrest him just for being a lying asshole. If we could do that I would have arrested my mother years ago."

Snickers from the men filled the room as they all knew that Tess's mom had jumped ship the minute her husband, Tess's father, became diagnosed with early onset dementia, leaving a then teenaged Tess to fend for herself and care for her father alone.

"Okay, gentlemen, settle down. Back to the missing pregnant woman ...." Tess scolded gently, an amused grin on her face. "Back to reasons why I think Slaydon is lying."

She tapped the police file in front of her with her index finger for emphasis.

"Second, was the issue with the dog, Max. Neil claimed that the dog had passed away two weeks ago, and they were 'devastated' and yet Mr. Harold Newman, the next-door neighbor, claims he just saw the dog three days ago. I don't know where the dog is now, but I plan on calling all the veterinarians and shelters in the area until I find more information about his whereabouts."

"Let's not forget about the kitchen being staged and the blood being cleaned up," Miles grumped, rolling his eyes.

"Wait a minute. This guy cleaned up evidence?" Malone asked incredulously. Tess nodded, equally annoyed at Neil Slaydon.

"Yes. Mr. Slaydon claims he cleaned up the blood out of habit, because it was a mess. If you ask me, he has OCD or something. The house is spotless, and he seems to like things a certain way," Tess thought aloud, "Like some kind of cleaning compulsion. That's a thing, right?"

Miles and Malone shrugged.

"I don't really care if people are slobs or neat freaks, as long as they don't destroy evidence!" Malone frustratedly exclaimed, running his fingers through his dark blond hair.

"Well, he could have felt compelled to clean or he could have basically detailed his house in an effort to get rid of evidence," Tess sighed. "All I know is this. We have a missing pregnant woman, an unlikeable husband who's been caught in a couple of lies already and confirmed human blood spatter found at the scene. I think we need to call a press conference, get more uniforms out there pounding pavement looking for her. Thoughts?"

"I agree. I've already got an APB out for her within Swain County and surrounding areas but I've also contacted BCI and The Ohio State Highway Patrol to keep a lookout. Janet Carmichael will be doing a piece on the case tonight for the local six o'clock news, but I think you're right. This is bigger than just an overdue adult who decided not to call home. Jessica Slaydon is pregnant, missing, and we found blood at the scene," Malone sighed. "Let's call a press conference for this first thing tomorrow morning with the bigger news stations out of Columbus if we don't find anything by then. Jessica will have been missing for nearly 24 hours by that point. Hopefully though, she sees the local news segment tonight and decides to come home."

"We can only hope," Tess agreed. After canvasing the houses nearest to the Slaydons, Tess had requested a handful of other officers to continue the canvass onto other streets in the neighborhood as well as calling area hospitals inquiring about Jessica or any pregnant Jane Does. Tess had contacted Dr. Abby Summers, the ME, along with area funeral homes and county coroners but no one had come across anyone fitting Jessica's description.

Tess had even called Jessica's mother, Lydia Fontaine, but had to leave a message on voicemail.

"Also ... and say what you will about this ..." Tess said, "but I asked Slaydon if he or his wife went anywhere after you two left their house on the fourth. He said no. But ... he also looked familiar to me, like I had seen him somewhere. It's been running through my mind all day and then it finally hit me."

"Well ...?" Miles leaned in, curious for the answer.

"He's Mr. Pushy Pants," Tess announced, a look of smug satisfaction spreading across her face. A grin spread across her face as Malone's face lit up in understanding.

"Who?" Scafferty asked, wrinkling his nose and looking around at everyone sitting at the table, apparently lost.

"The pushy, rude customer at Piedmont's Pay Less," Tess reminded them. "You know, that guy that was all huffy and nervous sweating all over everything? When I met Neil today, I noticed he looked familiar and when it finally clicked in my brain, I consulted the surveillance video from the store. It is definitely him. And he was even wearing the same gym pants today! Now, why would he lie to me about staying in all night unless he had something to hide? From the video, it looks as though he used cash to pay for his purchases, but I plan on tracking down Liam, one of the employees, to verify it was Slaydon."

Chapter Twelve

Friday, July 8th, 11:23 a.m.

Tess sat working at her computer, trying to finish up her report from the grocery store robbery. Her stomach was growling, and she was slightly annoyed with herself for not letting Deputy Cooper grab her some food when he offered. Instead, she took a swig of her tepid coffee and was abysmally disappointed.

Sighing, she leaned back in her chair and stared up at the ceiling, frustrated and stressed. She had reports to finish and a missing woman to track down. Where had Jessica Slaydon gone? Was she and her baby safe?

When Jessica failed to call home after the local news did their segment on her the night before, Malone had held a press conference with several of the news stations out of Columbus and surrounding areas in an effort to garnish more information about her whereabouts. Neil, still distraught, had stumbled his way through pleading with the public for any information about his wife's whereabouts. Moments after the segment ended, tips came flooding into the police station. Several officers had been tasked with manning the phones while others began following up on possible new leads.

Someone had called in claiming to have seen Jessica in a bright beam of light and being sucked up into a flying saucer. Another had claimed to have seen her as far away as Flagstaff, Arizona. Glad she wasn't meant to handle the tipline, Tess continued on with her investigation. If the officers answering the calls felt any tips seemed pertinent, then she would follow up on them.

Tess was still waiting on the warrant to come through for the Slaydons cell phone records. Hopefully they would shed some light on the whereabouts of the young mother. The Slaydon's bank records hadn't shown anything out of the ordinary. Just a mortgage on their new home, a car payment on Neil's two year old Chevy Silverado, and roughly $13,000 in credit card debt. What Tess found interesting was that according to the financials, all the credit card accounts had both partners' names on them ... except one. That particular credit card was only in Jessica's name and Tess wanted to know why. Curious, Tess had obtained the proper paperwork and had contacted the credit card company for the account only in Jessica Slaydon's name. Hopefully she would be able to glean some important information from it that would point her in the right direction.

As she sat at her desk, thinking about it, she hit the refresh button on her email to see if she had any updates. Nothing. With a frustrated sigh, she picked up her cellphone and was about to text Denny when her office phone buzzed. It was Bertie, the receptionist.

"This is Dane. What's up, Bertie?"

"Detective Dane, there is a woman here to see you. Lydia Fontaine. Said she's Jessica Slaydon's mother."

Surprised, yet please, Tess said, "Awesome, I'll be up to get her. Thanks, Bertie."

Friday, July 8th, 11:35 a.m.

"Mrs. Fontaine?" Tess inquired as she approached an older gray haired woman standing in the lobby absently looking at an anti-drug poster. At the sound of Tess's voice, the woman turned, a small, sad smile crossing her face. She wore a fuchsia knee-length dress and matching sandals, her white purse tucked under her arm.

"Detective Dane?" she asked, looking Tess up and down. Tess nodded and offered her hand.

"No offense, but I thought you'd be older," Lydia said, a spark of humor in her pale blue eyes. She shook Tess's hand and smiled.

"None taken," Tess smiled back. "My dad was the older Detective Dane. He's retired now though." She nodded to the woman to follow her. They quickly made their way down a narrow hallway to Tess's small office.

"Have a seat, Mrs. Fontaine. Coffee? Water?" Tess offered.

"I'm good, thank you," Lydia said, taking a seat in the chair in front of Tess's desk.

"All right. If you change your mind, let me know," Tess encouraged as she slid into her own seat behind the desk. "I'm guessing you got my voicemail yesterday and are here to talk about Jessica," she added as a statement rather than a question.

"Yes. I forgot to charge my phone yesterday and just got your message this morning. I was so worried I didn't even catch you saying that you were the detective! I just heard that Jessica was missing, and I panicked. I don't think I've ever driven that fast. Have you found her yet? Found anything?" Lydia asked, tucking her chin length gray hair behind her ears. Her eyes were red and puffy as though she'd been crying recently. Tess could imagine that this wasn't easy for her.

"No, we haven't found her yet. When was the last time you heard from your daughter?"

"She called me on the Fourth of July sometime in the morning. You see, I live up near Cleveland and Neil and Jessica usually come up there to visit over the holiday weekend. Well, this year, she didn't want to because of being so far along in her pregnancy. I told her that was fine, I understood. Besides, I am ... was ... planning on coming down for the birth and staying a few weeks. You know, to help out."

"That's kind of you to do. I'm sure she could use the help." Tess commented, making sure she spoke of Jessica in the present tense, as though everything was fine. She did not want to snuff out the woman's hope without having any hard evidence pointing to her daughter's demise.

Lydia smiled slightly, her face sad. "It's just not like her to run off, like some people are suggesting. Jessica isn't like that. She wouldn't put her baby at risk either." She sighed then, covering her face with her hands for a moment and then looking back up at Tess. "If anybody did anything to Jessica, it was him."

"Him?"

"Her husband, Neil," Lydia said, her mouth puckering up like she'd tasted something sour.

"Oh? And what makes you think that?" Tess said, grabbing a pen and some paper, jotting notes down to herself.

"He's a liar and an asshole," Lydia Fontaine accused bluntly. Tess looked back up at the woman, surprised at her open disdain for her son-in-law.

"Okay ... and what makes you feel like that?" Tess asked, watching the woman closely.

"I've never liked him, not one bit," the woman admitted, staring at Tess in earnest. "I know, I know ... no one is good enough for your baby, but before you judge me, hear me out."

When Tess nodded in understanding, Lydia continued, "When she brought him home one year for Thanksgiving, I thought he was okay at first. You know, a little quiet, maybe slightly backwards but I just chalked it up to him being nervous because he didn't know any of us yet. But then ..." she paused, looking down at her hands for a moment.

"Then?" Tess prompted gently.

"Then I heard him talking to her when they thought they were alone," she paused for a moment, thinking. "I'd asked Jessica to go to the garage and grab another carton of eggnog from the fridge we have out there—Costco overflow, you know—and so she did. After a few minutes of waiting, there was still no Jessica or the eggnog. I went to look for her and that's when I overheard them talking."

"What were they talking about?"

"It was more that *he* was doing the talking. She sounded like she was trying not to cry. She kept sniffling. They couldn't see me from where I was standing but I heard him. He was telling her she was going to do something–what I don't know–but from her tears I got the distinct impression that she wasn't comfortable with it."

"Do you have any idea what it could have been?" Tess asked, jotting down more notes.

"Who knows. The man is a neat freak, one of those OCD people," huffed Lydia. "Jessica was the opposite, so he was probably yelling about something not being clean enough."

"Well, having a documented medical diagnosis of OCD does not make someone a criminal," Tess inserted, trying to refrain from rolling her eyes and letting her frustrations at the comment show.

"I know that!" Lydia lightly snapped. "I'm just telling you that because ... well, he was always making snide remarks about how she went about doing things. Like nothing was good enough, or clean enough."

"Did you ever see him be violent with her? See marks or bruises anywhere?"

"No, nothing out of the ordinary, but then again, I only saw her a handful of times a year because we live a few hours away from one another."

"Did she ever confide in you? About the state of their marriage? If she was happy or not?" Tess asked, taking a quick sip of her water while watching Lydia over the top of her water bottle.

"We aren't overly open with each other like some mothers and daughters, but we are close. She never said she was unhappy or anything. When I did get to see her, she always seemed sad. I honestly don't know if it was because of Neil, or the fact that they lost Adam."

"Adam? Their son, right?" Tess asked, empathy filling her voice.

"What about him?" Lydia breathed, suddenly looking as though she'd start crying again.

"Tell me about that, about when you found out he'd passed."

"I was devastated. Completely broken, " Lydia nearly whispered, her eyes filling with unshed tears. "We all were excited for his arrival. Had the nurseries all decorated. There was one at my house and one at Jessica's. Mine was decorated in John Deere tractors with cow stuffies ...." Her voice trailed off, her thoughts caught in the past. "When they said that he was born ... dead ... I didn't know what to think. I thought it was all some sick joke someone was playing on us. Adam couldn't be gone, but he was. Whether we liked it or not, Adam was truly gone forever before he'd even arrived." Her voice broke then, the tears finally coursing down her cheeks.

Tess silently handed her a tissue and gave her a moment to compose herself before pressing on.

"How did Neil seem during that time?" Tess asked after the woman had calmed down enough to continue.

"He seemed just as upset as the rest of us. Maybe even more so. He just isolated himself, kept to the bedroom for days. I stayed at their house for a couple of weeks to help them out. Jessica was trying to recover physically and emotionally, so I was trying to make it as easy on her as possible. I'd cook and clean, take food up to their bedroom because Neil rarely came out. Jessica would come down occasionally and spend time with me. Most of the time, we'd sit in silence, and she'd be staring straight ahead like she was in some kind of trance. It was a dark time for our family."

"Did Jessica ever seek professional help after the loss of Adam?"

"Yes, she started going to therapy. The doctor put her on some antidepressants. At first, I thought it might have helped a little, but she never seemed to recover completely. My sunny daughter was replaced by a dark, moody one." Lydia paused to wipe her nose again. "Jessica was never the same again."

"I'm sorry to hear that. Truly I am," Tess gave the woman a sympathetic look. "I want you to know that we are doing everything possible to find your daughter."

"And what exactly are you doing now?" Lydia asked gruffly. She sighed and quickly added, "I didn't mean for that to sound so rude. I just want to know if I can help at all."

"It's okay," Tess assured, leaning back in her chair. "I am currently waiting for the cell phone records for both Jessica and Neil to come through. Hopefully that will shed some light on the days leading up to her disappearance."

"I tried calling the local hospital," Lydia offered, changing the subject. "You know, just in case Jessica had been in an accident or gone into labor early ...."

"We have, too. No luck," Tess agreed. "I have an APB out for anybody showing up at hospitals in the tri-state area with Jessica's name or any pregnant Jane Doe. So far, I've got nothing. We've called every hospital locally and in Columbus. She's just not there."

Tess watched as fresh tears pooled in Lydia's eyes. She felt horrible for Mrs. Fontaine, not knowing where her daughter was. Tess had no children of her own but knew she would be a basket case if she didn't know where her dog, Otter was. Which reminded her ....

"Do you know where Max is?" she asked Jessica's mother. The woman looked stricken and stared up at Tess.

"He's not at home? Jessica would never have left without him. He's her first baby, even before Adam." The tears finally spilled over and ran down her cheeks. "If he's not home, does that mean he's with her? Maybe if someone did take Jessica, they took the dog too? Or maybe, just maybe, Jessica left on her own volition to get away from her husband and took the dog with her? Maybe she's just laying low. Maybe she will call me." She pulled her cell phone out and began looking through it, most likely looking for any missed calls. Tess sighed. She hated to give the woman false hope, but the mystery of the dog's whereabouts remained concerning. Certainly, Neil wouldn't kill an innocent dog, if he had indeed killed his wife ... would he? Tess knew there was so much more to learn about the couple and as the days progressed, the case just got more and more disturbing.

"We will look for the dog, too," Tess comforted, leaning across the desk toward the broken mother before her. "He may be with Jessica. If we find the dog, maybe he will lead us to her. Don't lose hope."

"Now what do we do?" Lydia's shoulders sagged. "I have to do something or I'm going to go crazy."

"I get it," Tess empathized. "Are you staying in town for a while?"

The older woman nodded, "Yes, down at the Dew Drop Inn on Rte. 72. What a name for a motel ...." She shook her head, causing her earrings to dance on her lobes.

"If I find out anything, I will contact you. And if you have a picture of Max you could text me, I'd appreciate it," Tess stated. "Do you have the cell phone I called you on with you?"

Lydia Fontaine nodded, her face full of sorrow, her shoulders slumped.

"Thank you for coming by and speaking with me, Mrs. Fontaine. It's been very helpful."

"No, thank you, Detective Dane. For everything you're doing to find my baby." Fresh tears began sliding down

Lydia's face. She slowly stood up and, with another broken smile, she exited the office.

Chapter Thirteen

Friday, July 8th, 2:15 p.m.

As Tess wound her way down a rural route on her way to the dog shelter in search of the Slaydon's dog, her cell phone chimed from where it was harnessed to her dashboard. Denny was trying to FaceTime. Against her better judgment, knowing that distracted driving was against the law, she tapped 'accept' anyway as it had been way too long since she'd seen him.

His handsome face appeared on her screen as she greeted him with a smile.

"Hey there," he said, his smooth deep voice filling her Jeep.

"Hey yourself," Tess grinned, tearing her eyes from the road long enough to smile at him. "Whatcha doin today?"

"Paperwork mostly," Denny sighed. He appeared to be sitting in his Tahoe, but unlike Tess, was parked somewhere. "We are winding down the Cleveland case."

"We?" Tess asked, curiously, keeping her eyes on the road ahead of her.

"Yeah, Lindsey, my new intern," Denny responded. Turning to someone in his passenger seat, he said, "Say hello to Tess."

"Hi, Tess," came a sultry female voice that Tess instantly disliked. "I've heard a lot about you."

Tess glanced at the screen then to see a young, beautiful blond. Tess felt something stirring in her belly, and it wasn't good. Jealousy. How could she compete for Denny's attention when he was around *her* all day?

That's funny, Tess thought, *I haven't heard about you.*

Inwardly she was kicking herself for being a bitch. She wasn't usually one for being petty, but this had caught her off guard and she wasn't too keen about it.

"Hi, Lindsey," Tess smiled, despite herself. "Are you learning a lot of hands-on stuff?"

"Yes! Actually, doing this stuff in the field is so much better than reading about how to do it in class. Haywood here is an awesome mentor," Lindsey complimented, casting a glance at Denny.

"Yeah, he is," Tess had to agree. "Did he tell you he was one of my instructors at the academy and then was my training partner rookie year?" *See Lindsey, Denny and I have a history together ....*

"He did. And he said you just made detective and caught The Torture Killer?" Lindsey exclaimed, "I'd love to hear about that!"

"Sure, we can do that," Tess agreed, determined to take some of the bite out of her voice. Lindsey, though beautiful and spending a ton of time with Denny, seemed to be genuinely interested in her job and remained professional, despite Tess's prickly demeanor. Tess was just being jealous, and she knew it. She wanted to be able to spend more time with Denny, and here Lindsey got to spend multiple days a week with him.

"I'll tell you one thing I've learned so far! Working the crime scene is way more interesting than doing all the paperwork. I'll just leave that part to my partner," Lindsey joked and grinned over at Denny.

He seemed oblivious and laughed, shaking his head as he picked his cup up from the console and took a sip.

Tess stared at the screen for a second too long and when she dragged her gaze back to the road, she realized she was left of center. Turning the steering wheel sharply, she over-corrected and almost went into the ditch looming at the side of the road. She righted the vehicle, her grip suddenly sweaty on the steering wheel.

Having had enough of the conversation, and her sudden jealousy and knowledge of Lindsey, Tess decided to end the call.

Even though the signal was perfectly fine, she said, "Ohhh ... I can't hear you ... you're breaking up ... dead spot ...." and then hit the end button.

What the hell had just happened? When did Denny get an intern? Why hadn't he told Tess sooner? And why did she have to be smart *and* beautiful? Tess felt her temperature rise, her pulse pounding in her head.

A text came through then causing her phone to beep but Tess ignored it. She needed to clear her mind. Think about finding the Slaydon's dog instead of Lindsey and Denny.

With a scowl on her face, and determination in her heart, Tess pressed the accelerator toward the floor and raced down the road.

Chapter Fourteen

Friday, July 8th, 2:39 p.m.

The glass door of the Swain County Dog Shelter closed abruptly behind Tess as she stepped into the lobby and made her way across the chipped linoleum. From deeper in the building, the sounds of multiple dogs could be heard barking and baying. Tess could only imagine how loud it would be in the actual kennel room.

Walking up to the deserted counter, Tess glanced around at the photos of dogs and puppies lining the walls that were currently up for adoption. She made her way over to the dog wall and slowly walked along it, taking in each and every one, yet looking for one in particular. She was so lost in her thoughts that she didn't hear someone enter the lobby behind her.

"Can I help you ma'am?" came a female voice over Tess's shoulder. Tess turned and smiled in greeting at the young woman now standing behind the counter. Her shiny red hair was pulled back in a messy bun on top of her head and her blunt cut bangs accented her chunky black framed glasses and nose ring. She looked comfortable wearing a pair of worn jeans and a green Swain County Dog Shelter tee-shirt with a mysterious wet spot on the front. Her name tag read "Kaylie".

"Hello. I'm Detective Tess Dane with the Swain County Sheriff's Office and I am looking for a dog that was a possible witness to a crime."

"Oh! That sounds terrible!" the woman exclaimed, her green eyes going wide. "Do you have a name or description?"

"I'll do you one better. I have a photo," Tess held up her phone with Max's face on display. "His name is Max, and he would have come in sometime around July fourth."

"Oh, we always get an influx of dogs around Fourth of July on account of the fireworks," Kaylie explained as she began scrolling through her computer. "A lot of them are afraid of the fireworks so they run away from the sounds and end up lost or worse." She scrolled for a few more seconds. "You said his name is Max?"

"Yes. Apparently he's a Newfoundland mix, around four years old," Tess offered, consulting her notes.

"So ... what do you think he saw?" Kaylie asked, trying to act nonchalant.

"His owner is missing, and so is he," Tess said, flipping to another photo on her phone, this time one of Jessica Slaydon. "Have you seen this woman?"

Kaylie leaned in to look at the photo that was zoomed into Jessica Slaydon's face and shook her head. "That's the lady that's been all over the news, isn't it?"

Tess nodded grimly. Kaylie made an empathetic face and went back to scrolling on her computer. Suddenly she exclaimed, "Aha! We do have a large, brown Newfie mix here. Castrated male ... no collar. Just came in on ... July 5th."

Tess's heartbeat climbed. That was it! Had she found Max?

"You say he's here now? Do you know who brought him in?" Tess asked, trying not to shout with excitement.

"He's here now ... in the holding room. Dogs go there for ten days if they come in as a stray. Once the ten days are up, they are put up for adoption if they are healthy and doing well," Kaylie said, clicking some keys on her computer. "It looks like ... Ashley was the intake person on his case. She's here now. Let me get her so you can talk to her." Kaylie picked up the phone and talked to someone on the other end for a moment. Hanging up, she turned back to Tess. "She'll be right up. You can have a seat over there if you'd like."

Tess nodded and made her way over to a trio of sun-faded red plastic chairs, and selecting one, had a seat.

A few moments later, a thin blond woman wearing a pair of green scrubs came into the lobby. "Detective Dane? Hi, I'm Ashley."

Tess shook the woman's hand and asked her about Max. Ashley nodded enthusiastically as Tess explained why she was there.

"You bet, Detective! I'm pretty sure this guy is the dog you're looking for. Looks just like him!"

"And do you remember who brought him in? Was it this woman?" Tess asked, holding up her phone once more to the zoomed in picture of Jessica Slaydon.

Ashley shook her head. "Sorry. I'd like to help you find the missing woman, but the person that brought the dog in was a man. Said he found the dog running loose after the fireworks."

"A man? Can you describe him?" Tess asked, flipping through to a photo of Neil.

"Oh, um ... he was tall, dark hair, kinda hot actually." Ashley shrugged with a grin.

"Did he look like this?" Tess pressed, flashing the photo of Neil Slaydon.

"That's him!" Ashley exclaimed excitedly, "How did you know?"

"I can't really say at the moment, but can you show me the dog?" Tess asked, a ball of anxiety churning in her stomach. Why had Neil Slaydon dumped the dog at the shelter, claiming that it had been a stray? This turn of events didn't sound good for Jessica. Surely she would have put up a fight if she'd known he was going to dump her dog somewhere.

Ashley led Tess through the kennel room, and just as Tess feared, the noise volume increased exponentially. Deep barks, high pitched yips, even some low moans, assaulted her ears as they quickly made their way down the cement hallway. On either side of her, Tess could see dogs of various sizes and colors moving around. Most seemed to be at the front of their kennels, watching who was coming down the aisle and barking. Others stood quietly, tails wagging, eyes alert.

Tess, always a dog lover, tried to keep her eyes straight ahead as she followed Ashley to the holding room. If Tess looked at all of the dogs that were currently available for adoption, she'd either have a broken heart or would feel compelled to adopt them all and she didn't think Otter would like that much. He loved playing with other dogs but sharing his house with a whole pack of them? Not a chance.

Finally, Ashley swung a right and headed down a much quieter hallway before stopping in front of another metal door with a window in it. Through it, Tess could see it was another room of kennels. Following Ashley inside, they walked down a short aisle in between six dog runs. All of them were currently empty except for the last one.

And there he was.

Max lay curled up in a tight ball in the farthest corner of his kennel, his food bowl next to him still containing his breakfast. When the two women came to a halt in front of his door, the dog just lay perfectly still, staring up at them.

"Hey Max, you have a visitor," Ashley announced in a sing-song voice. The dog just looked at her and then at Tess. Opening the gate, Ashley motioned for Tess to step inside if she wanted to say hi to the large brown dog.

Tess stepped inside, making herself as less threatening as possible, and squatted down. "Hey buddy, I've been looking for you. What do you think about that?" She kept her voice light. The dog began to shake, and Tess's heart broke for him. What had he seen? What had he endured?

"When is he supposed to be put up for adoption?"

"Not until July 15th. Why?" Ashley asked curiously.

"I'd like to take him with me. He has a family waiting for him at home. I can sign all the appropriate forms. He was a potential witness to a crime and was brought here under false pretenses."

Ashley's eyes rounded. "Okay, sure. I can print off all the documents now and get you guys going." She paused, letting out a sigh. "He really is a sweet dog. I hope you find his mom."

"So do I," Tess nodded, "So do I."

Chapter Fifteen

After all the legal paperwork was signed and witness statements were made, Tess confiscated Max from the dog shelter and loaded him up in her car. The dog was hesitant at first but then, realizing they were going for a ride, decided it was fun and stuck his head out the window.

While driving down the road, Tess dialed Lydia Fontaine's number to let her know she'd found Jessica's dog. The older woman immediately began sobbing and thanking Tess profusely. Tess told her that she'd keep Max at her house to play with Otter until Mrs. Fontaine was able to head back to Cleveland or until Jessica was found, whichever came first. The hysterical mother was a blubbering mess of gratitude but finally calmed down enough to comprehend that Tess was asking her to meet her at the dog park later that evening to visit. After confirming the time, Tess disconnected the call and drove through afternoon traffic toward her home.

Just as predicted, Otter was beyond excited to meet a new friend, but Max seemed to be unsure of the situation at first. Deciding to give the two dogs some room to roam and explore, Tess led the duo out onto her small patio while she sat and watched them play. Although seemingly nervous at first, Max soon started wagging his tail and engaging with Otter. Tess watched the dogs play and roughhouse for a few moments before checking her email once again on her phone.

The detailed credit card statement had finally come through for Jessica's account. Excitement coursing through her, Tess quickly opened the link provided and read the list of purchase transactions. There were only two listed, both from the same website. Tess furrowed her eyebrows, deep in thought, as she quickly opened her internet browser to confirm her suspicions. Typing in the name of the online retailer and pressing 'search', she waited as the website loaded.

The color drained from Tess's face as she scanned the website's listings. This changed everything.

The dogs continued to roll around and chase each other as Tess made a quick phone call to the crime lab, but the detective barely noticed them. Her mind was reeling.

"Hey, Seawell, this is Detective Dane. You know that blood sample I sent in from the Slaydon case?" A pause. "That's the one. I need you to add on another test."

Chapter Sixteen

Saturday, July 9th, 10:42 a.m.

Neil Slaydon sat on the edge of the bed, his shoulders hunched in dismay. He felt so alone even though he wasn't. His front sidewalk was teeming with media personnel, nosy neighbors, and random gawkers that he didn't recognize.

Jessica had been gone for two days already and it felt like forever. The house, once full of laughter and chaos, now sat quiet and somber, as though a dark cloud of sorrow had spread over it.

He'd thought about visiting his best friend from childhood who lived in Pennsylvania, just to get away from the media storm camped out in his front yard but figured that wasn't a good idea. The police already treated him like a suspect. The media too. How would it look if he just gallivanted out of state while his pregnant wife was still missing? He just wanted things to go back to the way they used to be, even if it meant the house going back to the messy conditions Jessica brought to their home life. Back when Jessica was there with him, and they'd snuggle on the couch watching old movies or go on hikes on the weekends. It was nothing like the current state of the house— orderly and sterile like a hospital.

Of course, there were still pieces of her around the house. Her smiling at him from a photo on the mantle from their wedding day. Her hairbrush and makeup strewn about in the drawer in the bathroom. Her old leather sandals were thrown haphazardly by the back door. God, those sandals! He'd told her numerous times that they just needed to be tossed because they were so worn out, the tread smoothed from use. She'd always look at him and roll her eyes, saying they had character.

He looked around the bedroom now, the one they'd shared for such a short period of time. They'd only lived in this house for a couple of months and boxes still sat, unopened, around the edges of the room, as well as in the closet.

The closet.

He got up and padded across the room to the walk-in closet they shared. Opening the door and flipping the light switch on, he looked around. His clothes hung to his left, separated by colors. His jeans, sweaters, and gym clothes were nicely folded on the shelf. Even his shoes were neatly arranged on a low shelf near the floor. It was quite different from Jessica's half of the small space.

He glanced at her side. It was in disarray, a pile of chaos. The closet bar was crammed with hangers of various colors and hung in no particular order. The floor beneath her hanging clothes looked as though a laundry basket had vomited up its contents into a heaping pile of fabric.

He shook his head, a sad smile crossing his face. Jessica had been a messy, chaotic person from the day he'd met her.

He'd been sitting at a park in downtown Columbus, working on his computer and enjoying one of the first warm days of spring. The birds had been out early, their warbling and singing making a musical soundtrack to Neil's mundane workday.

The park was empty, except for a random jogger, that early in the morning. Shivering against a light chill that still lingered from the night before, Neil zipped his blue hoodie up farther and took a drink of his hot coffee.

Just then, a large brown dog of indiscriminate breed came barreling down the path toward Neil's table, trailing a long blue leash behind him.

"Max! Get back here you big fur ball!" came a loud female voice from farther down the trail.

The dog ignored the woman's pleas, too eager to climb up next to Neil and lick him. Neil, unaccustomed to large dogs, especially large dogs that were aggressive with their affections, began pushing the dog away, desperately trying to avoid the drool.

"Down, boy!" Neil said, with another gentle shove. The large dog begrudgingly obliged and stood whining up at him, tail wagging. Neil reached out and gingerly patted the dog's head.

"Oh! Sorry!" came the female voice again, this time from right behind Neil. He turned then and saw a young woman, her long blond hair pulled up in a messy bun on top of her head. Out of breath after giving chase, she bent at the waist and grabbed the dog's leash.

"Max, you *cannot* take off like that, bud!" she gently scolded. The dog just looked up at her with loving eyes then came back over to sniff at Neil's coffee cup.

"He really is a good boy," the woman said apologetically. "He just took off when he saw a s-q-u-i-r-r-e-l", spelling out the word as though the dog could understand what she was saying. Neil laughed at the situation, even though he was desperately wanting to wipe his hands off to rid himself of the dog hair and drool.

"It's okay, really" he said, meaning it. It wasn't that he didn't like dogs. It was that he didn't care for big, ill-mannered, drooly ones.

"I'm Jessica," the woman introduced herself as she pulled some hand wipes out of her pocket and offered Neil one. "He drools a lot. Sorry," she apologized again. Neil smiled at her and accepted her peace offering.

"Neil Slaydon," he offered as he wiped his hands off. "And this is Max?"

"Yep, my one and only," Jessica boasted proudly. "I don't think I could handle two of them! Could you imagine all of the drool?"

Neil made a face and Jessica laughed, her voice slightly sultry. He grinned then, intrigued by the woman in front of him. That day was the beginning of something amazing.

Until it wasn't.

Now, as he stood just inside their shared closet, looking at their things, his heart hurt. He missed his wife. Missed her laughter, her singing off key when she didn't think he was listening. Hell, he even missed her whining about small home projects he'd yet to finish.

He sighed, his shoulders drooping. Until his eyes fell on the box, its contents taunting him, even from the back of the closet. Neil felt bile begin to rise in his throat just at the mere thought of what it held. No. No. He wouldn't let it stay here another day.

With fierce determination, he quickly grabbed the offending box, torn and battered with "Winter Clothes" scrawled on the side. Ha! Lies, all lies. And he'd fallen for every single one. At the thought, Neil angrily grabbed the box flaps and refolded them, hiding the contents from his view. He'd dispose of it so he wouldn't have to think of it ever again.

Except he would. Because finding the items hidden inside would forever be seared into his memory.

Chapter Seventeen

The weekend had been spent canvassing the neighborhood and interviewing coworkers and friends of Jessica's. According to her coworkers at Sanderson Family Dental, where she was a hygienist, Jessica was a well-liked and reliable employee. Everyone seemed to have assumed that her absence at work was due to going into labor and that she was at home enjoying motherly bliss. The sad thing was that no one at her job had seemed to talk with Jessica and just assumed someone else had, therefore it was a great shock to them to see her face plastered across the six o'clock news.

As for friends, close or otherwise, it seemed that Jessica was somewhat of a loner. The one friend that Tess was able to track down, Avery Coleman, didn't have much to share as she herself was a new mother and hadn't been social in a few months. She'd told Tess that the few times she'd texted or spoken with Jessica over the phone within the past few weeks, she hadn't gotten the feeling that anything was amiss. Avery did say, however, that Jessica had made an offhand comment about feeling lonely at home and that Neil seemed to be emotionally pulling away at times. According to Avery, Jessica had made comments to her about attending swingers parties at Neil's insistence. When Tess asked about the Slaydon's open marriage arrangement, Avery had made a face and told Tess that Jessica had never fully been into it, that she'd only agreed to it to keep Neil happy but had since come to regret it. Avery and Jessica had shared many things, but when Neil had once suggested that they share partners, the two women had decidedly said no.

Tess found this all to be interesting as Neil had made it sound as though Jessica had been on board with the idea from the beginning. Had Jessica really been having extramarital affairs like Neil had suggested? Or had he only claimed they had an open relationship to justify his wandering eye? Falsely blaming her for things to alleviate his own guilt?

Now, as Tess drove toward her next stop, she let out a long sigh, thoughts rolling around in her head as different scenarios, different possibilities, played out.

"In one quarter mile, turn left onto Finch Street. Your destination will be on your right—54 Finch St," Tess's iPhone GPS directed.

Tess slowed to make the turn, worried as to what she'd find. It had taken her a while to track down Norma Slaydon, Neil's mother, as she was a bit of a recluse. No cell phone. No social media. And, surprise! No death certificate. According to Neil, his parents were dead. Now, it's a funny thing indeed that Tess herself was able to speak with the woman and schedule an interview.

When Tess had finally tracked down the woman's unlisted landline phone number, she'd called her, explained who she was and why she was calling and surprisingly, Mrs. Slaydon seemed eager to speak with her.

As she pulled up in front of number 54 Finch Street in a Columbus suburb, Tess began rethinking her plan.

The house in front of her was in severe disrepair. Piles of junk and overflowing storage bins littered the front and side yards as far back as Tess could see. There was an old wooden swing attached to a sagging porch, the seat of which was laden with a pile of old newspapers. Christmas lights still hung from the gutters despite it being the middle of July and a plastic Easter Bunny leaned up against the crooked porch railing, cracked and forgotten.

Tess sighed. The house looked so depressing and she hadn't even been inside yet. She turned off the ignition and then got out, closing her door behind her. The smell of cat urine hit her before she even made it to the front steps. Wrinkling her nose against the smell, she took a gingerly step onto the uneven porch, feeling the boards give under her weight.

Movement out of the corner of her eye made her jump. Whirling around to look, Tess caught sight of no less than five cats diving for cover as she approached the front door.

Bracing herself against the smell, and what she was starting to fear was a hoard situation, Tess knocked on the front door of the small single-story home. Within moments, she heard movement and a voice from within the home. The front door opened, revealing a large woman wearing a shapeless dress that fell to her knees. Her lack of a bra was very evident as she swayed back and forth trying to catch her breath. Graying hair trailed down her back in wilted clumps.

"You the detective out of Crawley?" she asked, finally catching her breath. She smiled at Tess through the screen door. Opening it, she beckoned Tess to come inside.

"Yes, I'm Detective Dane with the Swain County Sheriff's Office. We spoke on the phone about your missing daughter-in-law." Tess took a tentative step into the dark interior of the home and the cat urine smell only increased. This time, however, it was mixed with the stench of moldy food, unwashed bodies, and something unpleasant that Tess couldn't quite name. Plastering on a polite smile, she followed Norma Slaydon into what was possibly meant to be the living room although Tess couldn't be sure.

This was due to the fact that the first room, nearest the front door, was stacked floor to ceiling with ... junk. Bags of mystery items, piles of clothes, stacks of newspapers and magazines sat everywhere. Cats, dozens of them, crept around, some hiding, some sniffing the air curiously. Cobwebs hung from the ceiling and light fixtures while patches of mold crept across the ceilings and down the walls.

A narrow path through all of the clutter led from the front door on toward the back of the small house.

"C'mon through to the kitchen," Norma instructed as she slowly plodded her way through the mess. Tess, keen not to fall or touch anything, kept her eyes on the floor ahead of her, except there was no actual floor, just a layer of newspapers, magazines, and ... was that cat stool?

Tess swallowed down the bile that was churning in her stomach from the smell and sights of Mrs. Slaydon's home. It was only then that she realized how hot it was inside. There was no air conditioning, and as far as Tess could tell, no fans.

By the time the two women made their way to the kitchen at the back of the house, both were sweating. Norma Slaydon heaved her way to the cluttered table and lowered herself onto one of the grimy wooden chairs. Gesturing for Tess to follow suit, she took in large gulps of air and made a few hacking sounds from deep within her chest.

Tess, desperate to finish her business here as soon as possible, remained standing. "Oh, I'll stand if you don't mind. Long car trip had me sitting too long." Norma shrugged with a smile. She didn't seem to be bothered by Tess's decision.

"So, as I told you on the phone before, and I'm sure you've heard on the news, your daughter-in-law Jessica has gone missing. And I've been tasked with trying to track her down."

"Don't know why you came all this way," the older woman hacked, "I didn't even know I had a daughter-in-law until you told me—never mind a pregnant one. I haven't seen my son in over ten years." This was news to Tess.

"You haven't seen Neil in over a decade? Care to share why?"

"I honestly don't know why. It was the morning of his eighteenth birthday. I found a note on his bed. Said he was moving out and that I shouldn't try to contact him," the older lady remembered, "So I didn't." She shrugged her shoulders, a saddened look crossing her plump face.

"Did that strike you as strange?" Tess asked, wondering what kind of family dynamic the Slaydon's had. From the sounds of it, Tess was starting to feel that perhaps it wasn't a loving, nurturing one. And the condition of the house was not suitable for raising children in, for sure. Had it always been at this level of decay? Or had that only started in more recent years after her son had deserted her suddenly and her health declined?

"No, not really." Norma shrugged. "I was a single mom. I wasn't around too much when he was growing up. He acted like a selfish little prick most of the time, always wanting this or that, complaining all the time and I didn't want to hear it. I had to work two jobs just to support him and still he'd complain." This statement caught Tess off guard, and she tried to school her features. If that was how Norma felt about her son—treated him, spoke about him—no wonder he left as soon as he could. But, in Norma's defense, Tess had spoken with Neil herself and found him to be disagreeable and prickly. No one, it seemed, was innocent in this situation.

"Where was his dad? You're husband, Jim, right?"

"Dead. The dummy got himself killed in an accident on the job when Neil was just three years old. I kept telling him to wear his safety helmet, but did he listen to me? Hell no. Serves him right if you ask me."

Tess, taken aback by the way Norma spoke about her son and deceased husband yet again and was at a loss of words for a moment. She decided to change course.

"Do you think that your son, Neil, could ever hurt anyone?"

This caused Norma to burst out laughing. Slapping her knee, she hooted until she caught Tess's gaze and quieted. "No. That boy might be an asshole, and he might have done some pretty self-serving shit in his past, but I couldn't imagine he'd ever have it in him to hurt someone." She paused for a moment and then sucked in a breath, "Why? Do you think he killed her? His wife? What's her name again?"

"Jessica."

"Yeah, Jessica. Do you think that he killed Jessica?"

Tess sighed, "It's too early to know for sure. At this point, we are just trying to get a feel of who Neil and Jessica are as people. As a couple."

"Well, Detective, I'm sorry I couldn't help you out more, but I truly don't know my son anymore. He was rarely here as a teenager and since he officially left at eighteen, I haven't seen hide nor hair of him since."

Chapter Eighteen

Tess patted Otter's head as she ushered him and Max back into the house. It was nearly 3:00 in the afternoon but she'd been hungry and had decided to take a lunch break and spend the time with the dogs. Of course, instead of playing ball with her, Otter had just sat there and stared at Tess while she ate a sandwich and some chips, hoping she'd drop one. She didn't. Once the sandwich was gone, the dogs decided that it was finally a good time to play ball and Tess had spent the last of her lunchtime throwing a soggy tennis ball for them.

Now, as she let them back into the house, Tess's cell phone alerted to a new text coming through. Pulling it out of her pocket, she saw it was from Denny and her mouth turned up into a grin. As she read the message, however, her smile disappeared.

He was canceling their date yet again. This time the excuse was work. He'd been going back and forth to

Cleveland, working a case involving a police shooting at a meat packing plant. He hadn't been able to tell her much about it but from what she'd seen on the news and learned from him, it sounded as though a drug cartel had been working out of the meat packing plant. When local police had swarmed the building, a shootout had occurred, leaving three people dead and four others injured. The aftermath had caused a rift in the city as some people claimed the killings were justified while others claimed police brutality. Now it was Denny's turn to be impartial and process through the evidence and interviews to determine if the police were in the right.

Tess sighed now, as she read the text and then shoved her phone back into her pocket. A gnawing feeling of dread began pulsing in her belly. This was the third date he'd had to cancel in as many months. She was angry, hurt, and saddened that yet again she'd been put on the back burner yet at the same time, she understood completely.

As she locked her front door and made her way back to her Jeep, she thought about why it hurt her so much that Denny had canceled. It was because of Lindsey, his new intern. Ugh. Just the thought of Lindsey made Tess's irritation shoot through the roof.

Slamming the Jeep's door a little more forcefully than she needed to, she slid it into the driver's seat and pulled out of her driveway, headed back to the station. The whole time she was driving, she was stewing over Lindsey and

Denny and the fact that they got to spend all day every day together working on cases. Lindsey, with her keen eye for law enforcement and bubbly personality.

"This is dumb," she muttered to herself as she pulled into the Swain County Sheriff's Office parking lot. Tess was the only one who could let herself feel inferior. She normally had a thicker skin and didn't really care what others thought of her, but when it came to Denny, she did. She knew she was being ridiculous, jealous even, but she also felt hurt. She'd had a crush on him since the academy and that crush had slowly turned into more, especially while they were working together on the Torture Killer case. She knew he had feelings for her, he'd as much as said so, but she was afraid that maybe, just maybe, hers were deeper for him than his were for her and that's what scared her.

Taking a deep breath to clear her mind, she forced herself to stay positive. Denny had his reasons for canceling and she would have to try her best to not let it get to her. Grabbing her phone, she tapped out a response to his cancellation text. "It's okay, I get it. Will miss you. Stop by if something changes. The dogs and I will have to get pizza tonight and watch movies without you." After a second, she added a smiley face emoji and then hit Send.

Almost immediately, his response came: "Don't give up on me yet. If something changes, I'll stop by. Tell the boys to save me space on the couch just in case." Tess read the message and grinned, her spirits already lifting. See? She was just overthinking things. It would be fine ... right?

Heading into the station and casting a wave at Bertie, the receptionist for the past forty years, who was deep in conversation, Tess quickly made her way down the hall to her office.

Setting her coffee pot to brew something to get her through the rest of her day, she quickly went to work going through the files and paperwork on her desk. She currently had three open cases, but none were as severe or dire as that of the missing pregnant woman, Jessica Slaydon. She worked on writing the final reports for two cases she'd closed recently and set them aside to fill her coffee cup before sitting back down to review the interview with Neil Slaydon. Suddenly there was a knock at her opened office door.

"Hey, Dane, I have some results from the crime lab. About that missing lady," Deputy Drew Tanner said, sticking his head into Tess's office. She looked up from her desk with a smile.

"Perfect!" She accepted the folder from the young deputy. He'd been with the department for only two months and seemed like a kid to Tess, even though she herself was only a few years older than him. She'd graduated from the academy almost six years ago and felt old compared to the fresh faced nineteen-year-old standing in front of her.

"Thank you so much for bringing it over," she dismissed him as she eagerly opened the file and began to flip through the blood analysis results from the Slaydon's home. Deputy Tanner nodded and then left Tess alone to read.

Because of the nature of the case and the immediate need to find the missing pregnant woman, the lab had put a rush on the samples. Speed, and accuracy, were needed to gain a better understanding of what had happened in the days and hours leading up to her disappearance. Luckily for Tess, the crime scene technicians had found multiple blood traces throughout the house; on the picture frame, inside the sink drain in the master bathroom, and–when sprayed with Luminol–the area on the floor in front of the kitchen sink—the area that Neil Slaydon claimed to have cleaned up himself.

The first page of the report highlighted the victim's name and demographics. Jessica Elizabeth Slaydon, age twenty-nine, white female. An analysis had been performed on the blood sample found at the crime scene and had been compared to a known DNA sample from Jessica Slaydon from hairs taken from her brush. It was a match. The blood was indeed that of the missing woman.

The toxicology screen was next. It was simple and to the point–no drugs or alcohol found in the sample.

It was the third page, however, that caused alarm to flood through Tess's body. She had not been expecting it. Suspecting it, maybe, but hoping it wasn't true.

She slammed the file shut, her mind racing. Grabbing her phone, she dialed a number and as the person answered, Tess was already halfway out the door.

Chapter Nineteen

Wednesday, July 13th, 4:02 p.m.

Tess made her way swiftly up the front steps of the Slaydon home, set on getting some answers. Enough was enough. She was tired of Neil's lies.

She rang the doorbell and waited for a few moments. When no one came to the door, she raised her hand to knock but the door suddenly opened, revealing a tired and disheveled Neil Slaydon.

"What do you want?" he asked brusquely, keeping the door closed behind him as much as possible.

"Don't you mean 'have you found my wife?' or something along those lines?" Tess snapped, staring him squarely in the eye. His shoulders sunk slightly at that, his cool guy facade slowly crumbling.

"Did you? Find my wife?" he asked, seeming to let his guard down, but still not willing to be too amiable.

"No. Not yet," Tess answered more kindly, watching him closely. "I did find something out though that we need to discuss. May I come in?"

He stood there, reluctant to move. Finally, with a slight huff of impatience, he stepped back and opened the door for her.

"What did you find?" he asked as they went into the living room. Tess sat down on an old armchair next to the couch and was about to speak when a woman walked into the room from the direction of the kitchen.

"Hey, Neil, was that the pizza guy?" the woman asked but came to an abrupt halt when she saw Tess sitting in the living room with Neil. She eyed Tess's gun and badge hooked on her waistband suspiciously.

"Who are you?" she asked Tess, a look of confusion crossing her face. "You the cop?"

"I'm Detective Tess Dane with the Swain County Sheriff's Office. And you are?"

"I'm Annie."

"My sister, Annie," Neil said, smiling over at the woman. "She came to see if she could help with anything to find Jessica."

"Nice to meet you, Annie," Tess said, quietly sizing the woman up. She had long blond hair that fell to her waist and long thick bangs framed her face. Her resemblance to Jessica was uncanny and left Tess feeling uneasy. "Do you live locally?"

"I drove in from Columbus," Annie said, casting a glance at Neil, as he sat down on the couch with a defeated sigh. Tess eyed the two of them, skepticism etched across her face.

"What's your last name, Annie?" Tess asked curiously.

"Baldwin," Annie said, eyes moving back to Tess. "Annie Baldwin."

"And when was the last time you saw your sister-in-law?"

"Who?" Annie said, but then realizing, quickly added, "Oh Jessica? Not since ... Christmas?" she added thoughtfully.

"Yeah, Christmas. Jess and I met up at Annie's," Neil said, leaning back on the couch. "Look, Detective, I don't mean to be impatient, but why are you questioning my sister when my pregnant wife is missing? Shouldn't you be looking for her?"

"Well, I'm just coming from different angles, Mr. Slaydon," Tess said slowly, avoiding being baited by the impertinent man in front of her. "You never know what someone might say, the one thing that cracks this case wide open."

"So, it's officially a 'case'? Not just a missing person who failed to show up on time, like an overdue hiker?" Neil said with a sigh. He leaned forward in his chair and hung his head. Running his hands through his wavy, dark hair, he sighed again.

"Yes, Mr. Slaydon, this is an actual missing persons case. Your wife has been missing for over a week now. No cell phone activity, no credit card or bank activity. She is simply gone," Tess said, gaze bouncing between the two siblings. She paused for a moment. "Where is your wife, Mr. Slaydon? I think you know, and you just don't want to tell me."

"I don't! I don't know where she is!" he hissed, his head snapping up and glaring at her. "If I knew where she was, I'd tell you!"

"Just like you were going to tell me about the baby?" Tess said, raising a dark eyebrow at the man.

"What about the baby?" Neil asked, "The baby that you guys don't even seem to be worried about?"

"Sir, I can assure you, we are doing everything we can to find your wife and baby. We've called in BCI to help with the investigation and have a statewide APB out for them. But I need you to come clean with me and tell me the truth."

"What truth? My wife is missing."

"Let's cut the shit, Mr. Slaydon. I don't have the time or the patience to deal with any more of your lies." Tess snapped, her temper flaring. "We can do this here or down at the station. You pick."

"I have nothing to hide. Jessica left. She's gone. Or somebody took her. I don't know."

Annie just stood there hovering in the middle of the room, eyes large and round, as though she were unsure of what to do.

"Annie, why don't you have a seat?" Tess said, distractedly. Annie quickly sat down next to Neil, practically on his lap, letting out a nervous giggle.

"Sorry," she mumbled as Neil scooted over, giving her the side eye.

"I visited your mother. You know, the one you said was dead and buried?" Tess's voice was full of sarcasm. "Funny. She seemed pretty alive to me. Although she didn't seem to know anything about Jessica or the upcoming arrival of her grandbaby. Why lie, Neil?"

"Because to me she *is* dead," he muttered, his handsome features darkening. "I haven't spoken to her since I left that rat's nest on my eighteenth birthday."

Finally, Tess thought, *a truth.*

"And why was that?"

"Because the woman is a bitch and the house should be condemned," Neil snapped. "The last time I was there, I saw at least two mummified cats and enough excrement to fill five litter boxes to the brim. It's disgusting and no matter what I did, or what I said to her, she'd never clean it up."

"Is that why you seem to like things so clean now?"

He nodded, "I decided I wasn't going to live in a slob's hovel like that ever again. I deserved better. So now I clean all the time and avoid messes at all costs." He shrugged then, almost looking embarrassed at sharing something so personal.

"That explains a lot, Neil," Tess encouraged, "I mean that. I saw the condition of the house and I don't blame you for wanting to leave it as soon as you could."

He nodded at her, acknowledging that he heard her but not fully meeting her eyes. Annie just stared at her lap, her shoulders sagging. Tess decided to change course.

"Neil, do you and your wife have a Mastercard? Ending in the numbers 548 ... 6?" Tess asked, consulting her notes.

"No. We don't have any Mastercard accounts," he answered, watching Tess, a look of confusion wrinkling his forehead. "Why?"

"Well, that's interesting. Your wife, Jessica, has an open Mastercard account with a balance of ... $925.62. Ring a bell?"

"That can't be right. We only have our Visa debit cards and an American Express for emergencies," Neil said, his brows pushing together.

"I can assure you, it's correct. We've run financials on you and your wife. Why do you think she didn't tell you about that account?"

"I don't know. It's probably some department store card and she didn't want me to know how much underwear or perfume she was buying. Why do women do anything they do?" Neil deflected with a shrug. Absently picking at the seam in his pants, he seemed to be getting more agitated as the conversation progressed.

"There were only three transactions on it," Tess stated, ignoring his sexist remark, "One of which caught my eye. Have you ever heard of Joyful Journeys, LLC?"

"No. Should I?"

"It's a company that sells pregnancy props. You know, like fake sonogram photos, recordings of fetal heartbeats, or in Jessica's case, rubber pregnancy bellies."

"Rubber pregnancy bellies?" he asked, confusion still evident on his face.

"Yes. The kind women wear on television or in movies. Or when they are faking a pregnancy," Tess said, staring Neil in the eye.

"Faking a pregnancy! What?" Annie exclaimed, whirling around to stare at her brother. "What is she talking about, Neil?"

Neil sat there speechless. When his mind finally seemed to process what Tess said, he looked up at her, incredulously. "My wife *is* pregnant! I've seen the ultrasounds. I've seen her vomiting. Her belly is getting bigger. Even her breasts are filling out more. How can you come here and say such horrible things?"

"Mr. Slaydon, where are the ultrasound photos? The receipts from the doctor's appointments?"

"The picture is on the fridge. As for the receipts, it's all on her patient portal."

"Have you ever actually gone to the OB with your wife, Neil?" Tess asked, making notes to herself.

He was silent for a few moments, and then mumbled, "No. I was always working when she had her appointments."

"And who is your wife's OBGYN?"

"Dr. Chloe Cornecelli over on Fremont and Elm," Neil supplied distractedly, running his fingers through his hair.

"And when was the last time you saw your wife naked? Fully naked?"

"That's really none of your business."

"Answer the question, Mr. Slaydon. When was that last time you actually saw your wife's naked abdomen all at once?"

Neil just sat there, staring straight ahead, saying nothing. Annie looked down at her hands and absently picked at a cuticle, while muttering comments to herself.

"I think we are done here, Detective," Neil finally said, breaking the silence. "The past week has been hard on all of us, and I need some time to process your allegations. Either arrest me or leave, but we are done talking."

Tess stood, knowing she couldn't continue questioning him in their current situation without harassing him. She had nothing to arrest him on, and he knew it. She didn't trust him, or his sister. They knew something. Far more than what they were saying, and Tess was hell bent on figuring it out.

Chapter Twenty

Wednesday, July 13th, 5:15 p.m.

Thoroughly pissed off at Neil and Annie's attitudes and their unwillingness to tell the truth, Tess slammed her car door as she left the Slaydon's house. Perhaps it was good that she was driving a department car today and not her Jeep.

Calling Denny's cell as she made her way through traffic back toward the station, Tess took deep calming breaths.

"Hey, Tess!" Denny greeted her on the second ring. "This is a nice surprise. What's up?"

"A lot of new information has come to light regarding the Slaydon case, and I'm just frazzled. I just got done speaking with the man and I want to throat punch him. He's such a combative ... creep."

Denny's low chuckle filled her ear. "He must be bad. You don't usually let people get to you like that."

"Well, this guy seems to know how to push my buttons," Tess grumped, pulling into the station's parking lot. Finding a spot to park, she quickly did so and turned off the ignition. The car's interior immediately became muggy in the July heat.

"Do you need any help? I just got a call from my boss. He's headed up to the Cleveland office for something else so now I don't have to go to deliver the evidence and stuff myself. I'm in between things at the moment if you need extra hands or just want to hang out."

"What about Natalie?"

"She's at her new friend Lucy's grandma's house for the next two days. There are horses there and the girls are going riding every day."

"Oh! Enough said!" Tess laughed, remembering her own childhood obsession with horses.

"Yeah, it's all I heard about for days until I finally caved. Apparently Lucy's grandma runs a horse riding facility for handicapped children. All the horses are super chill and gentle. Grandma told Lucy and Natalie they were welcome to come out for a few days and learn to ride but they had to muck the stalls and feed the horses."

"Sounds fair," Tess grinned, "And sure, if you want to come hang out at the station with me, there is plenty to do. Maybe we can even get some food at some point."

"Nice," Denny said, a smile in his voice. "I'll head that way then. See you soon." Tess grinned to herself as she disconnected the call.

Getting out of the now stifling car, Tess walked swiftly into the cool interior of the Swain County Sheriff's Office and made her way down the corridor toward her office and the audiovisual room.

She could hear voices coming from the AV room and as she approached, Malone stuck his head out of the doorway and motioned for her to join them.

Inside the cramped room sat Deputy Cooper, the AV Guru, along with Malone, who was holding a large neon green slurpee in his hand. As Tess unfolded a metal folding chair to sit on, Malone went back to watching the video, as he absently chewed on his straw. Tess tried not to cringe at the irritating squeaking sound that the straw made when rubbed on the styrofoam cup. Malone seemed oblivious.

"A neighbor from four houses down the street from your vic sent this video over just now," Cooper explained to Tess. "Somehow it was sent to me, not you, by mistake. But that's your guy, right?" He pointed to the screen in front of him.

"My guy?" Tess asked, confused, "You mean Neil Slaydon?" Cooper nodded.

"What's he doing with the baby stroller? Did his wife have the baby before she went missing? If so, I'm confused. He sure takes that kid on multiple walks a day. Father of the year award," Malone said as he watched the surveillance video.

"What stroller?" Tess asked as she turned to view the screen to see what the men were talking about for herself.

"Slaydon took his kid on multiple walks the days before his wife went missing," Malone said, pointing at the screen as a grainy video showed Neil Slaydon pushing a stroller out of his garage and down the driveway. The stroller, covered in blankets to shield the baby from the midday sun, was nothing special. Just a mid-grade jogger stroller with three wheels. "He's taken the kid out like four times already."

"Four times?" Tess asked, her mind beginning to work in overdrive.

"Yeah," Malone answered, casting a slightly confused look at Tess. "Why?"

"Well, for starters, there isn't a baby," Tess stated. "There never was."

Chapter Twenty-One

Wednesday, July 13th, 5:33 p.m.

"What do you mean, no baby?" Malone asked, his brows furrowed as he stared at Tess.

"There never was a baby, at least not this time around," Tess said, moving her chair closer to Malone and looking at the video feed of Neil on repeat. "The lab results came back earlier today. No signs of pregnancy hormones were found in Jessica's blood. I have an appointment with Jessica's OB later today. There was a baby, two years ago, but the pregnancy ended in a stillbirth at 23 weeks gestation. Jessica Slaydon never seemed to get over it well despite therapy and medications. I believe she faked this last pregnancy for the attention and the desire for a child. Neil Slaydon apparently knew there was no baby from the look of this video, though. He seemed pretty surprised when I hinted at it just now when I spoke to him. How could I have fallen for his lies? He had to have known."

"Maybe he didn't know for sure, just suspected?" Cooper asked with a shrug.

"But he'd have to have known when this video was recorded," Tess pointed out. "I mean, who practices pushing around a stroller? Maybe he found out about the pregnancy and was in denial. He confronted her, they fought, she left him?"

"Unless he found out and snapped?" Malone supplied, leaning back in his seat. "Is that enough to want to kill someone over, though?"

"To have a spouse, someone you trusted, fake an entire pregnancy?" Tess asked, "Yes, I'd say so." She paused for a moment, thinking. "Having a baby is a huge life altering situation. It's something that changes the way you think, plan, and live. If Neil really didn't know that the pregnancy was fake until recently, he very well could have hit the roof."

"How could he have not known? He hadn't been intimate with his wife these past few months? Never touched her belly and realized it was fake? Never wanted to feel the baby kick?"

"I've been doing some digging through their finances and there have been a couple of online purchases that I've flagged," Tess said. "It seems as though Jessica had a credit card her husband knew nothing about. At least, his name is nowhere on the account. The purchases were from an online vendor for pregnancy props, like ultrasounds, or fake rubber bellies. Some of them look quite real. Why these sites exist, I'm not really sure, but Jessica seemed to know about them. I'm waiting to hear back from the online store about what exactly it was that Jessica purchased. But, I'm assuming it included a mid-pregnancy sized belly."

"That's just kinda messed up," Malone said, shaking his head. He turned back to the computer screen, thinking. "It's hard to believe that they hadn't been intimate though. You'd think, laying next to your spouse night after night, that there'd be some kind of hanky panky. He never touched her? Saw her naked?"

"Chances are, no," Tess answered. "I've never been pregnant, but listening to other women talk, it sounds like as the pregnancy progresses, you feel huge and uncomfortable. Maybe Jessica would brush off any advances Neil made, claiming she was nauseous, tired, or uncomfortable. Who knows for sure."

"So, if there was never a baby, then where is Jessica? And why is Neil pushing a stroller around multiple times a day?" Malone sighed. "It seems dumb."

"Not dumb," Tess said, the puzzle pieces suddenly fitting together at last. "Ingenious."

"Why?"

"Jessica was in the stroller."

"Tess, she's an adult. Jessica would never fit in that stroller," Malone said, making a face.

"She would if she were in pieces."

Chapter Twenty-Two

"Detective Tess Dane, I'm here to speak with Dr. Cornecelli," Tess said, flashing her badge. She had an appointment to speak with Jessica Slaydon's OB. She'd called the office only moments after receiving the lab results from the blood sample found at the Slaydon home. She had questions and hopefully the good doctor could give her some answers.

"She'll be right out for you, Detective," the receptionist answered before picking up the phone receiver and relaying Tess's arrival to the doctor.

Tess took her time, slowly walking around the nearly empty waiting room. The room itself was painted in a neutral cream color with navy blue chairs lining the walls. A few magazines lay scattered on an end table along with a crumpled pamphlet that read, "Syphilis: A Silent Killer."

On the walls hung various cheap works of art typical of a doctors office waiting room as well as some office policy signs. Advertisements for various birth control methods and women's health medication were displayed around the lobby as well.

She finished her slow circuit of the room and then decided to have a seat and wait. However, almost as soon as she sat down, a nurse came out of a door across the lobby and called her back.

They wound their way through a couple of hallways before stopping in front of Dr. Cornecelli's private office. The nurse knocked lightly on the door and a muffled, "Come in," came from the other side.

"Ah, Detective Dane, it's a pleasure to meet you," Dr. Chloe Cornecelli greeted with a smile. Her long blond hair hung down past the shoulders of her spotless white lab coat and her captivating smile revealed a row of perfectly white, straight teeth.

"Thank you for seeing me so late in your day, Dr. Cornecelli," Tess said, taking the other woman's proffered hand and shaking it. When indicated, Tess sat down across the desk from the doctor and glanced around the small room. A window took up most of the wall behind the desk, the windowsill covered in an assortment of houseplants in various degrees of health. Hopefully Dr. Cornecelli took better care of her patients than she did of her plants, Tess mused, eyeing a haggard looking snake plant.

"Oh, no worries. I had some files to finish up with and my last patient just left. Wednesdays are my late nights," the doctor smiled. "So, how can I help you, Detective?" she asked, taking a sip of herbal tea from a mug on her desk.

"I am here to inquire about a patient of sorts," Tess began.

"You know I can't tell you anything about a patient. It's privileged information," Cornecelli said, not unkindly. Tess nodded with a sigh.

"Yes, I understand that, but please hear me out," Tess said, hoping this meeting would finish better than it was starting. "I am currently working on a case. You might have seen it on the news. The missing woman from Crawley."

"Oh, yes. Jessica Slaydon. I've seen the reporting on it."

"Yes. That one," Tess confirmed. She pressed on before the doctor decided to kick her out. "It is my understanding that Jessica was a patient of yours a few years ago, and again during her current pregnancy."

"I'm not at liberty to tell you the names of my patients, Detective, but I will say that I don't recognize the woman on the news as a current patient of mine," Dr. Cornecelli offered, giving Tess a knowing look.

"So, you know that she is not currently pregnant?"

"I honestly can't say that one way or another. She might have gone elsewhere, but as far as I know, she is not a current patient here."

"Exactly," Tess mumbled to herself, somewhat relieved her hunch was right. "I'm going to tell you a story, hypothetically of course, and if you have anything positive to say, take a drink of your tea. If not, say nothing."

"Sounds easy enough. I like a good story," the doctor said, grinning over her cup.

"So, say a woman came here two, maybe three years ago for prenatal care and delivered a stillborn baby at 23 weeks gestation. Would that baby have had an autopsy to determine what had caused the death?" Tess asked.

The doctor took a sip of tea. A yes, Tess noted.

"And as far as you can remember, there was nothing untoward about this random woman and the stillborn two years ago?" Tess asked. The doctor just looked at her. A no. So the good doctor thought something seemed off? This didn't bode well for Jessica Slaydon.

"It's recently come to light that this random woman has been faking a pregnancy and is now currently missing," Tess said as she pulled out the lab results she'd stuffed in her pocket. "These are the results of an analysis of a blood sample taken from a recent crime scene."

The doctor leaned in to view the creased document that Tess had laid on the desk.

"As you can see, the sample came from a female victim and showed no signs of pregnancy. The DNA from the sample is a direct match for Jessica Slaydon," Tess said, watching as the doctor read the document. Dr. Cornecelli looked up at Tess with a concerned look on her face.

"So, what are you saying?" Chloe Cornecelli asked, her brows knitted together.

"I'm saying a woman who has gone to great lengths to fake a pregnancy has suddenly disappeared, leaving behind multiple blood stains at her house. Someone tried to clean up the scene but apparently forgot to check everywhere as we were able to find multiple samples throughout the house. Something is very off in that house and I am trying to figure out what happened. I need to find Jessica Slaydon."

Chloe sighed then, a look of fear and concern clouding her pretty face. "Well, I know that I typically can't speak about a living patient, but I can discuss a dead one. And since you are investigating a missing person, I'm legally permitted to talk to you."

Tess waited patiently for the doctor to continue, though she was excited to learn some new information.

"The baby, the one that passed away in utero, was named Adam," Chloe said with a sigh. "I always remember the ones that don't make it for one reason or another. Someone has to." She looked down with a saddened face. With a sigh of resolve, she began again, "Everything about the pregnancy had seemed completely normal, every milestone was met with flying colors. I had no concerns for the mother and baby. Until ...." She paused, staring off into the corner of the room, deep in thought.

"Go on," Tess encouraged.

"It was late at night when I got a call from our answering service. There was a mother in distress, bleeding profusely and had been admitted to the ER. It was one of my patients, so I responded immediately. By the time I got there, they had the mother stabilized—IV, monitoring—but the baby was ... gone. Unresponsive, no heartbeat."

"What made you suspect something was amiss?" Tess asked.

"Well, for one, there were strange bruises on the woman's abdomen and extremities. When asked, the woman said she fell down the stairs, but I'm not entirely sure I believed it," Cornecelli paused. "When a woman is pregnant, their body begins to make a hormone called relaxin. It helps make their joints and ligaments loosen as their bodies prepare to go into labor. That, coupled with the fact that someone late into a pregnancy is off balance because of their pregnant belly, makes a fall plausible."

"Well, then why did you suspect it was faked?" Tess asked again.

"I'm not really sure, to be honest," the doctor said. "The husband seemed very distraught, beside himself. She did too, but there was just this nagging feeling that something wasn't right."

"Did the baby's autopsy reveal anything suspicious?"

"Not really. Everything looked fine. He was anatomically perfect. He just came too early," Dr. Cornecelli said with a sigh. "There was some bruising noted if I remember correctly but nothing that couldn't be explained away given the traumatic birth."

"Did the police question them at all?" Tess asked. She hadn't seen any police reports, but that didn't mean that law enforcement hadn't been called.

"Not that I'm aware of," Chloe Cornecelli said. "You'd know better than me."

"There is no record of it that I've seen," Tess offered. "Did you verbalize your feelings with anyone? That something wasn't right?"

Chloe sighed again. "I offhandedly said something to a coworker, one of the delivery nurses, that something felt off. She just nodded and shrugged. That was the end of it." The doctor got up then and stood to look out her window at the small pond just beyond the parking lot. "Now that the woman is missing, I wish that I'd pressed the issue further. That I'd spoken up earlier. I had no proof of anything untoward. Just a feeling, and you can't really make a big deal over a feeling, can you?"

"No, I guess not," Tess agreed. "But you are speaking up now and that is helpful."

The doctor nodded, a sad smile crossing her face. "Do you think she's dead? Jessica?"

"I'm not sure," Tess said honestly. "It's not looking good though. No one has seen her in over a week. There is no activity on her credit cards, phone." She sighed. "We are just trying to put the puzzle pieces together at this point."

"Well, if there is anything else I can do to help, please let me know," Dr. Cornecelli said as Tess stood to go. "I hope you find her. Alive."

Chapter Twenty-Three

Wednesday, July 13th, 8:12 p.m.

After the meeting with Dr. Cornecelli, Tess and the team reconvened in the meeting room from earlier. Deputy Cooper had gathered together all the pertinent surveillance footage from the neighborhood surrounding the Slaydon's home. Now that it was highly suspected that the man had used the stroller as a means of transport to dispose of his wife's body, the team needed to make a video trail of exactly where he'd been going on his daily 'walks'.

The team sat around the conference table, everyone leaning in to watch the computer screen. Denny had arrived, bringing Detective Aaron Claybourne, a fellow BCI detective with him. Tess was happy to have the help. Sheriff Malone had contacted BCI earlier in the day and asked for additional manpower for this investigation considering the extenuating circumstances.

As the group sat around the table now, getting reacquainted since originally meeting during the Torture Killer case, Tess hungrily ate the sub and diet Coke that Denny had brought her, all while keeping her eyes on the screen in front of her.

The surveillance video showed Neil Slaydon leaving his home late the night of July fourth. Well after Miles and Scafferty had gone to question him and his wife, Jessica. The time stamp read 4:42 a.m. so technically it was early Tuesday morning. As the video played, the team watched as Neil walked to his shed at the side of the house and then back around to enter through the garage. It was hard to discern what he was carrying, but something black filled his hands.

Tess paused the screen and zoomed into the dark frame. It did nothing but make the photo grainier and more pixelated. With an irritated huff, she pressed 'play' again and the video resumed.

The detectives watched as Neil left the house again and was seen pulling his large black trash can into the garage from where it usually sat next to the house. Once he was back inside, the large garage door began shutting, leaving the house dark from the street view.

"This doesn't look good," Denny sighed, from where he observed next to Tess. The others around the table nodded in agreement as they continued to watch the screen.

"I bet he's putting her body in that trash can right now," Malone muttered, pointing to the screen. Tess moaned, somehow knowing that he was probably right.

"Cooper, did you say we got some more emails from neighbors with surveillance videos? Let's watch them. See if we can catch Neil's progression from the house. See where he goes with the stroller," Tess said, rubbing a hand down her face. She was tired—mentally and physically. It had been a long few days, and the sooner they found Jessica Slaydon—dead or alive—the better.

"Already on it, Detective," Cooper said as he changed video feeds to show another view, this time one of Neil Slaydon pushing the baby stroller down the road two streets over from the Slaydon's house during daylight hours.

"Why is he transporting her body parts in the stroller? Why not put her in his trunk and drive her somewhere?" Denny mused out loud.

"He knew that the moment he called us with his concocted story about finding her missing, we'd be watching his every move, searching his vehicles. Any time he leaves in his truck, either we are following him, or the media is," Tess said. "When this was recorded, he had to have just found out that Jessica was lying about the pregnancy. My guess is that he didn't want to be seen by anyone, so he casually told neighbors, if they asked, that Jessica was recovering from giving birth, so he was taking the baby on walks. Like does he think we wouldn't check with the hospitals to verify any of this? Or his relatives? It's absurd."

"People like to see new babies," Claybourne commented, glancing around the table. "How'd he keep people from looking under the blanket and seeing body parts of his dead wife?"

"Germs," Tess shrugged. "Most parents are very protective of their newborns and refuse to let anyone hold them. My guess is that, if asked, Slaydon would have said no, the baby was sleeping, and they didn't want to take the risk of getting it sick. Crisis averted. Most people would take the hint and not press the issue."

The others around the table nodded as they mulled it over. Finally, Malone sighed.

"Okay, so we've got a guy, finds out his wife is lying about a pregnancy, kills her, cuts her up, carries her around in a stroller to dump her somewhere. Now we just have to figure out when exactly, how, and where. The why seems pretty obvious."

They sat in silence for a few moments, watching Neil Slaydon pushing the three-wheeled jogging stroller over cracked cement sidewalks and past fire hydrants. Each officer was keenly aware of the grotesque contents of the stroller, as evident by the silence that seemed to suddenly fill the room.

Once Neil was out of view for that particular video feed, Cooper pulled up another email, searching the contents. Within moments, the video played, showing nothing exciting except for a few random cars making their way through the neighborhood. A couple of teenagers could be seen walking a small dog, and a mail carrier was dropping off mail to the different houses in the video frame. But there was decidedly one thing missing. Neil Slaydon.

"Okay, so, according to the map of the neighborhood and the time stamp on this video, we could assume that Neil should be crossing through the camera's view at any moment. Assuming that he's still walking at a leisurely pace," Denny commented. Tess and Malone nodded in agreement. They all turned and watched a few more minutes but still didn't see Neil Slaydon or the baby stroller.

"Come on, where are you?" Tess muttered to herself as she continued to watch the video feed. After slowly speeding up ten additional minutes of footage while waiting for Neil to come into the frame, Tess gave up with a frustrated sigh.

"Unless he's walking at a snail's pace, I don't think he came down this far." She stood up and walked over to the map of the neighborhood that someone had taped to the marker board. Using a Sharpie marker, she put an "X" on the locations where Neil Slaydon had been caught on video. On the address of the home where the most recent video was, she placed a circle.

Pointing to the circled location, she said, "So, according to that last video, Slaydon didn't come this far. He did, however, come past this address." She pointed to the last X she'd drawn. "Since there are no cross streets in between the two houses noted, we have to determine where he went."

"He'd have to have gone to someone else's house?" Malone suggested, almost as a question rather than a statement. "What else goes through there?"

"I think there is a nature trail somewhere around there. I can't remember for sure," Claybourne commented. "I took my niece and nephew there to ride bikes once."

"Wherever he is taking the body parts has to be somewhere easy to get to since he's pushing a stroller. Surely he's not parking the stroller somewhere and then lugging bags of body parts around like it's trash," Denny said with a grimace.

"True," Tess agreed as she looked the map over closely. She noticed a thin strip of green between some houses. "Does anybody know what this is?"

The others looked where she was pointing.

"That may be the trailhead I was talking about," Claybourne said, deep in thought. "Only one way to know for sure."

Chapter Twenty-Four

Thursday, July 14th, 10:39 a.m.

The July sun beat down on the officers as they walked down the street that just last night they'd been looking at on the map. In reality, the green strip Tess had pointed out had indeed turned out to be a trailhead for a nature preserve just outside of Crawley city limits. It was surprising how close it really was to the Slaydon's new house.

"This trail looks wide enough for a stroller to pass through," Denny said as he followed Claybourne, Tess, and Malone down the crushed gravel path.

Tess looked over at Denny and smiled, glad that he and Claybourne had driven back down earlier in the morning to help aid in the search. Catching her smile, he returned it, his dark blue eyes sparkling.

"Yeah, I was thinking that too," Tess agreed as they made their way into the trees. The trail wound through the woods, with houses butted up against it on one side, and forest on the other. Today, with the temperatures creeping higher, the trail was littered with joggers and bikers alike keen on staying in the shade.

"Does anybody know where this thing goes?" Denny asked, trying to bring the map up on his phone.

"I think it goes all the way to Camden Town and then eventually ends up in Columbus," Malone said. "It's part of the Rails to Trails that the state of Ohio started. You know, where they turn old railroad tracks into hiking trails?"

"Oh, yeah, I've heard of that," Claybourne commented. The group continued in silence for a few moments, the four law enforcement officers getting some stares from people walking toward them on the trail. They all wore dressy casual clothes, but their guns and badges holstered at their sides left little to the imagination. Tess was just glad she wasn't wearing a long-sleeved shirt like she had thought about doing that morning. The morning had started out cool but had quickly warmed up, causing Tess and the others to sweat.

A few moments later, they found themselves at the old Crawley Bridge, the Camden River swirling below. Downriver, Tess could see two men fly fishing and in the other direction, a woman was walking a Golden Retriever.

As the group got closer to the river, the sound of the rushing water became a roar, drowning out any attempts to talk. The group broke up and began looking around, trying to discern any areas where a body or body parts could be dumped out of view of passersby.

There were little tracts on either side of the trail that circled around to the shoreline under the bridge but they were narrow and plagued with tree roots. Hardly passable with a stroller in tow, especially if you wanted to go unnoticed. Looking at the area, Tess supposed that if someone was dedicated enough, they may be able to maneuver a stroller by but it would be difficult.

She turned around and made her way back up to the bridge and started across it. The bridge frame was old and metal but still in good condition considering. Once painted white, the paint was now chipped in some spots or covered with spray paint in others. The floor of the bridge was new, however, the boards having been replaced just last year thanks to a levy being passed.

Tess's steps echoed over the wooden planks as she slowly made her way over the bridge. This had been the place of a few suicides over the years, the most recent being Maggie Sloane, the center of the Torture Killings.

When she was halfway across the bridge, Tess paused and looked down at the churning river below. Had Neil Slaydon thrown his wife's body over the edge of the bridge and into the dark waters below?

Leaning out some to get a better vantage point of the turbulence below her, Tess had a dark feeling that yes, it was possible to throw something over the railing without causing too much fanfare. The moving water made enough roar to drown out the splash made by a falling object, and the barrier railing was designed in just the right way so that someone could stand close to it and be partially hidden from view.

"Whatcha looking at?" Denny said, coming up behind Tess and looking over the barrier to the river below.

"Just thinking about how easy it would be to nonchalantly drop bagged body parts over this railing that were transported here via a baby stroller," Tess said with an ornery grin and a shrug. Denny smirked and rolled his eyes.

"You joke, but I think you might be onto something," he said. "Looks like we might have to drag the river."

"Do you really think that Neil Slaydon has it in him to kill his wife, hack her into pieces and then throw her away like that?" Tess asked, serious once more. "All because she lied?"

"It was a pretty big lie. Not that it makes it right or anything," Denny said, as he continued looking over the railing. "I'd be pretty upset too if my partner or spouse lied like that. Not enough to kill because of it but I can see how someone could snap."

"Well, looks like we better call in the dive team and get the cadaver dogs down here. See what they can find," Tess said with a sigh. "I want that bastard in cuffs."

Chapter Twenty-Five

Thursday, July 14th, 1:45 p.m.

In the time it took the dog teams to mobilize and arrive at the old Crawley Bridge, the summer sun was getting relentless. The cloudless sky was cerulean, the air static and humid.

Tess took a long swig from her water bottle and tugged at the brim of her black Swain County Sheriff Department ball cap. Her sunglasses helped some but the sun's reflection on both the river and the various law enforcement vehicles parked haphazardly on the shore were intense.

Another vehicle pulled up and the loud baying of a Bloodhound emanating from it announced yet another cadaver dog's arrival.

"Hello there," one of the dog handlers said as she approached Tess, her German Shepherd by her side. "I'm Kathy and this is Tara," she said, indicating the dog.

"Where would you like us to start?" She flashed a bright smile at Tess.

"Hi, Kathy, I'm Detective Dane," Tess said with a smile. "I've been looking over a map of the river and discussing 'sciencey' stuff with some of the other handlers and officers. You know, things like river currents and water levels." She made a face. "Variables like that. The stuff that is out of my pay grade."

Kathy laughed, relieving some of Tess's anxiety. Tess had only seen one other incident of a swift water rescue involving a young boy who'd fallen into a river while fishing two years ago. Luckily the kid had made it but Tess was glad she'd never had to be involved in something like that again. As for a body recovery search in water? Well, she'd learned about it in the academy but had never needed to use the skills in real life.

"It'll be fine," Kathy said with a shrug. "This isn't our first rodeo, is it, Tara?" She patted her dog on the head. "Just tell us where you want us to start, and we'll get to it."

"Thank you. I'm sure you know how stressful these things can be," Tess sighed, biting her lip and then looking back at the map. "I have the river and shorelines sectioned off in chunks. A grid." She pointed to the map and indicated where they currently stood and where the grids' boundaries were.

"How many dogs are coming today? Last I heard, we had four available?" Tess asked, surveying the parking area for more search dogs.

"Yes, there were four dogs that are available today," Kathy agreed. "We have almost twenty dogs in our SAR group but not all of them are trained in human remains detection. Some just do trailing, some just do wilderness or area searches."

"I see," Tess nodded, listening intently. "Well, I appreciate all the help we can get! Thank you." Her thoughts were interrupted by the arrival of a man and his Golden Retriever, Dugg. The Bloodhound came up to the group shortly after and the handler, Jayne, introduced Tess to her dog, Romeo.

When introductions were made Tess was relieved that the SAR team seemed both capable and at ease with the job set before them. She'd never been in charge of something like this but she was determined to succeed.

While the SAR teams got ready to start, Tess made her way over to where Denny stood talking with one of the deputies. She was glad he was there, even though technically she was the lead detective from Swain County. Since Jessica Slaydon had been missing for over a week, and now, most likely buried in trash bags at the bottom of the river, BCI had officially stepped in to help. Multiple counties had been looking for the woman and even though Tess had been keeping Denny up to date on her investigation, he'd stood back and let her spread her wings.

Since the Torture Killer case nearly eight months ago, so much had changed. Back then Tess had been a deputy, cruising around looking for traffic violations and answering service calls. It was after her help closing the Torture Killer case and the restructuring of the sheriff's department's remaining staff, that Tess had decided to take her detective's exam. She'd received good letters of recommendation from the superiors at BCI for her attention to detail and ability to remain level-headed even under duress. It was their support, along with encouragement from Denny, that pushed Tess to sit for the exam and advance in her career.

Almost as though Denny could sense her eyes on him, he glanced over his shoulder at Tess and smiled. She smiled back and was about to go join him with the other officer but was interrupted by the arrival of Lydia Fontaine, Jessica's mother. Tess watched as the woman parked and got out of her car, quickly scanning the scene. When she caught sight of Tess, she made a beeline to her.

"Hello, Mrs. Fontaine," Tess said, trying to smile warmly at the grieving mother. Even though Jessica had not been proven to be dead yet, all indications pointed to the fact that she most likely was. There'd been no credit card purchases, no phone calls, no sightings. Jessica Slaydon, for all intents and purposes, had simply vanished.

Tess felt deep in her soul that something darker was at play but until she had something concrete on which to base her theories, she kept them to herself. No need to start a panic if one wasn't necessary.

"Hello, Detective. Any word?" Lydia Fontaine said, an ever hopeful look on her tired face. She stood before Tess, looking up at her expectantly and Tess sighed.

"Nothing official to report, ma'am. We've been interviewing neighbors, checking CC video ...."

"You're looking for her body. Aren't you?" Lydia said, casting a glance around at the chaos along the bridge and riverbank. "I was headed to talk to Neil, and I saw all the police activity. I thought maybe you'd found her." The woman's voice broke, and she held in a sob. Tess noticed that her eyes were red and puffy as though she'd been crying recently. Tess wouldn't have been surprised if the woman had been crying ever since she'd found out that her only child was missing.

"It's just a precautionary search, Mrs. Fontaine," Tess said sympathetically. "I'm not going to lie to you. You deserve the truth. But yes, we are looking for possible remains in an effort to rule out different theories. Hopefully our theory is wrong, but we won't know unless we look."

Large tears ran down the older woman's face. Tess watched as Lydia's expression crumbled and she let out a wail. Without thinking, Tess leaned forward and wrapped her arms around Lydia's shoulders and held her while sobs wracked her body. The two women stood like that for a few moments, Tess noticing some of the curious looks they were attracting from her colleagues but ignored them. Finally, Lydia pulled away slowly and dabbed at her face with a tissue. She looked embarrassed, heartbroken, and shattered.

"Thank you. For everything you're doing to bring my Jessica home," Lydia said, her small smile broken. "And I'm sorry about your shirt."

Tess looked down at her tee shirt and the teary wet spot on it. "No worries," she reassured with a nod. She watched as Lydia made her way back to her car, got in and sat there, staring out the window.

"Okay, people!" Tess called to the SAR and law enforcement personnel around her. "Let's get this started." They gathered around the fold up table she'd set up and looked at the maps of the river and surrounding area.

"I've broken down the river into smaller search areas. As you all can see, the current here at the bridge is rather swift, but as you head down river, it does seem to slow gradually before it makes it all the way to Camden Town." She indicated the areas of discussion with her marker. "Right about here," she said, circling a bend in the river, "is a rather large log jam. It's my opinion, along with some of those in the SAR group, that because of the water current under the bridge in relation to the log jam just a quarter of a mile down, if human remains are to be found in the river, they will most likely be found there." She tapped the circled area where the log jam was. "I would like some of the dog teams to work the areas I've marked off, starting with the area under the bridge. We will work our way down river, searching methodically, sending divers down when needed. While the dogs search the river, I'd like the other volunteers and law enforcement to perform line searches on either side of the riverbank."

A couple of people nodded, some whispered among themselves. Tess continued, her voice reaching the group but quiet enough that spectators at a distance wouldn't be able to hear. "We are officially looking for human remains, specifically those of Jessica Slaydon. Her family is present, so please be mindful of how we conduct ourselves and what we say. Should anyone find anything of interest, please radio to base 'Code Black', and then change to channel nine. For our search, please everyone, have your radios on channel eight. Be mindful that this is open communication with all searchers and should only be used for official use. Basically, don't be joking around and hogging up the channel." She looked at the group before her. Most of them acknowledged what she'd said, some seemed bored. Groaning inwardly, Tess kept her expression schooled, trying to appear confident and sure of herself, even though deep inside she was nervous as hell.

"Okay, any questions?" she asked, grateful when there were none. "I've asked James with the SAR group to break everyone into groups. If you're here as a canine handler or as canine support, please see James for your posts. All others, please stay here for your instructions." With that, the group dispersed, half seeming to go with the dog teams. Tess looked at the remaining search volunteers, mostly consisting of retired or off duty law enforcement and even some students from the criminal justice department at the local community college.

Tess quickly set about dividing the non-canine volunteers into groups of four and sending them to their various posts to begin their searching. Each group had one radio, various flags and trailing ribbon to mark items of interest, and plenty of snacks and water. They were instructed to check in with base every hour, on the hour.

Glancing at her watch, Tess noted the time. It was a little after 3:15 p.m. and the sun was relentless.

As Tess watched the search groups head toward their respective areas, she began to pace, her mind racing. She was a tangle of nerves and excitement. Not that finding a murder victim's body was exciting, but at least then, they'd have some answers.

Jessica Slaydon had been missing for days now, and even though Tess felt some relief that there was no baby to worry about, she was still distressed to find the young woman. Based on things that Lydia Fontaine had said about her daughter, Tess felt that if Jessica had left of her own volition, she would have contacted her mother by now. Perhaps she and Neil had fought one too many times and Jessica had left in a huff, but surely she'd let her family know she was okay, right? The silence, both via phone and social media, coupled with the lack of movement of Jessica's credit cards or bank accounts did not bode well.

Tess felt someone walk up beside her and she paused her pacing long enough to determine it was Denny, a concerned look etched into his handsome face.

"You doing okay?" he asked, standing still, hands in his pockets. He wasn't wearing his usual dress slacks and button-down shirt as he was off official duty today. He was clad in jeans and a navy blue BCI tee shirt that complimented his eyes.

"I'm okay, just anxious," Tess admitted, looking up at Denny from under the brim of her baseball cap. "Thanks for coming here on your day off. I feel bad taking you away from Natalie."

"Nah, it's all good. She got home from Lucy's grandma's horse farm and decided I was uncool and wanted to stay with my sister and play with cousins," he grinned. "I knew she'd grow up someday and not want to hang out. I didn't think it would be so soon though." He paused, looking over his shoulder distractedly at the river and the search parties in the distance. "I just hope they find Jessica. This doesn't look good."

"Right?" Tess sighed quietly. "Her mom is here." She nodded inconspicuously toward Lydia Fontaine's vehicle, still parked in the shade, the air conditioner running. Denny's face looked grim.

"I thought that's who you were talking to a bit ago," he commented with a sigh. "I can't even imagine what she's going through. Not knowing. The feeling of dread."

"On one hand, I'm glad she is here. On the other hand, I'm worried what they will find and if it will be too much for Lydia to handle."

"It's a valid feeling. We'll just try to shield her from seeing anything if we can help it." Denny shrugged, his hands still in his pockets.

The two stood in silence for a few moments, watching the searchers in the distance, waiting for the radio to crackle to life.

Eventually, each team reported into base. As of yet, no one had found anything suspicious, anything that would point them in the direction of Jessica Slaydon's whereabouts.

The afternoon ticked by, and as each hour passed, the searchers would report in with nothing. Tess was determined not to feel defeated. Maybe they had it all wrong? Maybe they just needed some more time?

As the sun dipped low in the western sky, igniting the horizon in beautiful shades of pinks, oranges, and purples, Tess was eventually forced to call off the search for the evening. The terrain was uneven, the river swift and unyielding. It was just not worth the risk of the searchers, both human and canine.

After thanking everyone for their help, Tess announced that they would be continuing on downriver in the morning, paying special attention to the log jam farther down. Some of the faces in the crowd of volunteers looked exhausted, some defeated, while others looked like they were ready to search again. Hoping that they would all return in the morning to continue the search, Tess bade them all goodbye and went to find Denny.

"Hey, you all set?" he asked as she approached him. He'd been talking with two other officers near the vehicles when she'd found him.

"Yeah, I guess so," she sighed. "I was really hoping to find her today." Her shoulders slumped. Absently she brushed the back of her hand across her sweaty brow and glanced around for more water.

"I know, me too. We just started searching too late in the day. Tomorrow will be productive ... I hope," he smiled warmly at her.

"So, uh, I know we were talking about getting dinner together but then Claybourne ended up riding down with me. We can still go if you want, we'll just have a tagalong," Denny sighed, his frustration evident on his face.

"It's okay, I get it," Tess replied, even though inside she wanted to scream. She just wanted to spend time with

Denny without work and others getting in the way. "I need to let Otter out anyway."

"You want to let him out and then meet us somewhere?"

Tess paused, seeming to mull it over, and then grinned. "Sure. Meet me at Ida's Diner in an hour."

Chapter Twenty-Six

Thursday, July 14th, 8:52 p.m.

It was almost 9:00 p.m. when Tess was leaving Ida's. She was exhausted, but her belly was full of good food, and her heart was happy considering the darkness of Jessica's case hovering over her like a dark cloud. Having dinner with Denny and Claybourne had been good for her soul and the trio had swapped stories and laughs to the point Tess's sides hurt.

Denny had sat next to Tess in the booth, and though they hadn't defined their relationship, much less announced it to anyone one, Tess was pleased when she felt his hand slide under the table and graze her thigh. He'd taken her hand in his larger one and interwoven their fingers, sending a warm sensation coursing through her and she finally felt herself relax. The stress of the past few days, tirelessly searching for Jessica Slaydon, was wearing on Tess, both physically and mentally.

Now, as she got into her Jeep, Denny came up and grabbed her door before she could shut it. She looked up at him and grinned in the darkened parking lot of the restaurant.

"You better watch it, mister. I'll call the cops," she played along, not wanting the evening to end. She knew tomorrow would be spent back at the river, dredging it for a body, but for the moment, she just wanted to turn that part of her brain off.

"I *am* the cops," Denny's deep voice suddenly husky, his heated gaze sliding from her face down her body. "I think I need to search you, ma'am. Please step out of the vehicle." A sly grin crossed his handsome face and Tess raised her eyebrow at him. A bemused expression on her face, she slid back out of her seat to stand in front of Denny, anticipation filling her eyes.

"What about Claybourne?" Tess asked, trying to glance over Denny's shoulder, searching for Aaron Claybourne's red head among the cars parked in the lot.

"Don't worry about him. He went back inside to use the bathroom," Denny said, gently pulling Tess closer to him. "Trust me, he'll be gone for a few minutes. I told him not to get the cheese sticks." He shook his head slowly. "He knows he can't eat dairy."

When Tess made a face, Denny let out a low chuckle and pulled her even closer to him. He looked down at her for a moment, his deep blue eyes searching hers for a moment before he lowered his lips to hers.

Tess moaned quietly as she slid her arms around his neck, pressing herself into his embrace. It had been too long since they'd seen each other, much less alone, and Tess felt as though she were starving. She wanted to be with him, every moment of every day. He was the one person left in her life who always seemed to get her, who seemed to truly care about her feelings and well-being. In short, Denny was her person.

It was at that moment, standing next to her Jeep, in a crowded parking lot of Ida's on that hot July evening, that it hit Tess like a ton of bricks. She loved him. She loved Denny, plain and simple. She'd known it for a while, deep in her soul, but had pushed the feelings down, not ready to admit them out loud, much less to him. The thought of him not reciprocating her feelings kept her mouth shut. It would crush her soul irrevocably if he didn't love her back. Until she was sure, without a doubt, she'd keep her feelings to herself.

The sound of someone clearing their throat caused Denny and Tess to pull apart. Claybourne stood next to Denny's black Tahoe, a grin spread across his face.

"Well, I guess that clears up my suspicions," he laughed, as Tess subconsciously ran her hands through her hair and felt her cheeks turn bright red. She was also keenly aware of Denny's hand on her ass and was sure that Claybourne had noticed that as well. Denny just cast a glare in Claybourne's direction, which in turn just caused Claybourne to make a kissy face and laugh harder.

"Relax, Haywood. Your secret is safe with me," he called over to Denny. "And Tess, it was a pleasure having dinner with you tonight. We'll see you tomorrow at the river. C'mon, Romeo," he beckoned to Denny. "Let's hit the road."

As Tess pulled away from the restaurant, her lips still tingling from Denny's kisses, her phone rang. Glancing at the lit-up screen, her spirits wavered.

"Hello, this is Tess," she answered, her mind racing. It was well after 9 p.m. now, and the lateness of the call didn't bode well.

"Hey, Tess, it's Angela, at Toliver Care Home. I swear, I have to quit calling you late like this!"

"It's okay, Angela. You know I'm always up late. Is everything all right with Dad?"

"Yes, actually. That's why I'm calling you. He's suddenly *very* lucid, talking my leg off, demanding to see you." Angela's soft chuckle filtered over the phone. "Would you like to talk to him?"

"Even better. I'm like two minutes away," Tess was hopeful, "Can I stop by? I know it's not official visiting hours, but I promise to be quiet ...."

"Girl, you do not have to sneak in here to visit your father." Angela's smile was evident in her voice. "Come on over. I'll meet you at the front door."

The one person she wished she could tell about her detective exam was her father. Of course, she could tell him just fine, but the retired cop wouldn't remember what she said. He couldn't. He'd been diagnosed with early onset dementia nearly nine years ago and had been living at the Tolliver Care Home for the past three. Tess tried to visit him a couple of times a week but sometimes got tied up late with work or her dad wasn't lucid. Regardless of if he knew who she was or not, Tess always made an effort to see him. And recently, he'd been forgetful, even kicking her out of the room in a panic. Tess was emotionally frail when it came to her dad. Seeing him like that, being forgotten like that, was so hard. She'd often find herself sobbing when she got home from visiting him these days.

Hopefully tonight would be different.

Chapter Twenty-Seven

Thursday, July 14th, 9:23 p.m.

"Hi, Dad!" Tess greeted as she walked into his bedroom at the care home. The room was dimly lit by a bedside lamp, and the TV was on, but muted. Sparsely decorated, as Tommy Dane preferred, the room was nice and orderly. Tess grinned when she noticed one of Natalie's school pictures taped crookedly to his dresser mirror. Denny and Natalie must have stopped by to visit recently, the thought warming Tess inside like a hug. She had made sure that only certain people were allowed to visit her father as his dementia progressed and he got confused so easily. Denny and his young daughter Natalie were most definitely on the short list of approved visitors though.

Tommy Dane turned and looked at his daughter and a huge smile spread across his face. Reaching for her, he moved like he was going to try to get up.

"Don't get out of bed, Dad. I'll come to you," Tess quickly went to his bedside and enveloped him in a big bear hug. His arms, weakened from underuse, squeezed her back gently.

"How are you doing, Bug?" Tommy asked, using the nickname he'd made for her when she was two. He was the only one allowed to call her that.

"I'm well," Tess smiled, sitting on the edge of his bed, fighting back tears that her dad was there mentally and knew who she was. "I made detective," she blurted out, excited to share the news.

"That's my girl!" he smiled, his eyes glistening with unshed tears, "I always knew you were destined for great things, Tess. I mean, *somebody* had to fill my shoes."

"Oh boy, somebody's feeling their oats tonight," Tess laughed. "But yes, Dad, I had some big shoes to fill. You were always my role model. My everything."

"You better not make me cry, Tess," Tommy commanded, even as his tears threatened to spill. "I'm proud of you, baby. I really am."

Silent tears slid down Tess's face, her heart in turmoil. This is how things should be. She should have her dad around, talking shop, swapping stories, giving and taking advice. And yet, these moments were few. And getting fewer as his disease continued to ravage his body.

"You marry that Haywood guy yet?" Tommy asked, startling Tess out of her thoughts.

"What? No, Dad." She felt herself blush, even as she tried to play off her father's sudden interest in her love life. Where had that come from? How did he even know anything about her and Denny?

"Just curious. I saw how you were last time you talked about him. All moony eyed and dreamy," Tommy grinned, watching his daughter for a moment. When she said nothing, he went on, "You think I don't notice stuff. And sometimes I don't. But on the days that I can think straight, I write down the things that stand out. That way, I can read it later, if I forget, and remember. And I wrote down something a few months ago that I just reread tonight. Remember when you came and told me about Sheriff Burrows? And what had happened to Maggie Sloane? How you finished what I couldn't? I wrote that all down in my journal. I wanted to remember that, because it is important. Because *you* are important." Tommy grinned. "And well, I happened to also put a note about how much you blushed when you talked about Denny, and then when he came in here that day, too? You two couldn't take your eyes off of each other. So, I repeat, have you married him yet?"

"No, not yet." Tess grinned, somewhat embarrassed but also amused. "We don't get to see each other much because of work." She sighed, her frustration evident on her face.

"You working a case now? Tell me about it—I want to live vicariously through you," he grinned, leaning back into his pillows to get comfortable.

"I don't know if you've been watching the news, but I'm working on the missing person case. The pregnant woman, Jessica Slaydon."

"I saw you guys at the river today. It was on the news," Tommy nodded, reaching for his water glass on his bedside table. Tess helped him and as he sipped, she told him how the search had gone.

"I'm just frustrated, Dad. I really thought we'd find something today. I ... I feel like I have to prove myself, somehow, you know? Being a new detective, and a female at that, it's kinda hard at times to be taken seriously. And when we came up empty handed today at the river, I just felt defeated," Tess admitted for the first time out loud.

"You're doing well, Tess. You broke the volunteers up into manageable teams, made a grid of the search area, approached it professionally. Don't lose heart. If the woman is there, you'll find her."

"How do you know all of this?" Tess asked, eyeing her father suspiciously. "About the grid and search teams?"

"You aren't my only visitor, you know," Tommy grinned. "I've known about the detective exam for a while—I wrote it in my book. But I'm glad you told me."

"Who—"

"Doesn't matter, Tess. Let me keep my secrets." Tommy Dane smiled. "But you are doing great things. You're an excellent cop, and I am so very proud of you. Don't lose heart, Bug. Find the woman, get justice." He reached out and took her hand, his skin cool to the touch. Giving her hand a small squeeze, he yawned. "Sorry about that, kiddo."

"No, don't apologize. I should let you get some sleep," Tess glanced at her watch. It was almost 11 p.m. "I should go." She stood to go, but not wanting to leave her dad, especially when he was lucid.

"Give me a hug, sweet girl," he said, reaching up for her. Tess bent down and hugged him back. "I love you, Tess."

"I love you too, Dad."

Chapter
Twenty-Eight

Friday, July 15th, 2:45 p.m.

It was nearly 3:00 p.m. the next day and the sun was relentless, just as it was the day before. So far, nothing had been found except a broken flip flop, two used condoms, and enough empty pop cans to fill a recycling bin. Tess was getting discouraged. Had they got it all wrong? Was Jessica really off living her life somewhere? Or was she dead and they were just looking in the wrong spot?

With a sigh, Tess took a long drink from her water bottle, contemplating how much longer she should have the search continue. She was about to confer with Denny when the radio on her shoulder came to life.

"Base, this is Dog thirteen. Code Black. Repeat Code Black," came a female voice over the radio. "Changing to channel nine."

Tess's heart rate picked up. They'd found something! Quickly turning to the correct channel, she spoke into the receiver, "This is Base. Go ahead, Dog thirteen."

"Yeah, this is Jayne. I'm down at the log jam and Romeo is giving some strong indicators of human remains under the surface." Tess could hear the Bloodhound baying loudly in the background.

"Copy," Tess said, excitedly waving for Denny and Claybourne to come closer. "We will be down at your position shortly." She changed her radio back to channel eight and radioed to all the search parties, "This is base. All teams, stand down until further instructed."

"They found her?" Claybourne asked, a look of relief crossing his face.

"Possibly. Bloodhound alerted at the log jam. Let's go," Tess urged, already halfway to her vehicle. Leaving Malone in charge at base, she, Claybourne, Denny, and Lindsey headed toward the bend in the river. Lindsey had come with Denny to help with the search as well, and even though Tess was less than excited to see another woman hanging out with Denny, she was grateful for another pair of eyes.

As they pulled in, Tess could see the dog and handler off to the side playing with a tennis ball. She'd learned in watching the canine SAR groups the previous day that dog handlers always had a reward session after the dog was done working, whether they'd been successful in finding their subject or not. To the dogs, it was simply a game of Hide and Seek so to keep them motivated each handler gifted their efforts with a game of frisbee, tug, or snacks–whatever was the dog's favorite. Watching Romeo run back and forth, drooly tennis ball in his lips, Tess smiled despite the grave reason for her being at the river that day.

When Tess, Denny and Claybourne approached Jayne and her canine support volunteer, Lucas, they greeted each other.

"So, what did you find? And where exactly?" Tess asked, directly. Lucas pointed out toward the middle of the log jam.

"We were about there when Romeo started signaling and alerting us that he'd detected something. We then circled around and made another pass. Sure enough, he alerted again. Same spot," the young man said. "I marked the area on the jam with the pink tape." He pointed to a piece of neon pink trailing tape tied carefully to a tree branch sticking out of the log jam near the water's surface.

"How does the dog smell something that's dead and sitting at the bottom of the river?" Claybourne commented, "This whole river smells like fish and mud."

"You really want to know?" Jayne asked, coming over to stand with the group near the water's edge. "The remains give off gasses that float to the surface, sometimes even an oily residue. The dogs smell it and alert. You gotta remember, dogs' noses are like up to 10,000 times better than a human's. So, if something stinks to us, you can only imagine how it smells to them."

"How deep down can they smell?" Tess asked, truly interested. The river, at its deepest, was only 10 feet or so in the drier summer months.

"I've heard of dogs finding remains almost 80 feet down or more. It's crazy if you think about it. This river is nothing compared to a search we did out of state a few years back. Romeo found the guys remains two years after he'd drowned. They sent divers down and found him nearly 52 feet below the surface," Jayne said, bending to give Romeo a good head rub. "Dogs are pretty amazing if you ask me."

Chapter Twenty-Nine

Friday, July 15th, 4:04 p.m.

A while later, the divers arrived. As they readied themselves, Tess almost felt envious of them as the sun's rays beat down on them. At least the divers got to cool off a bit in the water.

Except Tess didn't want their grisly job. The thought of looking for a dead body in the murky depths of an underwater grave touched Tess in a way that sent shivers down her spine. When she was younger, she'd gone on a kayaking trip with some friends and had almost flipped over near a log jam, much like the one she was currently looking at. Then, her mind had wandered, and she'd thought what if there was a dead corpse floating just below the surface, its bloated, fish-eaten flesh caught in the branches.

Just thinking about it now sent a shiver down Tess's spine, causing Denny to glance over at her.

"You okay?" he asked, giving her a questioning look. She shrugged and tried to play it off.

"Yeah. Just thinking about what they might find under there." She took a few steps closer to the riverbank as the small Jon boat made its way to the log jam. Two divers sat on the edges of the boat, watching as they got closer to the pink trailing tape tied to the tangled branches where Romeo had signaled.

"Hopefully we get some answers," Denny said, watching as Lindsey came over to stand with them. Tess felt her hackles come up but schooled her features. She wouldn't let Lindsey know about her insecurities. Keeping them from Denny was hard enough.

The trio watched as the divers disembarked the boat and then slipped under the surface. Tess was unsure how deep exactly the river was at the bend where the log jam was, especially this time of year. Normally the hot summer sun would cause the water level to evaporate, but recent summer storms had caused a deluge to swiftly fill the river basin. This in turn pushed more branches and detritus onto the tangle of floating logs.

The moments passed slowly. Everyone on the bank stood quietly, murmuring amongst themselves, all eyes on the water. Dave, the search volunteer playing the part of "boat captain" sat at the helm of the Jon boat and squinted overboard. The tension was palpable, and time seemed to stand still. Would they find Jessica Slaydon today? Would they find her at all?

Suddenly, one of the divers emerged from the surface and looked toward Tess and Denny standing on the shoreline. Tess's shoulders slumped as the diver shook his head. They'd found nothing. A frustrated growl quietly emerged from Tess's throat. Where was Jessica Slaydon? The river seemed to be the perfect spot to dispose of her body, if in fact Neil had killed her. If he had dismembered her and transported her away in the baby stroller. But what now? What leads did she have to follow up on? She felt like kicking something like a petulant child who'd been told they couldn't have candy.

Tess's hand was on the radio, about to call base and give them an update when the second diver popped up from the water, holding a small black trash bag. She'd found something!

"Get me out there!" Tess commanded as she made her way over the riparian terrain and climbed onto the second awaiting boat. The volunteer at the helm nodded and, putting the motor in gear, headed toward the divers.

Within moments, Tess's boat sat next to the diver's. The two divers were still in the water, watching her approach, while hanging on the side of their boat.

"Great work!" Tess commended, "Is there more down there?" She watched as the female diver brought the trash bag to Tess. Donning rubber exam gloves, Tess took the bag and laid it in the bottom of her boat.

"Yeah, I found more," the diver nodded, watching as Tess took a folding pocket knife from her pants pocket and was about to cut the bag open. She paused though and looked at the diver.

"How many?" Tess asked as she decided to take photos of the trash bag as it was when it came out of the water, sealed tightly with layers of duct tape. Snapping a few photos on her phone, she waited for the diver to answer.

"I saw at least three more, but they were caught deep in the branches of the log jam. The rain really didn't help make this easier on us."

Tess nodded, absorbing the information. As the divers watched closely, along with the people on the shoreline, Tess stuck her phone back into her pocket and went to work making a slit in the plastic bag just under the duct tape. At the first puncture, they could smell it. The stench of death emanated from the bag and as Tess pulled it open, her heart hurt. They'd found Jessica Slaydon. What was left of her at least.

Pulling the bag open, Tess looked down at the contents. Two human feet, complete with pink nail polish, lay severed in a puddle of congealed blood mixed with water. The smell was overpowering, and Tess's throat began to close up as her brain processed what she was seeing ... and smelling. Grabbing the bag closed with her hand, she looked over at Denny on the shoreline and nodded. He nodded back in understanding and pulled out his phone to place a call.

Turning to the divers, she said, "Thanks guys. Unfortunately, this is what we are looking for. Are you able to bring up the other bags or do we need to call in more help?"

"Nah, we can do it. It'll take a few minutes to get to them," the female diver said confidently. "I'll have Jim take underwater photos if we can." She nodded at the male diver. "It's pretty murky down there." Jim nodded in agreement.

Within moments, the divers disappeared under the surface once more and the waiting began again. To use the time well, Tess radioed to base to let them know what was found. Malone took the information down and told Tess he'd deal with the searchers that were standing by waiting for instructions. He also mentioned, much to Tess's annoyance, that the media had started to converge at the bridge. Luckily, police barricades were in place to keep them at bay for a while. It was just a matter of time for them to find a breach and sneak down to the river to take photos. Tess rolled her eyes inwardly at the thought. She did not want a media circus until they verified that the remains were indeed that of Jessica Slaydon. The county, even the entire state, had been watching the case upfold, photos of a smiling Jessica Slaydon plastered all over every window of every gas station and diner in the tri county area. A missing pregnant woman was big news.

Chapter Thirty

Friday, July 15th, 7:09 p.m.

Later that evening, hungry and exhausted, Tess and Denny, along with his new sidekick, Lindsey, stood around the exam table in Dr. Abby Summers' morgue. Summers, the medical examiner, had agreed to do a cursory autopsy on the body found in the bags in the river. She would do a further, in depth one, of course, but Tess needed answers sooner rather than later. The media and her superiors were breathing down her neck to catch a break in the case.

"So, is this all of the bags?" Dr. Summers asked, laying out the severed body parts as anatomically as she could. The divers had found a total of eight bags caught in different tangles of the log jam. The initial bag holding the feet was quickly joined by two holding a pair of legs, cut into four pieces at the knees, and two bags each holding an arm, with hands still attached, bent at the elbows. One had held the lower half of a torso, the spinal column severed just under the ribs. Another bag held the top of the torso, including ribs, sternum, and shoulders.

"So far we've got arms, legs, and a torso," Dr. Abby Summers. "Any guesses what's in the last one?" she asked with a bit of gallows humor to lighten the mood as she lifted the last black bundle out of the body bag and laid it on the exam table. Taking a pair of scissors, she sliced open the bag and pulled out the contents: a woman's severed head.

Tess felt her stomach lurch at the sight, but when she caught Lindsey taking a step toward the table, a look of curiosity on her face, Tess felt a surge of spite to show her up in front of Denny. Juvenile, she knew, but she just couldn't help it. Lindsey, with her flawless skin and bubbly personality. Tess groaned inwardly just thinking about the other woman spending her days with Denny, getting too close to him just to spite Tess. But was that *really* what she was up to? Tess wondered if maybe she was just playing the jealous girlfriend, being ridiculous, making tension when there wasn't any. If Tess would get her head out of her ass and be honest with herself, she'd have to admit–Lindsey was very smart and seemed capable. She asked appropriate questions, carried herself professionally, and Tess *really* hadn't seen her flirt with Denny, right?

Tess glanced over at Lindsey and saw the woman's hand covering her nose, despite the mask she wore, to avoid the smell of decomposition that permeated the room. Also wearing a mask, Tess forced herself to ignore the smell and focus on the decapitated human head staring blindly back at her. God, how awful.

Long blond hair lay in limp chunks around the woman's bloated face but Tess was sure it was Jessica Slaydon. The scar through her left eyebrow was evident still, even during this stage of decomposition. Tess sighed, knowing it would be her job to tell Lydia, Jessica's mother, that her daughter was indeed not coming home. Telling Neil Slaydon would be a whole other issue. They would be asking him to come down the station under the pretense that they had some more questions about Jessica and the days leading up to her disappearance. Tess wanted Neil's reaction to his wife's death recorded. She knew that he'd killed his wife, everything was pointing that way. She just needed more proof. Determined to see him pay for his crimes, Tess steeled herself for the inevitable confrontation. But for now, she leaned closer to the body, making sure that Lindsey saw, and inspected the cut marks on the body parts.

"Chain saw? Reciprocating saw?" Tess asked Dr. Summers, "Or one heck of a knife?"

The doctor leaned closer and moved a light with a magnifying lens attached to it over the body to inspect it further. Once she seemed to find something, she leaned back and gestured for Tess to have a look. "See the jagged markings?" Abby asked as Tess leaned in to have a look.

"Those are cut marks from a saw, not a knife. You can tell by the marks on the bone. Saws make pretty smooth cuts whereas a knife would cause a mix of shallow and heavy cuts."

"Shallow cuts?" Lindsey asked, still standing close to Denny. Abby nodded and pointed to a piece of bone sticking out from the victim's left leg.

"If someone uses a knife to cut through bone, there would be ... skip marks, you know, from the knife slipping or moving out of the previous cut groove. Imagine the killer's hands or gloves are wet with blood. When they put pressure on the knife handle to make a cut, the blade can slip some, causing shallow, more superficial cuts."

"And you're not seeing those here?" Tess asked as she moved around the table to inspect the body parts from various angles. She tried breathing through her mouth as the smell of the decaying flesh hung in the air.

"Not so far. I'll inspect each piece further in the morning when I'm fresh but tentatively, I'm pretty sure the cause of death is a gunshot wound to the back of the head. And if that didn't kill her, then getting cut up definitely did," Dr. Summers said, pointing to a large wound in the back of the woman's skull. Tess looked at the decapitated head in surprise, noticing the wound through the sodden hair for the first time.

"Any idea if the gunshot wound was accidental and then maybe somebody panicked and cut her up? Or was she murdered and then cut up?"

"This is definitely murder. See those marks on the skin around the wound?" Summers asked, pointing to dark speckled markings around the gaping hole. "That's stippling from gunpowder. Your 'vic' was shot from behind at close range."

"Stippling? From GSR?" Lindsey asked, daring a small step closer to see what the doctor was talking about. By the look on her face, she was both horrified and curious.

"Yes, exactly right. Stippling is the type of gunshot residue made from close range gunshot wounds. The closer the shot, the more clustered the marks are. As the distance increases from the victim to the gun, the stippling widens. The gunpowder makes shallow, superficial marks on the skin around the wound that helps us determine distance of the shot," Abby explained to Lindsey.

Lindsey nodded but remained quiet. Tess continued to investigate the hole in Jessica's severed head.

"Is there any chance at all this could have been self-inflicted?" Tess asked, glancing up at Dr. Summers. "I have to ask even though I'm pretty sure you're right."

"Unless Mrs. Slaydon could extend her arms like Inspector Gadget and reach around her head, I seriously doubt this was self-inflicted."

"Inspector Gadget?" Lindsey wrinkled her nose in confusion.

"An old cartoon from back in the day. Way before our time," Tess offered, barely giving Lindsey a glance, unable to look away from the autopsy table. She heard Denny chuckle softly as he listened to them.

"Gee, thanks," chided Dr. Summers. "Now I feel old. But seriously, Jessica Slaydon was shot in the head and then dismembered. I'll have to do my internal examination, get her cleaned up, but I'm pretty confident in what I'm seeing here. I'll confirm ID with dental records so you can make an arrest."

"Well, thank you, Doc," Tess said, somewhat relieved at finally getting some answers. "Please let us know if there is anything else you need. I look forward to your final report."

Summers nodded and then led them out of the morgue and down a well-lit corridor to the lobby of the Medical Examiner's Office. It was after hours, everyone was gone for the day except for Dr. Summers, the janitor, and the dead people in the coolers.

Tess typically didn't like going to the morgue during the day. But at night? She'd been ready to go before she'd even gotten there.

The trio said goodbye to Dr. Summers and then walked to their cars. Tess's Jeep Wrangler was parked next to

Denny's black Tahoe. Other than Dr. Summers' vehicle, the parking lot was empty.

Tess tried not to let her frustration show when she realized that Lindsey must have ridden with Denny. Tess saw green, the dark feeling of envy curling itself around her throat and chest.

Resisting the urge to say something snarky, because it would accomplish nothing but hurt feelings, Tess crushed her molars together and headed toward her Jeep. She was almost there when she realized that Denny was talking to her.

"What did you say?" she asked with an aggravated sigh. It had been a long and arduous day and she just wanted to get home to Otter.

"I asked what your plans were for tomorrow," Denny repeated, giving Tess a confused look. Lindsey just leaned up against the Tahoe's front passenger door, checking something on her phone.

Tess rolled her eyes at the other woman's back and continued to get into her own car. She lowered the window when Denny approached, his face in shadow. Behind him, a street light illuminated the dark parking lot, making a buzzing sound.

"What's wrong? You seem mad all of a sudden," Denny asked, placing his hands on the door of Tess's Jeep.

"It's just been a long day and I'm over it," Tess stated, putting the Jeep in gear. "I'm grouchy, hungry, and I just want to get home to my dog."

"Okay ...." Denny said, carefully watching Tess. "I just wanted to make sure I hadn't done something to tick you off."

"If only it were that simple," Tess snapped. "Look, I'm sorry. I have to go. Have fun with your little shadow." She cast a look of disdain at Lindsey and quickly backed out of her parking spot and headed home, leaving Denny standing there wondering what had just happened.

Chapter Thirty-One

Friday, July 15th, 9:45 p.m.

Tess shoved the last bite of her leftover beef stroganoff into her mouth and began chewing. Closing her eyes, she willed the tension and stress from the day's event to leave her body. She was exhausted, both mentally and physically. A hot shower had helped, along with food in her belly. Now she just needed some sleep.

Swallowing her food and then sipping the last of her water, she gathered up her plate and cup and headed toward the sink. The house was quiet and dark, except for the light over the stove. Tess sighed as her bare feet padded across the room.

Suddenly, the kitchen was lit up by headlights turning into her driveway, followed by a car door shutting. The dogs started barking as a knock was heard at the front door. Tess sighed. It had to be Denny, and she just didn't have the energy to deal with work or anything else tonight.

She headed to the door and peered out, and sure enough, Denny stood in the shadows of her front porch, a concerned look on his face. She felt bad for the way she had left things and opened the door.

"Hey," she mumbled, trying to grab the dog's collars as they full body wagged in an effort to get to Denny.

"Hey, yourself," he greeted, bending down to look her in the eye, "Mind if I come in?" Tess nodded for him to enter and stepped back, a collared dog in each hand.

"These two knuckleheads have way too much energy for me tonight," Tess commented, forcing a smile across her tired face. She watched as Denny squatted down to the dog's level and the two canines went crazy snooting and greeting him. Tess couldn't help but laugh then.

"You hungry?" she offered over her shoulder as she made her way back into the kitchen. She was already pulling out the rest of the beef stroganoff from the refrigerator knowing he'd be hungry. He always was.

"You know I'd never pass up food," came his muffled answer from under the dogs in the entryway. Tess rolled her eyes, a smile crossing her tired face, as she watched the three of them playing on the wood floor as she waited for the microwave to ding.

When it finally beeped, Tess set the warmed plate of food on the table as Denny went to wash his hands at the kitchen sink. Tess plopped down wearily on the chair opposite Denny's seat.

"So, where's your shadow?" Tess asked, nonchalantly, as she flipped through a pile of unopened mail.

"Shadow?" Denny asked as he sat down at the table, "Oh, you mean Lindsey? I dropped her off at her car down at the station." He took a bite of the food and grinned as he quietly chewed. After swallowing, he commented, "This is amazing. Did you make this from scratch?" Tess nodded as he took another bite.

They sat in silence for a few moments, Denny lost in his dinner and Tess trying to decompress after a long and stressful day. After a few moments, Denny pushed his empty plate away and leaned back in his chair.

"Thanks for dinner, Tess. That was delicious," he complimented and then watched her silently for a few moments.

She could see him watching her out of the corner of her eye but was so tired she didn't even know what to say to get things off of her chest. To talk to him about her feelings, her needs.

"About earlier, at Dr. Summers' office ...." he asked tentatively. When Tess turned to him, he continued, "I ... I don't know what I did, but I feel like I made you angry—like I upset you somehow." He stared down at his empty plate for a few moments and when she said nothing, he looked back up at her exhausted face, at the tears that seemed to be threatening to fall from her blue eyes.

"Tess …" concerned filled his face as he reached across the table to wipe her cheek under her eye. "Honey, what's wrong?"

"Nothing," Tess mumbled, pulling away to dab at her own eyes. "It's just been a long day."

"Yeah, it has," Denny sighed in agreement, letting his hand drop to the table. "I'm exhausted, too. But what I'm worried about is that you seem angry with me. Like there is a rift between us somehow and I don't like it."

"There's a lot of stuff I don't like right now," Tess scowled. "I need a vacation."

Pushing back from the table, she quickly grabbed his plate and fork and headed for the sink. Plugging the sink drain and running hot water, she added some dish soap with a huff.

"Don't we all," Denny commiserated. She could feel his eyes on her from across the room. "I haven't been anywhere in … six years? It's just part of the job, I guess."

"Well, you know what, Denny?" Tess snapped, turning to glare at him, "I would just like to spend some time with you. Without work getting in the way. Without having to share your attention with Natalie or Otter or fucking Lindsey!" The last part escaped her lips, and she was immediately wishing them back in. Shit.

Tess turned around, her back to Denny, as she began scrubbing at another plate. She had a dishwasher but at that moment, she was agitated at Denny and embarrassed that she'd said too much. Tears threatened the back of her eyelids, and she resisted the urge to sniffle. She would not let him see her cry. If he wanted to cast her off, make excuses not to see her, then fine. She wasn't going to fling herself at him and embarrass herself further.

The soft scraping sound of the kitchen chair pushing out from the table told her he was standing up. Would he leave, angry and annoyed at her? Surely, after her snide comment. Tess hated the thought of them fighting and she shoved her shaking hands into the hot dish water, feeling the bubbles popping around her wrists.

She nearly jumped when he came up behind her and gently laid his hands on her shoulders. Sucking in a deep breath, she stood still, her hands still fully submerged.

"Is that how you really feel, Tess?" Denny asked softly, "Like I don't want to be around you? Spend time with you? Is that what's been bothering you?" he sighed. She remained quiet, tears silently coursing down her cheeks.

"Tess, I need you to turn around. Please talk to me." She felt a light tug on her shoulders, but remained still, not wanting him to see her tears.

"Tess? I'm sorry. I'm sorry you feel this way," he said softly, moving closer to her still. "It was never my intention. If I could spend everyday with you I would. You should know that."

"Then why am I always the lowest priority?" Tess asked, her anger and frustration swelling again. "Every time we make plans, you cancel them. How can I not think that you don't want to spend time with me?" She grabbed a towel and wiped her hands off, dabbed her eyes quickly before turning around and facing him. Bad move. Her heart began to race, just looking at him. He was closer than she thought he'd been and now she was practically standing nose to nose with him.

Sensing she was about to bolt, Denny stuck his hand out and held her in place gently. She stopped moving, her eyes remained on his throat, his shoulder, his chin. Anywhere but his face.

"Tess ..." he said, gently lifting her chin to make her look at him, "Tess, you are never my lowest priority. Ever. And I'm so sorry that I made you feel that way. I had to cancel twice because of work, once because of Natalie. I'm a father. I have responsibilities. Surely you can understand that?"

Tess slowly looked up, her gaze resting on his mouth and then moving up to his eyes. So blue. He was watching her intently, a look of concern and something else she couldn't quite discern etched into his handsome features.

"I would never come between you and Natalie. Period," Tess said, looking him in the eye. "And I understand work. It's always there. One case finishes, and then somebody does something else and another case lands on your desk." She sighed. "I just ... I'm just frustrated."

"Me too," he murmured. Reaching up, he gently pushed her long dark hair behind her ear. "I hate canceling on you. It kills me to hear the disappointment in your voice each time it happens." He paused then, bending down a couple inches to look her straight in the eye. "But what was that about Lindsey?"

"Nothing," Tess muttered, turning to move away from him. He stopped her, a light grasp on her arm.

"You think I'd rather spend time with Lindsey?" he asked incredulously. When Tess didn't say anything, he stood back up but not before Tess saw him grin.

"Yes, Lindsey!" she snapped, pulling her arm away from him. He immediately let go but said nothing, his eyes still sparkling with amusement. "Lindsey with her bubbly personality, super smarts, and perky breasts. She's really good at her job, she's beautiful, and you let her flirt with you! Right in front of me!"

And then she heard it. He was laughing quietly to himself. She looked up at him, a glare darkening her face. "Seriously?" she seethed.

"You're jealous," he grinned, still standing much too close to her. She was torn. On one hand, she wanted him even closer to her, but on the other, she was mad and wanted to be as far away from him as possible.

"I am not. You're just naive," she said with a huff. God, why did she have to find him so attractive when she was so angry?

"No, you're jealous. And I think it's cute," he grinned. She scowled. He continued, "For the record, she talks a lot—she doesn't know half as much as you do. And she chews her gum like a horse, which drives me insane."

Tess rolled her eyes, still unwilling to let him know that he was correct. She was jealous, and she hated herself for it.

"As for her breasts," he continued, looking down at Tess, "I wouldn't know if they were perky or not because there is only one pair that I'm interested in—and they aren't hers." As his gaze slid lower, Tess felt heat rise up her neck, a blush covering her cheeks. She swallowed audibly, her words lost. Her breathing came in shallow gulps as she watched his smoldering gaze move up again from her chest and then pause on her mouth.

He stepped even closer, their bodies touching. She was gently pinned between him and the kitchen sink, and she felt her pulse quicken. Then he leaned in, and their lips met, his arms pulling her closer to him. She moaned lightly as he deepened the kiss, and she felt his hands on her hips. She leaned into the kiss, her arms reaching up to circle around his neck. He ran his hands up her sides then back down to her hips, his fingers gently exploring her body as they went. Tess pulled her hands free from his neck and moved them lower to his chest, his muscles firm under her touch. She could feel his heartbeat, racing to match her own. He pulled away from her just enough to see her face.

Resting his forehead on hers, he looked into her blue eyes and slowly caught his breath. She could feel his hardness pressing into her waist.

"See what you do to me?" he whispered. "You're the only one I notice. The only one I want to spend time with. You're the only one that makes me think dirty thoughts, thinking about all the things I can't wait to do to you." He watched as Tess blushed all over again and he grinned.

"What did you have in mind?" Tess asked curiously, their foreheads still touching. She looked up at him then and saw the heat in his gaze as it slid over her. She gulped, suddenly both embarrassed by her bravado but also turned on as never before. She wanted his hands on her, to feel him around her, in her, but she was too shy to say anything.

His hand came up and cupped her cheek and said, "All in good time. I don't want to rush this. You mean too much to me for me to mess this up just because I want you so bad."

He wanted her? Really wanted her? Tess couldn't suppress the grin she felt crossing her face. She leaned up into his embrace again and pressed her lips to his neck. He seemed to like that as his hands tightened their grip on her hips and a mumbled sigh escaped him. Turning to press her lips to his again, Tess deepened the kiss, and he responded.

Suddenly the blaring alert of an incoming call filled the kitchen, breaking the tension that filled the room. It was Tess's phone.

With a sigh, she went and answered, "This is Detective Dane."

"Hi, Tess, it's Angela, over at Tolliver Care Home. Sorry to call you so late again but I thought you should know."

"What's happened to Dad?" Tess asked, her mind reeling. She heard a sigh on the other end of the phone. "He was perfectly fine last night." She could feel panic rising in her chest.

"Well, there was another incident tonight. Your dad is fine. For now. But he fell and hit his head earlier this evening. We checked him out and his vitals seemed fine, so we put him back in his room. A short time later though, the bedside alarm went off and well ...."

"Yes? Is he okay?" Tess asked, casting a worried look toward Denny, who was now standing next to her, an expression of concern on his face.

"He is now. It seems that he had some kind of seizure. He was in the middle of it when they responded to the alarm. We got him stabilized and everything is fine now, but we are going to be transporting him to OSU first thing in the morning for some more scans to see what caused it. Obviously, if something changes before then, we will take him sooner."

"Thank you, Angela. You've always been a good lookout for Dad," Tess said, emotion filling her voice. She tried to swallow down a sob as she processed what had happened to her father.

"Anytime, Tess," Angela's smooth voice filled her ears. "You know that you and your father are important to me. I got you. My shift is over at 6:00 a.m. and I wanted you to know what was going on."

"Should I come down now?"

"Nah, sweetheart. Your dad is snoring comfortably. You get some rest. I'll call you if anything changes."

"Thank you, Angela," Tess sniffled before hanging up the phone. She set the phone on the table and her shoulders slumped. As Denny wrapped his arms around her to comfort her, she felt herself shatter inside. He gently guided her toward the couch as sobs wracked her body.

He held her as she cried, her body curled up against his as her tears dampened his shirt but he didn't seem to mind. He started rubbing her back gently and as her tears slowed, he changed to lightly scratching her back and she felt herself relax. She kept her head on his chest, listening to his heartbeat while his hand continued to scratch her gently and with a sigh, she closed her eyes.

Chapter Thirty-Two

Saturday, July 16th, 6:44 a.m.

Morning sun streamed through the blinds of Tess's living room, and she jolted awake, only to find herself snuggled on the couch with Denny wrapped around her.

It was then that the events of the previous night had come flooding back to her. Her father, Denny's kisses, him holding her while she cried. Slightly embarrassed that she'd cried herself to sleep on him, she turned to look up at his face and found that he was still sleeping. She watched the gentle rise and fall of his chest as he slept, his arms wrapped around her from where they'd been asleep all night. They were covered with a blanket although she didn't remember covering them up. He must have, always one to make sure she was comfortable.

Worried that she looked atrocious from crying so much the night before and that she had morning breath, Tess tried to quietly sit up and disengage herself from Denny and the couch. No success, because as soon as she began to move away from him, his arms pulled her back to his chest.

"Please don't leave yet, Tess. I'm enjoying this," he mumbled as he snuggled into her again. Tess grinned to herself and when she reciprocated the snuggle, she heard him sigh contentedly.

"I could get used to this," he whispered in her ear.

"What? Falling asleep on the couch after I cry and snot all over you?" Tess teased.

"Nah, not so much the crying part," Denny smiled, rolling her so they were spooning. "I meant waking up next to you. It's a great feeling." He pulled her closer to him and she sighed.

His words caused Tess to feel giddy. Denny moved then, his hand slowly inching its way over her hip and down to the waistline of her pants. Tess's breath hitched as she waited to see what, if anything, he was going to do. Her backside was pressed up against his groin, her back to his chest. She couldn't see his face, but she could feel his eyes on her as he watched her reaction to his touch. His touch. She wanted to feel him touch her, but she was also so nervous and she didn't know why. It was Denny for crying out loud. Maybe it was because of the feelings she'd kept buried away for so long. Maybe it was just excitement, and she was overthinking.

Suddenly, she felt his lips on the back of her neck and as they slowly made their way down to her shoulder, she let out a contented sigh. Feeling emboldened, she gently pushed her backside up against him and felt his hardness pressing against her. She moved, just a little, and when she heard his quick intake of breath, she grinned to herself.

"Are you trying to make this difficult for me?" he said, his voice thick with emotion as his fingers moved again along the waistband of her yoga pants. He lightly let his fingers slowly dip below the edge of her waistband, up around her belly button and then back again.

Tess's breathing hitched as she felt her skin tingle from where he'd touched her. Where she hoped he'd touch her. She must have moved again because he let out a hiss and held her hip still against him. She froze for a moment and then she felt his hand moving back over her abdomen, this time sliding under her shirt.

The feel of his warm fingers slowly making their way upwards under her shirt was enough to make Tess sigh and relax. By the time his hand cupped her breast, Tess was ready to do anything to feel him touch her all over. She let out a soft moan as she turned toward his hand as it continued to explore her through her bra.

Suddenly, Otter, who'd been asleep on the floor, shot up and ran toward the front door, barking and carrying on, Max hot on his heels. Tess and Denny both jumped at the sudden chaos and Tess stood up and went to see what they were going on about. *It better be something important,* she thought to herself as she glanced over her shoulder and saw Denny headed for the restroom.

The dogs continued to bark and jump at the front door as Tess spied through the peephole. Nancy McCrae, her elderly neighbor, stood on Tess's porch, a mason jar full of something red in her hand. Slightly irritated that Mrs. McCrae had broken the spell with her and Denny, Tess begrudgingly grabbed Otter's green collar and opened the front door.

"Oh, hello, Mrs. McCrae!" Tess smiled at the little old lady standing before her. The older woman looked up at her through the thick lenses of her wire-rimmed glasses.

"Hello, dear!" Mrs. McCrae spoke loudly, as she normally did, yet still causing Tess to jump back at the volume. "I've brought you some of my strawberry preserves. It's like jelly!"

"Well, thank you, Mrs. McCrae. Otter and I love jelly," Tess said, taking the offered jar of preserves. The older woman stood there for a moment, blinking up at Tess, saying nothing.

"It's jelly!" she announced again, louder this time. "You put it on toast!"

Tess stifled a smile, wishing that Mrs. McCrae's family would invest in some hearing aids for her. "Oh, we will definitely put it on toast. Thank you so much for thinking about us."

"You're welcome, dear. You're welcome." Nancy McCrae was turning to go when something behind Tess caught her eye. She stopped, lowered her glasses down her nose, and squinted into the interior of Tess's house. "And who is that, dear? My, my, but he *is* handsome. I've seen him around here a lot recently," she stated in a loud stage whisper. "Go get 'em girl." With a wink, the woman returned her glasses to the bridge of her nose, grinned at Tess, and then left.

Tess stepped back into the house, shut the door, and then turned around to find Denny standing there with a bemused look on his face. They looked at each other and grinned.

"I hope you like preserves on your toast," Tess smirked. "It's like jelly."

Denny let out a low laugh, shaking his head at Mrs. McCrae's visit and evaluation of him. Tess gazed over at him, took in his bare feet, jeans from yesterday and his tee-shirt he'd changed into the night before. His dark hair was perfectly tousled and his face looked rested. She had to admit–Mrs. McCrea wasn't wrong–he *was* handsome.

Disappointed, though, that Mrs. McCrae had ruined the mood, Tess headed for the bathroom to see how atrocious she looked.

"C'mon, Otter, Max, let's go potty," she heard Denny say as she shut the bathroom door.

While Denny and the dogs were outside, Tess decided to grab a quick shower because, as feared, her makeup was smeared and her slept-on hair vaguely resembled Medusa. Besides, she had a morning briefing with Malone and the team soon.

Torn between staying in the hot stream of water and visiting with Denny, Tess turned off the shower, and quickly wrapped herself in a towel. Gathering up her dirty clothes and tossing them in the hamper, she opened the bathroom door to dart to her bedroom, and squealed.

"Sorry!" Denny exclaimed, jumping back from the bathroom door, his hand still up from where he had been about to knock. "I was just going to ask you if you wanted to go get some breakfast or if you wanted me to make something before your morning briefing."

Breathing and heart rate back under control, Tess looked up at Denny, her wet hair framing her cheeks and neck. He just gazed at her for a few moments, saying nothing with his mouth, but a lot with his eyes.

Tess gulped, blushing at the direction her thoughts were going, and finally blurted, "You pick. I'll just get dressed and we can do whatever."

"Or you can stay undressed, and we can do whatever ...." his eyes raked over her like hot coals. Tess sucked in a small gasp and felt her face flush.

"Relax, Tess." Denny softly chuckled. "I'm not going to eat you." He paused, and then added with a grin, "Yet.

But I will. Besides, Malone will be on our case if you aren't there in—" he glanced at his watch, "thirty minutes."

Tess gasped again, this time for a whole new reason, as she ran across the hall slamming her bedroom door behind her.

Chapter
Thirty-Three

Saturday, July 16th, 8:33 a.m.

Twenty-eight minutes later, Tess walked into the conference room, a gas station coffee in her hand. Malone looked up from his place at the head of the table and nodded at her as she quickly found seats next to Deputies Miles, Scafferty, and Cooper.

"Okay, what do we have, folks?" Malone asked as a way to start the meeting. "Has Lydia Fontaine been told that the body we found in the river yesterday is indeed her daughter Jessica?"

"Not yet, sir," Tess began. "We stopped at the morgue last night for a preliminary look at the remains. They visually appear to be that of Jessica Slaydon. Dr. Summers will be doing the official autopsy today as well as fingerprinting the remains and comparing dental records. As soon as an official ID is confirmed, I'll tell Lydia. She will have a million questions and I want to have as much information as I can going into it."

"I do not envy you of that job, Detective Dane," Malone empathized. Tess nodded grimly. She wasn't looking forward to the conversation at all.

"We have units camped out in front of Slaydon's house," Scafferty supplied. "The judge is waiting for the final go ahead to sign the arrest warrant for Neil Slaydon. It's all filled out except for the signature."

After finding the initial blood stain on the picture frame and the Luminol detecting the cleaned up blood in front of the sink, an official search warrant had been issued and the house searched top to bottom. Because of all of the search activity at the river and processing the remains of Jessica Slaydon, the team had each been tasked with a different area of investigation and now it was time to officially compare notes.

"Okay, so let's review one last time before we make idiots of ourselves," Tess cautioned. "We have proof that Neil lied about leaving the house that night to go to Piedmont's to basically get a kill kit–saw blades, cleaner, plastic bags. We have blood evidence in multiple spots throughout the house that belong to the victim. Even in an area where our suspect tried to destroy the evidence—the blood spot in front of the kitchen sink. We have multiple surveillance videos showing Slaydon's movements through the neighborhood with the stroller.

Do we have forensics back on the stroller yet?" she paused to ask Miles.

"Yes, just came in this morning," Miles opened a file in front of him. "There was a minuscule droplet of blood found on the fabric part of the stroller. The fabric was black, so it was easy to miss. However, Luminol doesn't lie. The sample's being processed now at the lab, but it has been confirmed to be from a female human. Official DNA results are pending."

"Good work, Deputy Miles," Malone commended. He turned back to Tess. "You mentioned in your text last night that Mrs. Slaydon was shot. Was any kind of firearm found at the Slaydon home?"

"No. And there is nothing registered under either of their names," Tess sighed. "So, if he killed Jessica he must have tossed the gun. It was either bought illegally, explaining why it's not registered, or it belonged to someone else."

Malone looked frustrated but nodded in understanding. He turned to the rest of the group. "Any word on the Slaydon's cell phone records?"

"So far, we still haven't found Jessica's cell phone," Scafferty offered, joining the conversation. "The records show no activity on it since the evening of the Fourth of July. It appears that the phone was at the Slaydon house all day. The signal stopped pinging around 2:15 a.m. on July 5th. It either ran out of juice or someone turned it off."

"We turned that house upside down and never found it," Tess thought aloud. "It had to have been dumped somewhere. Maybe it's wherever the gun is? Or it's still at the bottom of the river."

"In which case, we may never find it," sighed Miles. "What about Neil's phone?"

Scafferty grinned, "That was a little more enlightening. It appears that Mr. Slaydon forgot to leave his phone at home when he went to Piedmont's. That, coupled with the surveillance video from the store, proves that he lied about his whereabouts. As for the call log, it looks like he called his wife's number multiple times on the fifth, probably to make it look like he was concerned. Even left some voicemails. There are some texts to someone named "Peaches" and well ... let's just say, Neil and Peaches have been sending explicit photos back and forth for a few months now. I've seen more of Neil Slaydon than I ever wanted to."

"Gross," Tess said, wrinkling her nose. "Any clue who Peaches is?"

"No. I've literally seen her from every angle—and I mean *every* angle—except her face." Scafferty grinned as he watched Tess's face.

"Again ... gross." Tess shook her head. She heard Miles laughing quietly next to her and gently smacked at his arm.

"Did his phone ping anywhere close to the river on the days he allegedly dumped her body?" Malone asked, trying to get them back on track.

"The dump area and his house are too close together to determine exactly. Meaning, they use the same cell tower," Scafferty explained, watching the faces of his coworkers fall. Then he started to grin. "But, then our boy Neil decided he wanted to order some lunch. When his phone prompted 'use my location' he clicked yes without thinking. According to that, he was standing in the middle of the Camden River."

"Let's go get him," Tess commanded, already halfway out the door, "Get Judge D'Angelo's signature on that warrant now!"

Chapter Thirty-Four

Saturday, July 16th, 9:22 a.m.

"What do you mean, he's gone?" Tess nearly shouted. She shouldn't be surprised that Neil Slaydon was MIA, but she was. "He was supposed to be under 24-hour surveillance!"

"Well, he didn't come out the front door, that's for sure," Deputy Drew Tanner said over the phone, his voice strained and repentant. "I've been out here since early this morning. Deputy Greer was here before me, but he didn't see anything either." Tess knew Greer was the deputy tasked with the night watch over Slaydon and at the moment she wanted to throttle him.

"This is unbelievable," groaned Tess, her mind racing. "We have to find him! He's wanted for the murder and dismemberment of his wife Jessica."

"So, it was her body after all?" Tanner said with a sigh. "Look, Detective Dane, I really am sorry he slipped out on us. I've been sitting here staring at his house all day and haven't seen anything. Not even a curtain flutter. He must have slipped out the back sometime last night or someone would have seen him."

Tess sighed in agreement. "And you checked the house thoroughly? Every nook and cranny?"

"Of course," Tanner said, an edge of irritation in his voice. "As soon as Deputy Jefferies showed up with the arrest warrant we went to get him. He didn't answer the door and so Jefferies and I kicked it in. Searched everywhere but he wasn't there."

Tess gritted her teeth in frustration. She wanted to punch something but knew that it would help nothing.

"I'm on my way. Start canvassing the neighborhood. I want all eyes looking for Neil Slaydon." Tess hung up the phone without waiting for Tanner's reply. She knew she was being harsh on him, but she was frustrated and angry.

Calling dispatch, she updated them on the situation and put out an APB on Neil Slaydon and his truck. He could be anywhere, especially since they didn't even know when he'd escaped.

As Tess headed toward the Slaydon's neighborhood, she kept her eyes peeled for any signs of Neil or his vehicle. Where would he go? She was deep in thought and after a few seconds, she finally noticed her phone vibrating in the console. Grabbing it without looking at the called ID, she answered.

"Dane."

"Hey, it's me," Denny's voice came across the speaker. "I just heard about the APB. What happened? I thought he was under surveillance?"

"He was," Tess snapped, not taking her eyes off the road. "Apparently he slipped out the back door at some point and now he's on the run. Must have seen all the activity swarming the river and knew he was on borrowed time before we found her."

Denny swore under his breath. "Where are you now? I can meet you. Help you look."

"I'm headed back to the Slaydon house. Aren't you working today? You left my house when I did."

"Got an arrest first thing this morning. I'm back home now, just finishing up the reports," he said. "I know I'm not officially on the Slaydon case, but I'd like to help if you need it."

"Sure," Tess said, turning down a street in Slaydon's neighborhood, "I'll take all the help I can get." She paused for a moment, driving slowly and checking out people's backyards as she made her way toward Neil's house. "Where would you go if you'd just murdered your wife and the cops had found her dismembered body parts in the river?"

"As far from you as possible," Denny said. "I'll call the airport, put a flag on his driver's license and passport. We should get any info of him trying to run for it that way."

"We've already flagged his passport," Tess said, as she continued to search her surroundings for their suspect. "I took care of that pretty early on. I never had a good feeling about the man and now my feelings are validated."

"You do seem to have a good knack at reading people's characters," Denny said fondly, trying to distract Tess.

"I try," Tess sighed as she pulled up at the Slaydon house and parked next to Tanner's cruiser. "I just got here. I'll see you when you get here." They said their goodbyes, and Tess hung up.

Tanner met her in the driveway, his head hung low and his shoulders slunk. He reminded her of a child who'd just had his sandcastle stomped on and she had to remind herself to go easy on him. But not too easy on him—he was still a rookie, and this was a chance to learn from his mistakes.

"Anything yet?" she asked, coming to a halt in front of Tanner and looking around as though Neil Slaydon would just be hanging out waiting to be found. Tess groaned inwardly at the thought. This was a shit show. The media was already having a heyday over 'body parts in bags down by the river.' Just wait until they found out that the sheriff's main suspect was now on the run.

"No, ma'am," Tanner said, not quite meeting Tess's gaze. "Jefferies and two other deputies are currently canvassing the neighborhood. I've asked homeowners at the neighboring houses to check their CC video feeds for any signs of Slaydon."

"If his truck was parked in the garage, how did he get it out without you all seeing it?" Tess snapped, trying desperately to reign in her frustration and anger.

"He had it parked in the alley out back," Tanner said, pointing a thumb over his shoulder. "He hasn't parked it in the garage since this all began. There's too much stuff in there."

"What are you talking about? When I was here the first day, the garage was perfectly clean and his truck was in there," Tess called over her shoulder as she made her way up the Slaydon's driveway to spy in the garage windows.

Inside the garage, where Neil's truck once sat, the concrete floor was now piled high with cardboard boxes and various pieces of furniture. What on Earth was Slaydon trying to pull? Making an excuse for the rookie deputy so that he didn't have to park in the garage because he was planning on escaping?

Tess angrily smacked the windowsill with her hand as she pulled her cellphone out of her pocket to call into dispatch. It was time to set up an all-out search for Neil Slaydon.

Monday, July 18th, 10:32 a.m.

According to Neil's bank, there had been no activity on his account since two days ago, when he'd decided to make a run for it. To say Tess was frustrated was an understatement.

If Neil was running, he'd need to get gas soon if he wasn't already out. As of yet, there had been no sightings of his black pickup truck either. He could have abandoned it somewhere and hotwired another but no stolen vehicles had been reported in Swain County in the past forty-eight hours. Sure, he could have made it to Columbus easy enough where he'd be at an advantage. There were more places to hide, dump a car, and steal another in the big city.

Tess was waiting to hear back from the car manufacturer about the GPS data built into the truck's interior. Neil's phone was a bust as he'd turned it off, thus making it untraceable. Of course, Tess had someone watching for any signal from the phone pinging off a tower should Neil turn it on for even a moment. Then at least, they'd have an area to focus on.

Just yesterday, Tess had shattered Lydia Fontaine's world, as she'd told the woman that her daughter would not be coming home. The sounds of sorrow that had emanated from Jessica's mother would haunt Tess for years to come. Dr. Abby Summers had called Tess earlier in the day to inform her that she'd confirmed an ID of the woman in the bags by using dental records, sadly provided by Jessica's own place of employment. Dr. Emmett Sanderson, Jessica's boss and dentist, was heartbroken at the news of finding Jessica's remains, but had handed over her medical file in record time.

The day had been stressful and emotionally exhausting to say the least. Unfortunately, today seemed to be starting out the same way.

Tess was cruising down the main street in Crawley after visiting her father at Tolliver Care Home and the sadness from seeing her dad like that mixed with the frustration of having a killer in the wind had put Tess in a foul mood.

Since having his seizure a few days ago, Tommy Dane had been in and out of consciousness. The doctors apparently thought that this could be due to his dementia and how his brain was currently working. Things weren't looking good and Tess was heartbroken. She just wanted her dad home with her and have him like he used to be, before dementia had taken its toll on him. Her current house was the same one she'd grown up in with her mother and father and she had so many good memories of her childhood.

That was until her dad had become ill and her mom had decided it was all too much to deal with and had left, filing for divorce just two weeks later. Since Tess was sixteen, she'd chosen to live with her father and Tommy Dane had received full custody of her. He'd also retained possession of the house during the divorce, his now ex-wife wanting only money from him.

As his dementia progressed, slowly at first, Tess helped him maintain the taxes and mortgage on the property, made sure the bills were paid on time, and kept the pantry stocked. Though just a teenager at the time, she was thrust into adulthood much earlier than her peers. But it was her dad, the one person who had been there for her all those years, the one that loved her unconditionally, who went to all her high school soccer games and parent teacher meetings. Tess did not feel resentful of him in any way. She was glad to help him in any way she could.

The thought that he was now laying in a bed at Tolliver Care home, unable to get up broke Tess's heart.

When she'd visited him that morning, he'd seemed to recognize her for a short while but then quickly got confused and agitated. When Tess finally stood to go, he was resting comfortably, fast asleep under his covers.

Now, as she turned toward Camden Town to head back to her office, her phone rang from the console of her car.

"This is Detective Dane," she greeted, without a glance at the caller ID.

"Hey, Dane, it's Scafferty. We got a ping on Neil's phone. Looks like he turned it on for a few seconds, but it was enough."

"So where is he?" Tess asked excitedly, unconsciously speeding up on the highway.

"Looks like he's somewhere near the Yardley Game Reserve. That explains why he's been able to lay low and not use his debit or credit cards."

"He's probably been camping and making s'mores for the past two days while we've been looking for him," Tess mumbled, relief and agitation pumping through her. "I'll call BCI. We need more manpower to search the woods. Can you contact Miles and Malone, update them on the situation? I'll meet you at the station in like ... ten minutes. I'm in my Jeep so I can't do lights and sirens," she half joked.

"See you soon. I'll work on wrangling people here," Scafferty agreed before disconnecting the call.

Tess quickly dialed Denny's number and filled him in, requesting BCI's assistance to apprehend Neil. Yardley Game Preserve was a huge swath of forested land and finding one man, especially one who was keen on remaining hidden, would be like finding a needle in a haystack.

After assuring BCI would be able to provide additional manpower, Tess worked with her deputies and Sheriff Malone to organize a plan to capture Neil Slaydon. If everything went to plan, they'd have Neil Slaydon behind bars before nightfall.

Chapter Thirty-Five

Monday, July 18th, 1:02 p.m.

Within a couple of hours, law enforcement from multiple agencies surrounded Yardley Game Preserve. It was not lost on Tess that mere months ago she'd been to the same area to view the crime scene of one of the Torture Killer's victims. Then, the victim was displayed in a gruesome Blood Eagle. Tess hoped, prayed, that today's activities would not end in such a vile display of gore and depravity.

As the officers from BCI, Swain County Sheriff's Department, and even a few off duty Ohio State Highway Patrol officers took their positions to help flush out Neil Slaydon, Tess felt her anxiety grow. Would they succeed in capturing the wife killer? Or would he slip from their grasp yet again?

"In position. The dogs are ready," came a male officer's voice from over the radio. Tess was grateful to have multiple canine officers available and ready, positioned at different areas of the forest.

"Copy," Tess spoke into her radio, from her position near base. "All right boys, let's do this. Remember, it is unknown if our subject is armed or not, so proceed with caution. He is under suspicion for the murder of his wife and has little to lose. Stay alert. Remember to check in with base every sixty minutes or so. Any trace of human activity should be noted, but keep your eyes peeled for Neil himself. Consult the photo you have been given. Good luck out there."

With that, the officers moved in toward the woods, disappearing into the undergrowth within minutes. Tess, wanting to be in the field instead of being in charge of base, chomped at the bit.

She began pacing back and forth, searching the edge of the forest for any activity. Agitation coursed through her as she flattened a tract of grasses near the woodline from pacing so intently.

Deputy Miles came up to her then from where he'd been manning the radio and computer communications.

"Go. I've got this," he offered, giving her a small grin. "You weren't meant to sit around and wait. There are others here that can help me." He motioned with his hand at the two other officers milling around working on various things. They looked up at Miles and Tess and nodded.

"Yeah, we got this. Go get your man," the female BCI officers said with a smile.

"Am I that obvious?" Tess wondered aloud, relief crossing her face. All three of them nodded back at her with knowing grins.

"Go. Before the others get too far ahead," Miles commanded lightly. Tess didn't need to be told twice. Patting her radio and readjusting her duty belt to ensure her gun and everything were exactly where they needed to be, she grabbed a bottle of water before heading into the woods after Malone and Denny.

Once under the shadow of the trees, the forest was dark and cool. Swiftly looking about her, Tess could see a duo of officers to her left, up on a ridge. To her right, farther away, another small group and a German Shepherd dog were spread out searching.

Overhead, Tess could hear birds singing in the tree tops and a light breeze moving through the leaves. Trying to work her way through the underbrush and avoid tripping on exposed roots or rocks made for a slow pace. She couldn't see Denny or Malone from where she was but knew they should be close by. As long as she kept the other officers in her sights, Tess felt confident she'd be okay. Glancing over her shoulder every so often, she slowly made her way deeper into the forest.

Before long, sweat began to bead up on her forehead and she felt herself panting with exertion. A gnat buzzed around her face annoyingly as she swatted at it repeatedly. Pausing to take a quick sip of water, she nearly jumped when her radio crackled to life.

"We have movement! Subject has been spotted!" came a disembodied voice through the speaker.

"What is your position?" Tess asked, pressing the button on her radio.

"Northwest corner of the search area. He's running, headed southeast. Wearing a white tee shirt and jeans."

"Any dogs in the area, please respond," Tess commanded. Her radio beeped.

"This is K9 unit 503, Officer Spencer. We are in the area; dogs are alert and ready."

"Perfect Officer Spencer," Tess said, relief filling her voice. "If conditions are safe, feel free to release the dogs. Let's push this guy toward us."

"Copy," Spencer said. Tess could hear the dogs whining and barking excitedly over the radio. "Find!" Spencer commanded the dogs before the radio went silent.

Turning her trajectory, Tess quickly ambled over a dry creek bed and some fallen logs, headed toward the north west corner of the search area. Hopefully if Slaydon was running in her direction, she'd spot him before he spotted her.

Within a few moments, Tess could see other search teams slowly pressing in from other directions. Some were up on ridgelines, looking down into the ravine. Others were checking various rock outcroppings. Tess decided to veer left a little more and check out an area of thick undergrowth.

Brambles and thickets clawed at the exposed skin of her arms and face and she willed herself not to think about ticks as she pressed forward, gun in her hand. The forest floor was littered with fallen leaves from the previous autumn and did nothing to muffle her footsteps. Trying her best to be as quiet as she could be but also move swiftly through the foliage, Tess kept her eyes peeled for any signs of Neil Slaydon.

Pulling a large branch out of the way, Tess found herself at the edge of a small clearing in the woods. She quickly cast a glance around herself for any signs of movement or lurking shadows but saw none. Where was Slaydon?

All of a sudden, she heard a clicking sound from behind her and felt the cool muzzle of a gun press into her temple. The tiny hairs on the back of her neck rose as she came to an immediate halt, her breath coming out in uneven gulps.

"Drop your gun, Detective," Slaydon's voice whispered close to her ear. Tess held out her gun, willing her hands to stop trembling. She'd already seen what he'd done to his wife. What horrid things would he do to her if this went south? Where were the other search parties? Were they getting closer? The only thing she could hear at the moment was the sound of her own breathing.

"Stop wasting time. Hurry up," Slaydon commanded as he reached around her with his empty hand, yanked her gun from her hand and tossed it into the undergrowth at their feet.

"You don't want to do this, Neil," Tess negotiated, "These woods are full of law enforcement and search dogs. There's no way out."

"Shut up!" he snapped, wiggling the muzzle of his gun roughly against her skin. "I've tried talking to you guys in a civil manner, but nobody will listen to me. You thought I was guilty before you even showed up at my house!"

"And your current behavior is supposed to make me believe you're innocent?" Tess asked incredulously, turning her head to look at him. She knew he was lying about things. She'd already caught him in some lies already, but was he truly a wife killer? She had so many unanswered questions, so many lies to sift through. Calling his bluff was dangerous, but she wasn't about to go off into the woods with him. She'd go down with a fight if he was actually planning on hurting her.

"I just want to start over!" Neil snapped. "I love my wife! I just want her back. This whole thing is a huge nightmare, a misunderstanding. The kind of shit you see on an episode of Dateline. This wasn't supposed to end this way. *We* weren't supposed to end this way." A sob threatened to escape from his chest.

"How was it supposed to end?" Tess asked, slowly taking a step backward away from Slaydon. He was so wrapped up in his emotions that he didn't seem to notice. About to risk another step backwards, Tess halted when Neil looked up at her angrily.

"We were supposed to be happy! We were supposed to grow old together and get those matching rocking chairs for the porch. But that didn't happen."

"What happened to change all of that?" Tess asked, slowly resuming her backwards escape. Neil didn't let on if he noticed.

"I think it was when we lost Adam. I ... I closed up. Wouldn't talk to her or anyone. She went to therapy, but I wouldn't. I was too manly or some shit. It was my own ego," Neil sounded so deflated, "Jessica was upset at me for not getting help. She resented me for not trying to be a better husband after we lost our son. You see, before Adam, she and I were always laughing. We were super happy, and sure, we fought sometimes, like I told you before. When we fought, it was bad, but we always made up and it made us stronger. But after Adam, after things fell apart like that, she and I started to drift apart. I'd work more and avoid coming home. I just didn't want to talk to her. Avoidance was easier than working it out. Not that long after we lost the baby, I found out she was having an affair with someone at work, and you know what? I wasn't even that upset. I loved her, but I wasn't even upset that she was fucking her coworker."

"And why do you think that was?"

"Because I'd already been having affairs for years by that point. Marriage is strange if you think about it. Vowing to love only one person for the rest of your life. How can you even pledge that to someone when you will constantly meet new people all of your life? When Jessica found out about my ... second? No, third girlfriend, she was upset. She cried for days, saying she'd never trust me again. But when I sat her down and we discussed it, at length, she agreed with me to try an open relationship. We could screw whoever we wanted to, but we'd always come home to each other at night. It worked out well for us for a while and then something changed."

"What was that?"

"She lied to me ... again. Just like she always did. But this time ... it was different." Neil swallowed back emotion. Tess could tell that he was getting more agitated and emotional as the moments slipped by. She tried to be sly and glance around her, looking for anyone else that may be within shouting distance, but saw nothing.

Suddenly, Neil turned to her, anger and hurt clouding his once-handsome face. Now, his usually wavy, styled hair stood on end, jutting out in all directions. The stress of the past few days had definitely taken their toll on him. His clothes were dirty and torn, from hiding in the woods no doubt, and dark circles had taken up residence under his eyes. In short, he looked as though the whole ordeal had aged him quite a few years.

He stood there, watching Tess for a moment, seeming to size her up, weighing his options. Letting out a deep sigh, his shoulders slumped as though he had finally given up.

"She just couldn't be honest with me. Over anything," Neil whined, as though he were the victim—not his beautiful wife who was lying in pieces in a body bag at the morgue. "Jessica wasn't like that at first, when we first met. But over the years, I started to realize that she was a dishonest person."

"And that's worth shooting her over and cutting her into fish bait?" Tess asked, her anger over Jessica's unnecessary slaying obscuring her mind. "You couldn't have just asked for a divorce like a normal human?"

"You don't understand what it's like!" Neil lashed out angrily, pacing back and forth like a caged bear. "To be lied to, repeatedly, by someone you love. To find out all your hopes and dreams are built on lies. Made up stories!" Tears began to slide down his cheeks and he didn't bother to wipe them away. "Everything that came pouring out of her mouth was untrue. A full on river of lies!"

"When exactly did you find out that Jessica wasn't pregnant? That there was never a baby?" Tess said, as she slowly glanced down, trying to see where her gun had landed.

"A couple of weeks ago now," Neil sobbed as he squatted down, his gun still in his hand, and focused on his breathing. "I was putting some clean clothes away when I found the box in the closet." A sob wracked his body. "I opened it to organize the closet because I was sick of all the boxes still sitting around. We'd lived in that house for months already and she still had a stack of crap sitting in the corner." He paused, taking in a gulp of air, and then wiping his eyes with the back of his hand. "That's when I found the belly thing."

"The rubber belly? What did you do then?" Tess asked, trying to buy time for backup to show up.

"I confronted her," Neil snapped, as though he thought Tess was stupid for asking. "I carried the fake belly downstairs and threw it on the table, demanded she pull up her shirt and show me her stomach." He stood then and resumed his pacing. Back and forth, back and forth. Tess stood her ground, casually moving just her eyes, looking for any way of escape or signs of backup.

"She wouldn't show me. Said I was being ridiculous. We started fighting. It was bad, there was lots of yelling and name calling. She threw an apple or something at me, I don't even remember. It broke the window on the back door. Shattered the glass everywhere."

"Is that the shouting and glass breaking that your neighbor Harold heard on Fourth of July?" Tess asked carefully. Neil nodded but continued pacing.

"Yes. And then the bastard called you guys and the cops showed up, asking questions."

"I can see how you'd get super angry. I'd be mad, too, if I found out my spouse had been lying about something as important as a baby. I think I'd want to hurt someone. Did you hit her? Is that why she had a bloody lip?" Tess asked cautiously, watching as Neil seemed to be getting more and more agitated as the seconds passed.

"I hit her. The lying bitch," Neil muttered. He balled his hands into fists as he stalked back and forth, shoulders hunched. "She deserved what she got."

"Is that why you killed her?" Tess almost thought he wouldn't answer her but then he did.

"Yes. Because she was a cold-blooded liar."

"When did you do it? Right after my coworkers were there?"

Neil nodded glumly. "Yeah. They left and she ran to the bathroom, locked herself in. That made me angry all over again, so I banged on the door ... demanded she let me in."

"And did she?"

"Eventually. After I told her I was going to get my gun and shoot the lock out." He paused then, glaring at Tess, his eyes red and puffy. Spittle foamed in the corner of his mouth, but he seemed to not notice.

"And did you? Get the gun, I mean?"

"Yes. And I was about to shoot the lock out of the door, but she finally opened it," he said. He stood there a moment, as though remembering every detail. And then a dark look came across his face. "She was naked."

Caught off guard, Tess made a face. "Naked? Why?"

"I don't know. Maybe to taunt me? Make me change my mind and tell her I loved her?" He laughed, a bitter sound containing no humor. "Her stomach was flat, just like when I met her. There was no baby. There never was one. At least this time around." He paused again but kept pacing. Over his shoulder, Tess caught a glimpse of movement. Backup had arrived. She had to keep Neil talking. He was still armed and dangerous.

"Is that when you killed her?"

Neil nodded, a look of anguish crossing his once handsome face. A deep guttural sob erupted from him. Gun still in hand, he held his hands up to his ears, as though to block out all sound, and continued to sob, angry wet tears staining his shirt. "She turned her back for just a second and that's when I shot her. I didn't want to see her face when she knew she was about to die. I loved her. But she lied to me. She lied!" Neil collapsed then, laying on his side in a fetal position, arms around his head, sobbing. The gun had fallen and skidded to the side but still within reach of him.

Apparently, Malone and Denny had seen the gun tumble into the weeds from where they crouched in the undergrowth behind Neil. Malone nodded, signaling to Tess to make her move.

As Tess dove for the gun, Malone and Denny ran from the brush into the clearing, guns drawn and aimed at Neil. Slaydon seems oblivious to their arrival, so caught up in his own Hell.

He sat up, disoriented, tears streaming down his face. He gave no fight when Malone slid the metal handcuffs around his wrists, the latch making a satisfying click.

Monday, July 18th, 6:02 p.m.

Neil Slaydon was finally behind bars. The case of the missing wife, Jessica Slaydon, was closed. But something about it bothered Tess. Something wasn't right.

As she sat, curled up on the couch, Otter by her side, Tess began reading through all the case reports and witness statements again. She was missing something. But what? The nagging feeling wouldn't leave. Normally when she wrapped up a case, there was a feeling of finality, of accomplishment, but this time around, that feeling was nowhere to be found. A sense of dread flooded Tess instead. There were too many lies, too many unanswered questions. Neil Slaydon was a hot-tempered asshole, but did he really shoot his wife? Did he really cut her up into pieces and dump her remains in the river? Tess could see him doing it, based on her interactions with the man, but at the same time, he really seemed genuinely upset that she was gone. And where had he gotten the gun from? The one that he'd used to kidnap Tess today? Had someone given it to him or had he bought it off of the street? After Slaydon's arrest, it had been sent for ballistics testing to see if it was indeed the murder weapon. Only time would tell.

With a frustrated huff, Tess tossed the file onto the floor and rubbed her temples. Her head was starting to hurt, the stress and lack of restful sleep starting to take its toll. She unfolded her long legs and went to stand up from the couch when something caught her eye.

On the floor, scattered at her feet, was the report from the first responder to Slaydon's home. She remembered reading the report when it had first come through but now, a detail stood out at her in vibrant detail.

She needed to speak with Neil Slaydon's mother again. Something she'd told Tess just didn't add up.

Quickly finding Nora Slaydon's phone number in her notes, Tess dialed it, her mind racing. Finally, after the fourth ring, the older woman answered.

"Hello, Mrs. Slaydon. This is Detective Dane with the Swain County Sheriff's office. I'm sorry to bother you again but I just had one more ques—"

"You mean arresting my son, my only son, wasn't enough for you? You gotta call and harass me too?" the older woman snapped.

"Ma'am, your son is currently arrested under suspicion for the murder and dismemberment of his wife," Tess sighed, not willing to be cowed by the woman's aggressive greeting. "I have a question though that may help his case. Are you willing to speak with me?"

"If I must. Go on." Tess could hear some random background noises but couldn't distinguish what exactly was going on. "Well ... ? I ain't got all day."

"Mrs. Slaydon, what hospital was your daughter, Annie, born at?" Tess asked, silently crossing her fingers for a break in the case.

"My daughter? Ha!" Mrs. Slaydon erupted in laughter, which quickly turned to a hacking cough. "I don't have any daughters. Just Neil. Why?"

"Did your husband Jeff, Neil's father, ever have any other children with any other women?" Tess asked, still hopeful.

"Not that I know of," coughed Norma Slaydon. "We were high school sweethearts—got married right after graduation when I found out I was pregnant with Neil. Shortly after that, Jeff was killed in a freak accident at work ... some kind of chemical holding tank exploded. Unless he fathered a kid from beyond the grave, I'd say no." She laughed at her own wit. Tess had to smile too. Not because she found Mrs. Slaydon to be humorous in any way, but because she just cracked Jessica Slaydon's case open once again.

Chapter Thirty-Six

Monday, July 18th, 6:35 p.m.

"It's his sister, Annie! Except she isn't his sister! She's his mistress," Tess exclaimed. "How could I have been so stupid!" She gave a frustrated growl as she dropped into her office chair, the tiny wheels squeaking in protest at the sudden impact.

"We all believed him, Dane. He took us all for a ride," Malone said, sitting down more gently than Tess had, taking the seat across from her.

"Where is she now?" Tess asked, rubbing a frustrated hand down her face.

"We have units at her house now, but she's not there. Looks like she's been gone for a few days. Moldy fruit on the countertop, chunky milk in the fridge."

Tess made a face. "Gross."

Malone just shrugged. "We found a gun in the back of her closet: a 9 mm Glock."

"You found a gun? Why didn't you lead with that!" Tess exclaimed, leaning forward, nearly falling off her chair. "This is huge!"

"I found out like two seconds before you walked in here huffing about Neil," Malone grinned at her. Tess rewarded him with a playful scowl.

Turning serious, he continued, "The gun had also been fired recently. I'm guessing she killed Jessica and cut her up. This is only speculation, of course, until ballistics come back. According to Dr. Summers, Jessica was shot with a 9 mm."

"So now we have two guns in two different sizes: Neil's and Annie's. The gun Neil had in the woods looked smaller than a 9 mm. More like a .22."

Malone nodded, "Yeah, it was a .22, so not our murder weapon." Tess nodded grimly as she mulled over the information.

"And Annie's fingerprints were on the 9 mm, not Neil's," Malone continued, "I'm glad you thought to ask for her fingerprints to exclude her from possible perps at the crime scene." He gave Tess a wry grin, knowing that her way with words had worked in her favor yet again.

Annie Baldwin had agreed to offer up her prints voluntarily in an effort to exclude herself from the various fingerprints found at the house. But that had been days ago, back before Jessica's body had been found. Back before Neil had run. Back before Annie had vanished.

"But why get Neil roped into all of this?" Tess asked, leaning her head back and closing her eyes to think. *What a nightmare!* "Or ... or ... how about this: She shoots Jessica because she wants Neil for herself, and Neil, being the jerk he is, helps her dispose of the body?"

"You could be onto something," Malone allowed, "but do you think she knew about the baby being a lie? Would she be willing to kill a pregnant woman just so she could have her man? Seems extreme."

"It does, but that's because we are normal people, not heartless killers," Tess said with a frustrated huff. "I say we go back to the jail and talk to our boy again, now that we have this little tidbit of knowledge."

"I'll set up an interview with Slaydon for first thing tomorrow morning," Malone nodded. "We'll find Annie Baldwin. She doesn't have a record and hasn't shown any signs of violence until now. I'll get an APB out for her. But I need you to bring your A-game tomorrow with Neil, so go home, Dane. Get some rest. I'll deal with this mess tonight and see you in the morning, okay?"

Tess nodded glumly, wanting to stay and work, but also wanting to be at home with Otter to unwind. She vowed to herself to plan a vacation, even if it was a short one, once the Slaydon case was closed once and for all.

Chapter Thirty-Seven

Monday, July 18th, 9:15 p.m.

"It's a nice turn of events that you were able to come for dinner tonight," Tess commented as she turned off the kitchen light and made her way to the living room where Denny sat on the couch concentrating on his cellphone. The dishwasher made a low humming noise from the kitchen as Tess sat down next to him with a sigh of contentment. It felt good to relax, like Malone had told her to do. She'd come home, grabbed a hot shower, played with the dogs and then Denny had come over bearing food.

"Yeah, it was, huh?" he commented as his phone buzzed again. Tess glanced down at it and saw Denny's boss' name lit up. He sighed and read the message.

"Are you going to have to go?" Tess asked, trying to hide her disappointment. Grabbing a blanket off the couch distractedly, she watched as he slid his phone back into his jeans.

"Not to work, no. Just wrapping up some final things with the Cleveland case," Denny said, leaning his head back on the couch and then turning to look at her.

Tess could feel the heat from his gaze as he studied her intently. Her eyes were on his hand resting on the couch between them. Slowly she slid her gaze up his body and came to a halt on his blue eyes.

"I meant what I said the other day. About wanting you but not wanting to rush things," he began, his gaze never leaving Tess's. "I ..." he sighed, pausing for a moment as though he were unsure of how to go on. "I haven't been with anyone in over three years ... since ... well, before Cassie passed away."

"Denny—" Tess breathed, her hand covering his. He turned his palm over and grasped her hand, interlacing their fingers.

"No, I need to say this," he said, allowing their hands to remain on the smooth leather of the couch. He swallowed audibly, and he nervously pulled his gaze from hers for a moment before finding it again. "I haven't been with anyone since Cassie. For multiple reasons, but mostly ... because I'm scared."

"Scared?"

"Not scared like I won't know what to do. Trust me, that's never been the problem," he grinned in an effort to lighten the mood. "I guess at first I felt like I would be betraying Cassie, betraying our vows together."

Tess said nothing, just waited patiently for him to go on. With a long sigh, he did, "With Cass being so sick for so long, plus working long hours and trying to raise a young child, it was …. It was hard, Tess. My days became one dark never-ending expanse of time. I was lost, just going through the motions. But those months following her death, I poured whatever I had left into my daughter. Making sure Natalie was thriving and working through everything. I put my own needs and wants on the back burner, so to speak." He paused again, giving Tess's hand another light squeeze.

"But then something happened. I got a call about a dead guy found in a boat with your name written inside it. Yeah, I knew you when you were in the academy. I was your partner for your first two years on the force. I've always respected you and enjoyed your company. But it wasn't until we were partnered up again for the Torture Killer case that … well, I started seeing you in a different light." He turned his gaze back to her face, a whisper of a smile playing on his lips.

"A part of me that had laid dormant for so long suddenly seemed to be alive again. I finally feel like I have a chance at a happy future. All of that changed the night I got shot. I know it wasn't a bad wound, but it still got me thinking. It was there in the hospital bed that I really started thinking about my priorities, about the people who mean the most to me. I know that Cass would want me to live my life, move on, and find happiness again. My daughter is thriving now despite losing her mother, my career is going well, and I have you in my life." He turned to Tess then, facing her head on. "Beside Natalie, you are the most important person in my life. And I'm just afraid that if I rush things with you, that if you aren't ready for that, then somehow I'll screw this all up and lose you. I've already lost one woman I loved. I don't want to risk losing another one. I just wanted you to know that. To know all of this."

Tess, her mind reeling from what he'd just admitted, said nothing for a moment as she processed his words. He must have taken her silence as a bad sign, because his face fell.

He stood then, sliding on his shoes, silence filling the air. He paused for a moment, long enough to look down at her. "I'll let you get back to whatever you were doing before I barged in." He made his way over to the wooden front door slowly as Tess stood from the couch and followed him.

As he turned to leave, his hand on the doorknob, Tess reached out and lightly grasped his arm. "Don't go," she blurted. He paused, looking at her questioningly.

"Please ... stay the night," she said, looking up into his deep blue eyes. At her words, his pupils seemed to dilate, and he sucked in a breath.

"Like *stay the night*, stay the night?" he asked, almost in a whisper. A look of longing mixed with slight amusement crossed his face as Tess fidgeted nervously.

"Yes, like stay the night, stay the night," she said, still looking him in the eye. "With me. In my bed."

The words had barely escaped her mouth when he stepped toward her, dropping his car keys back on the hall table in his haste to hold her.

"You sure?" Denny asked, his arms wrapping themselves around Tess. She nodded and that was all it took. A huge grin on his face, Denny reached down and grabbed her ass, wrapping her legs around his waist. Tess slipped her arms around his neck, kissing him deeply as he carried her down the hallway toward her bedroom.

Chapter Thirty-Eight

Tuesday July 19th, 7:12 a.m.

The next morning it dawned overcast, the sky gray. Tess awoke and found herself entwined with Denny and her bed sheets. As her mind replayed the event of the previous night, a grin spread across her face. With a contented sigh, she snuggled in closer, her head resting on Denny's bare chest. He tightened his grip on her and snuggled her close.

"Remind me to send Natalie to her friend's house more often. I like having slumber parties with you," he said, planting a kiss on the top of Tess's head.

"Yeah, I could get used to this," Tess smiled up at him. He looked down at her, watching her intently. He trailed his fingers down her back in small circular motions across her naked skin, and then rested them on the curve of her hip.

"No regrets?" a slight look of apprehension shadowing his features.

"No regrets," she confirmed, with a contented sigh. "You?"

"None," he said, a look of longing crossing his face. "I've been imagining doing that with you for a while now."

"Oh?" Tess asked, an amused grin creeping across her face, "And what else have you been imagining?"

Denny leaned down and whispered something in her ear and Tess felt her skin warm at his words.

"Oh, like this?" she whispered as she slid her hand under the sheet and began exploring his lower half. When she wrapped her hand around him, he let out a hiss and she smiled. "Just wait until you see what *I've* been imagining."

An hour later, Tess stood in the kitchen, scrambling eggs and pouring orange juice for herself and Denny. She didn't even try to hide the ridiculous smile plastered on her face as she stirred the eggs around in the skillet. Her long hair was pulled up in a messy bun on the top of her head, and Denny's tee shirt she was wearing barely covered her rear end, but she didn't care. She was happy. Beyond happy, even though she knew she had to get dressed soon to go interview Neil Slaydon at the jail.

After she and Denny had spent more time in bed, she'd finally pried herself away from him long enough to grab a shower while he fed and let the dogs out. When he went to get a shower for the day, Tess had playfully grabbed his tee shirt and slid it on over her red lace underwear. He had yet to see them, of course, but just knowing she was wearing them was enough to make her feel like a goddess.

As the eggs sizzled in the pan, Tess replayed the events of the previous night in her mind over and over. The feel of his hands roaming her body, the feel of him moving over her, the things he'd whispered in her ears ....

"What did those eggs ever do to you? They smell burnt."

At the sound of his voice, Tess jumped and whirled around, her face hot from the memories that had just been going through her mind.

The subject of her thoughts, Denny, was standing in the kitchen doorway, wrapped only in a towel, fresh from the shower. Tess let her eyes roam over him, which just heated her more. His muscular chest, flat stomach—not a complete six pack, but damn he was rocking a dad bod. The scar from his gunshot wound, still puckered and pink, was visible on his hip, just above the low-slung towel. Tess gulped as her thoughts went wild.

"Tess. The eggs," Denny said firmly, with a nod to the stove. A small grin spread across his face when he took in the fact that she was wearing his shirt.

"Oh!" Tess exclaimed, reality finally dawning on her as she whirled back around to the stove to turn off the eggs. They were now blackened and smelled undesirable.

Denny's chuckle filled the room as he came over to the stove to survey the damage. "It looks like you were a little ... distracted .... What were you thinking about?" He raised his eyebrows at her, fully knowing where her mind had been, because his had been in the same place.

"Nothing," Tess mumbled, even though they both knew that wasn't true. Denny reached for her, pulling her to him.

"Come here, beautiful," he gently leaned down to kiss her deeply. She responded by wrapping her arms around his shoulders and moving closer to him. His hands slid down her body and grabbed her ass, pulling her legs up around his waist. He set her down on the countertop, and she shivered from the cool feeling of the granite under the backs of her legs.

"I came out to find my tee shirt. Seems to me that someone stole it while I was in the shower," he grinned, leaning into her, their foreheads touching. Tess looked up at him and raised an eyebrow.

"You can take it back if you want," she smirked, raising her arms. Denny's eyes flared as he watched her. Taking the hem of the shirt, he pulled it up and off of Tess, leaving her in nothing but the pair of red lace underwear.

"God, Tess. You're ... perfect," Denny breathed, his eyes taking her in. Feeling emboldened by his appraisal of her, she shimmied to the edge of the counter and leaned forward, her breasts pressed into his chest.

"If you're taking the shirt, then I get the towel," she whispered in his ear as his hands slid up her thighs toward the red lace.

"If you take the towel, then you're definitely going to be late for your meeting with Slaydon," he tormented her, even as a finger slid beneath the lace. Tess sucked in breath, not giving any further thought about Slaydon or work issues. All she wanted right now was Denny.

"Screw it," she muttered as she reached to yank the bath towel from around his waist.

Chapter Thirty-Nine

Tuesday July 19th, 9:30 a.m.

The jail was loud, a cacophony of sound: yelling, banging, movement. Tess and Malone sat in an interrogation room, waiting for Neil Slaydon to be delivered to them.

Suddenly, the gray metal door opened and the sounds from the jail increased as Slaydon shuffled in, hands cuffed in front of him. The guard nodded at Tess and Malone before shutting the door behind him. The room was instantly quieter.

"Orange looks good on you, Neil," Tess commented sarcastically, watching the man stand before her wearing a set of scrubs in Inmate Orange. Tess was rewarded for her wit with a scowl as Slaydon pulled out a chair with his sandaled foot and plopped heavily into it.

"What do you want?" he half growled. "Haven't you done enough? I'm locked up. What more do you want?"

"We want the truth, Neil," Tess said, leaning forward in her seat. "We have your girlfriend down at the station right now. Figured we could compare notes." The lie slid from her lips much easier than she thought it would.

"Girlfriend?" he asked innocently. Tess rolled her eyes at the audacity of the man.

"Annie. Don't even start with me today, Slaydon," she snapped. "We have Annie talking to us, telling us all kinds of things."

"Shit," Slaydon mumbled under his breath. Tess raised an eyebrow, staring across the worn metal table at Slaydon's slumped form.

"I'm sorry? What was that?" even though she knew exactly what he'd said.

"She doesn't know anything," Neil seethed. He stared straight ahead, avoiding eye contact with both officers. Malone leaned back in his chair, flipping his pen around his fingertips, watching as Tess continued.

"We know she isn't your sister. In fact, you don't have any siblings at all." Tess let the statement linger in the air for a moment. "How long have you been cheating on your wife this time, Neil?"

The inmate just sat there, staring straight ahead, his face placid.

"Cut the shit, Slaydon!" Tess snapped, her hand slapping the metal table in front of her and causing Slaydon to flinch. "How long have you been screwing someone else? Been lying to your wife about where you'd been?"

He finally looked at her, but still said nothing. Tess bristled, feeling the urge to scream in his face.

"You sat in your living room boo-hooing about how much you loved your wife. About how many lies she'd told you and how betrayed you felt. Now we realize that you've been lying just as much and yet she's laying, in pieces, in a body bag at the morgue." Tess stood up, frustration and anger coursing through her. Pacing back and forth across the small room, she kept her eyes on the orange clad man at the table.

Slaydon continued to stare back at her, arms crossed over his chest. Stubble darkened his usually clean-shaven face and his eyes appeared haggard.

"Here's what I think," Tess offered. "Correct me if I'm wrong. I think that you and Annie have been banging for a while, or maybe she's not the first side piece you've had. Regardless, I think she wanted you all to herself, but one thing stood in her way. Jessica. Maybe you told her that you'd found out that Jessica was lying about the pregnancy and that just pushed Annie over the edge? But why would Jessica lie about the pregnancy in the first place? In an effort to save your marriage, because in her mind, a baby would fix everything? Maybe Jessica had found out about your ... philandering ways and so she came up with the pregnancy scheme to get you to stay with her? How am I doing so far?"

She was awarded with a snort from Neil, followed by a slight shrug.

"You tell me, Detective, since you're so smart and shit," he finally said, his face becoming hard.

"Okay, I will," Tess countered. She paused at the table and leaned over, placing her hands on the cool surface. Her face was merely inches from Neil's cold blue-eyed glare. "I think that your girlfriend wanted you for herself, shot Jessica and then had you dismember the body and dispose of the pieces. Except you missed some evidence when you cleaned up the scene. Oh! And the security footage from neighboring houses! You forgot that we'd check that and find out exactly where you went each time you took the stroller out on your walks. It was just a matter of time until we found the pieces of your wife, sunk at the bottom of the river near Old Crawley Bridge. Are you really going to do this?"

"Do what?" Neil huffed, rolling his eyes toward the ceiling to avoid eye contact with Tess.

"Take the fall for Annie. Some stupid, jealous woman?" Tess hissed, playing into Neil's misogynistic persona. She knew he disliked pushy women, ones that thought they had something over him. "She killed Jessica, didn't she, Neil? Shot her in the head and then panicked. Made you cut up your wife's corpse and dispose of the pieces.

To what end? So, you two could run off to Canada or something and be together? She should have known that there was a good possibility that you'd be saddled with the blame and then what? She'd visit you in prison? Getting a little hanky panky up against the vending machine when the guards turned their backs?" Tess rolled her eyes at the idiocracy of it all.

Watching Neil closely for any cracks in his cool exterior that she could exploit, she stifled a grin when she saw his face twitch. He lowered his eyes, staring blankly at the gray metal table, and absently picking at some of the chipped paint on the edge.

"If you talk to us now, tell us the truth, then maybe the judge will see you in a more favorable light when sentencing comes around. Or, you can sit here, smug as a cat who caught a mouse, and take the fall for her. Because she's talking, Neil. Making up her own narrative as to her involvement in the case. What's it gonna be? Her word or yours?"

Slaydon let out a long sigh, his shoulders slumping slightly in defeat. He muttered something that was unintelligible to Tess.

"What did you say?" she asked, watching him closely. He finally looked up at her, his face now looking resigned to his situation.

"I didn't kill Jessica. I lied about that," he said quietly, his eyes growing moist. "It all happened so fast."

"Start at the beginning, please," Tess requested as she once again took a seat across from him. The room was quiet for some time, the only sound coming from a clock that hung over the door leading to the jail.

"I found the belly thing in a box in our closet one day while Jessica was at the grocery store. Apparently, she had multiple sizes. You know, so that it looked like her belly was growing as the pregnancy progressed. What she planned to do after the nine-month mark, I don't know. It worried me though, once the initial shock wore off," he paused then, taking a big breath and then wiping at his face with the back of his shackled hands. The metal sound of the cuffs scraping along the edge of the table echoed through the quiet room.

"At first I was in shock. How could she lie about being pregnant like that? Especially after we lost Adam?" The tears came then, two big ones, rolling down his cheeks. "I ... I just wanted a baby, but she never really recovered emotionally from the loss. I decided, once I'd found the rubber belly, that I would confront her. I was so upset and didn't know where to turn so I ended up calling Annie. Told her everything that I'd found out. It destroyed me. I felt so betrayed." His eyes became red and watery, and his hands began to shake.

"At first Annie was angry for me and said I should just leave Jessica. Get a divorce," he pressed on. "I didn't want that. Despite what you must think, how this must look,

I did love my wife." He paused, a shudder wracking his body.

"I told Annie that I needed to talk to Jessica. Confront her, hear her side of things. Her excuses," he eventually went on. "Jessica was always such a ... chaotic person. Very ... impulsive. The pregnancy wasn't the first thing she'd lied to me about in our marriage. Maybe that is why ... I don't know."

"What?" Tess asked, gently encouraging him to continue. Neil's eyes slid up to meet Tess's, his once smug look replaced by one of accepted defeat.

"Jessica got home that night. I helped her unload the groceries, so many thoughts running through my head. Part of me wanted to scream at her, hurt her. But then the other part of me wanted to know why." He leaned over and rested his head on the edge of the table for a few moments and then eventually looked back up.

"I finally just ... blurted it out. Said I had found the belly and that I was on to her lies. At first, she just stood there in front of the fridge, staring at me. I demanded she answer me, and when she didn't, I reached for her shirt to see her belly for myself. She let out a scream and jumped away from me, toward the garage door. At first I thought she was going to run out, but she didn't. She just lifted her shirt and started crying. I saw the rubber belly then and started sobbing, asking her why."

"And what did she say?" Tess asked. Malone sat quietly, still rolling his pen through his fingers as he took everything in.

"She said she knew about Annie. Just like she knew about Sofie before her, and Nikki before her. You see, Annie wasn't the first woman I'd had an affair with. But, then again, Jessica wasn't so innocent either. She's had her relationships over the years. At least two that I know of. Anyway, when it came to Annie and the pregnancy lies, Jessica said she did it to save our marriage. She said that if she was pregnant, then I'd be happy again like I was when Adam was on his way. That we'd be a stronger couple again, like we used to be. She lied to me to keep me with her. She knew that I was planning on asking for a divorce, so she came up with this scheme."

"To what end though?" Tess asked, carefully watching Neil. "Where was she planning to get a baby at the end of the nine months?"

"She hadn't planned that far, I guess. If she had a plan she never told me. That night, in the kitchen, when she told me what she'd done, I lost it. I remember starting to yell at her again. I got into her face and screamed. She hit me so I hit her back. That's how we usually ended our fights. Hitting each other, screaming, then making love," he sighed. "You must think we are crazy. We were volatile. It's almost like the more we fought, the more physical we got, the more passionate we were with each other."

"I'm not a psychiatrist. I can't speculate over the inner workings of one's marriage. I just want the facts," Tess said, her mind going into overdrive trying to sort through everything.

"We were in the middle of arguing when the door to the garage opened. It was Annie. She'd never been inside my house or met Jessica before as far as I know. I was shocked to see her standing there. She was glaring at Jessica. I asked her what she was doing there but she ignored me. Annie just started screaming at Jessica, calling her a lying bitch. They both started yelling at each other and then when Jessica turned away from Annie to confront me again, Annie pulled out a gun and fired." At his last words, Neil let out a sob from deep in his chest. Rocking back and forth in his chair, the handcuff chains clanging quietly together, the man sobbed.

After a few moments, the sounds began to be replaced by quiet gasps for air, yet the tears continued to fall.

"What happened then?"

"Jessica fell. Dead. I knew she was dead the moment she hit the floor. There was blood everywhere. Annie just stood there, staring down at her. I tried finding a pulse on Jessica but there wasn't one. And her head ... it was .... There was a huge hole and ...." Neil stood up then, making it over to the wastebasket just in time to empty his stomach. With a shaking hand, he wiped off the corner of his mouth and turned his red-rimmed eyes toward Tess again. The smell of vomit filled the small room, quickly making the situation more unpleasant. Tess tried to ignore it, keeping her eyes on Neil as he continued.

"I panicked. I yelled at Annie and asked her why she did that. She said because she wanted to be with me and wanted "that lying bitch" out of our lives once and for all. I couldn't believe it. I ... I was in shock. Annie had killed my wife."

At his admission, Tess's theory was substantiated. Now they just needed proof that it was Annie behind the trigger and not Neil. Hopefully the ballistics results would come through with the needed information.

"Then what happened?"

"We had to do something with the ... body. I went out to the garage and got my saw. I put a plastic bag over her head so it wouldn't leak everywhere, drug her to the bathtub, and began cutting her up. It was strangely harder than I thought it would be," he stated, distractedly.

"Where was Annie during all of this?"

"She was there for part of it but then said she couldn't handle it. I told her it was her fault and maybe she should be the one doing all the work, but she refused. She ended up leaving, so I just continued working, bagging up the parts. Cleaning up the house. I even had to stop to get more supplies."

That confirms the reason for the trip to Piedmont's, Tess thought as she listened to Neil.

"I knew I'd have to get rid of the bags but didn't want anybody to see me. So, I decided to drop them in the river," Neil confessed with a defeated sigh.

"And you used the baby stroller to transport her." Tess stated it as a fact, not a question. Neil's slight nod confirmed her suspicions.

"And where is Annie now?"

"Isn't she down at the sta—" he started to say and then realized his mistake. "Shit. You all lied, didn't you?"

"You actually fell for that?" Tess smirked. "We had our suspicions about what had happened. Now tell me where she is."

Neil Slaydon glared at her for a moment, saying nothing. Then, realizing that he'd been caught, he sighed.

"I don't know," he said simply. "I've only seen her once since she killed Jess. That day you came over and we told you she was my sister. She'd stopped by, trying to get me to come away with her, so we could be together. She knew I was under investigation but didn't seem to understand that the minute I ran away with her would be the minute you all would have tracked me down. She said she'd wait for me."

"Where?"

"I don't know."

"Stop bullshitting me, Neil."

"I don't know ... for sure. She said her family owns a log cabin down in the Hocking Hills somewhere. Said I should meet her there."

"Did she give you an address or anything?" Tess asked, getting more frustrated as the moments ticked by.

"No, sorry," Neil mumbled. He looked so forlorn that Tess almost believed him.

"There are hundreds, if not thousands, of log cabins in the Hocking Hills. It's a vacation renter's paradise. You have to give me something more than that."

"Honestly, I don't know. I just remember her saying that there isn't any cell service out there, but I should meet her at the Stone Glen Trailhead on Saturday the twenty-third at noon."

"Thank you. See? Was that so hard, Neil?" Tess said, nodding to Malone as he wrote down the meeting spot. Tess turned off the recording device and began gathering up her notes.

"So, what happens now?" he asked, suddenly looking worried, casting a glance around the small room.

"Well, you get to stay here, while Sheriff Malone and I go meet up with your girlfriend."

Chapter Forty

Saturday, July 23rd, 11:54 a.m.

The air was tense, all eyes watching for Annie Baldwin. Tess, having asked for some extra manpower from BCI and the local county deputies, had undercover officers positioned all over the Stone Glen trail and parking lot. Some officers posed as young couples getting ready for a nice hike. Deputy Miles, dressed in jean shorts and a Hawaiian shirt, wore a pair of binoculars around his neck. A tattered copy of an old wild bird identification guide was shoved into his back pocket. He was stationed walking along the trail, gazing up at the canopy of trees. Tess nearly snorted when he showed up in his ensemble, complete with a pair of black-framed glasses and a "Boise Rocks!" ball cap pulled down over his eyes.

Denny, wearing black running shorts and blue tee shirt, made a show of stretching as though he were about to run a marathon. Tess, sitting inside her Jeep Wrangler, watched his reflection out of the rearview mirror. Despite the dark reason for being there at the trail, Tess felt a grin slowly form on her face as she watched him. His subtle grin let her know that he knew she was watching him flex his muscles. Resisting the urge to shake her head, Tess pulled her eyes away from Denny's athletic form and surveyed the parking lot once more from the driver's seat of her car.

Her long dark hair hung down her back and a pair of sunglasses obscured her face from view. It was very different from how she usually reported to work. Then, her hair was either pulled back into a ponytail or a low bun. But today, things were different.

Annie, having met Tess before at Neil's house, would be tipped off in an instant if she saw her as she normally appeared.

Adjusting the rearview mirror, Tess took in the view behind her parked vehicle once more. All seemed to be quiet.

"Anything yet?" her walkie talkie crackled to life. Tess nearly jumped at the sudden sound but quickly replied. Sheriff Malone's voice sounded garbled for a second from where he took up position near the main road, posing as a dog walker, with Otter on a leash. Max had been left at home so that Annie wouldn't recognize him.

"Negative. You?" Tess asked the sheriff. She took a sip from her water bottle while she waited for his response.

"Not yet," came his answer, "I'm starting to wonder if we've been pl—wait." He paused and then, "Subject is arriving. White Honda, red stripe down the hood."

"Copy," Tess said. It was showtime. She rolled down her window and dropped a handful of sunflower seeds out, her signal to Denny that the subject was arriving. With a slight nod, he bent and tied his shoes, as a signal to the other officers who were milling around acting like hikers and tourists.

Just then, a white Honda Civic with a large red stripe down the hood came rolling into the parking lot and parked. Tess watched subtly as the woman flipped down her visor and plumped her lips in the mirror.

Suddenly the Civic's front door opened and out stepped ... someone else. It wasn't Annie, just another blond woman, clad in yoga pants and a sports bra. Tess sighed, her frustration growing. She watched as the woman headed toward another trail that led away from the Stone Glen trail.

"Stand down," Tess said into her walkie-talkie. "The subject was not in the Honda."

Glancing up into the rearview mirror, Tess watched as Denny stretched his neck and kept nodding to his left, his eyes darting to Tess's Jeep and back down to the ground. Suspicious, she glanced over in the direction that Denny kept nodding in and that's when she saw her.

Annie, on foot, had cut through from another trail and was now picking her way across the parking lot, while looking down at her phone. She glanced up as she put her phone to her ear and looked around. Tess watched out of the corner of her eye as the woman slowly approached the trailhead, walking past Denny, who was tying his shoes again. Two officers from BCI whom Tess hadn't met before, stood close together, seemingly discussing the map of the trail displayed on a brown wooden park ranger sign. They looked up as Annie approached and gave her a friendly smile. Annie, however, only nodded and then walked to stand off to the side of the trail, looking distracted.

"Waiting on a lover that isn't gonna show," Tess muttered to herself. She sent a quick text to Malone: "She's here. Came in on foot."

"Copy. En route," came his immediate response.

Tess knew that some officers, sprinkled deeper along the trail, had walkie-talkies so they could be alerted to be on the lookout if Annie made a run for it.

The plan, should everything go right, was for Malone to walk Otter back to the safety of the Jeep and once the dog was inside the running, air-conditioned vehicle, the others would know to act. If Annie did anything before Malone gave the signal, then Tess, Denny, and the 'couple' reading the map were to alert the other officers to act. Hopefully, the arrest happened without incident.

Annie, wearing a neon pink tank top and black leggings, remained standing to the side of the trailhead, absently glancing at her phone. Tess watched as she periodically looked up and surveyed the parking area, presumably watching for Slaydon.

Tess leaned back in her seat, trying to make herself small so that Annie didn't see her. Glancing up at the rearview mirror again, Tess watched Denny's reflection as he gave one final stretch and then started slowly jogging toward the trailhead where Annie stood.

Denny was nearly halfway across the parking lot when one of the police radios squelched out a loud sound. Annie's head jerked up from her phone, a look of panic etched onto her face.

Like a horse out of the starting gate, Annie bolted and disappeared down the trail, Denny and the other two officers in hot pursuit.

"We've been made!" Tess exclaimed into the radio as she leaped from her Jeep. "Repeat, we've been made! Subject fled on foot down the trail. All units respond. Subject is wearing a neon pink shirt and black leggings. Get her!"

Taking off at a sprint, Tess made good ground, narrowly dodging exposed tree roots and rocks along the trail. Up ahead of her, she caught glimpses of neon pink moving among the trees.

Somewhere up ahead, Tess knew Deputy Miles would be waiting in his birding ensemble. Chest heaving from exertion, Tess swiftly made her way down the trail.

Narrowly avoiding colliding with an Asian couple and their toddler standing to the side of the trail, Tess commanded them to leave the area immediately. With all the police activity on the trail, the family looked startled but quickly headed back toward the trailhead.

Tess continued down the trail, closing the distance. Her radio crackled to life as one of the officers further down the trail said, "Lost sight of subject. Officers standing by at Stone Glen. Two civilians here, being escorted to safety, but there are no signs of the subject."

Shit. Where had Annie gone? And where was Miles and Denny? Surely Malone was behind her, Otter safely tucked away in the protection of her Jeep.

Frustration growing, Tess continued down the root laden path as quickly as the terrain would allow. Coming around a large boulder at a curve in the trail, she found Miles, sitting on the ground, holding his ankle. His birding book and binoculars lay scattered next to him.

"Are you okay?" Tess asked, as she skidded to a halt to check on her coworker.

"I'm fine. Twisted my ankle," Miles moaned softly. "She came around this rock and ran right into me, knocking me off balance. Damn tree root."

"Which way did she go?" Tess asked, expecting him to point further down the trail. Instead, he pointed to her right, away from the trail.

"She took off that way," Miles said as he slowly tried to stand up on his sore ankle. Tess helped him, all the while looking over her shoulder for any signs of Annie.

"Are you okay to stay here for now?" Tess asked, impatient to be in pursuit again. Deputy Miles nodded, understanding the situation.

"I'm good for now. I'll try to head back toward the trailhead," he said. "You better not forget about me though," he added with a grin.

"Never," Tess smiled as she took off through the woods in the direction that Miles had indicated. "Radio in and tell everyone what's going on, please," she called over her shoulder.

The terrain began to ascend, moss covered boulders making climbing difficult. Tess's legs burned with exertion but still she pressed on.

Her radio crackled to life again as she listened to Deputy Miles relay the information about his fall and the position of the subject.

Damn Annie, Tess thought as her eyes continued to survey the horizon, looking for any signs of the woman. The only thing Tess could see in front of her was the steep incline covered in a thick layer of leaves and mud. Where did Annie go? There didn't seem to be many places to hide along this stretch of woods.

Just then, Tess's eye caught a flash of neon pink movement to her left. Turning her head toward it, she caught sight of Annie before she quickly disappeared behind a tall rock face in the steep terrain.

Altering her trajectory, Tess swiftly made her way toward the spot where Annie had just disappeared.

Below her on the trail, Tess heard voices and turned to look over her shoulder as Denny and Malone quickly followed her up the rock-laden terrain. Glad to see backup close at hand, Tess rounded the rock face and continued onward in pursuit.

There! Another flash of neon pink and the swing of a blond ponytail just thirty yards ahead. Tess pressed on, her lungs burning, legs aching.

"Stop! Police!" Tess yelled as she gained ground, closing the distance between herself and Jessica Slaydon's killer.

Annie paused for a moment, looking over her shoulder at Tess. With a smirk on her face, she turned back around and started running again. She quickly disappeared into the undergrowth.

Behind her, Tess could hear Denny and Malone making progress as their feet pounded up the forested terrain behind her. Knowing they were there gave Tess the energy to continue. They had to catch Annie!

Up ahead of her, Tess could see the thick undergrowth that Annie had disappeared into. Bursting through the bushes, sticks and leaves smacking her in the face, Tess realized her mistake almost too late.

As she broke through the undergrowth, the ground gave way and she felt herself falling through the air, down a steep embankment. Branches and leaves slapped her at her face on the way down as the hard packed dirt and rocks wreaked havoc on her body.

Finally, after what seemed like forever, but in reality was mere seconds, Tess skidded to a halt at the bottom of a moderately steep ravine. As the dust settled, Tess sat up, her face and chest covered in dirt and debris. Up the ravine behind her, she could hear Denny and Malone traipsing through the underbrush.

"Watch out for the ledge!" Tess hollered up at them as their voices came closer. They must have heard her because when she glanced up, she could see Denny looking down at her, a concerned expression etched into his handsome face. He bent at the waist for a moment trying to catch his breath.

Giving him a silent thumbs up sign, he nodded in relief and began searching the ravine for Annie from his vantage point. Tess looked around as well but saw nothing except dense woods and undergrowth.

Suddenly, Denny let out a low whistle and Tess looked back up at him. He pointed off toward Tess's right and nodded at her. Malone, she noted, was already picking his way down the ravine a few yards down the ridge from where she sat.

Standing slowly, testing her weight on her ankles, she realized, though sore, she was fine. Quickly dusting off her backside out of reflex, she made her way in the direction Denny had indicated.

The bottom of the ravine, littered with pebbles and sticks, appeared to actually be a dried up creek bed. Keeping a low profile, Tess quietly picked her way down the ravine toward Annie's last sighting. Hopefully they would have her in handcuffs soon.

Tess was exhausted, thirsty, and thoroughly pissed off. Come Hell or high water, she would catch Jessica Slaydon's killer and put her where she belonged. Behind bars.

Suddenly, a flash of movement caught Tess's eye again, this time much closer. Veering in that direction, Tess found Annie, sprawled out on her ass, her left shoe missing. Five feet away the missing shoe sat, encased in thick mud, from where the mire had sucked it off of her passing foot.

"Should have tied your shoes tighter, Annie," Tess growled as she leaped toward the woman. Annie rolled away as Tess landed on her, narrowly escaping. Tess, however, was quick, staying one step ahead of Annie as the killer looked for an escape route.

"Give it up, Annie," Tess said, grabbing at the other woman's arm to hold her still. "We have you surrounded. This stops here." She rolled Annie over onto her stomach and placed her knee on the woman's backside to hold her still.

Click. One handcuff was in place. Tess leaned over the squirming woman, reaching for her other hand.

"Not so fast, bitch," Annie seethed, throwing her head backwards, hitting Tess straight in the mouth.

Tess instinctively yanked her head back, pain coursing through her mouth and chin. She tasted iron and knew she was bleeding. In the back of her mind, she hoped her teeth were okay, but more pressing was apprehending Annie.

The other woman howled, wriggling to get away from Tess, but Tess just swung her leg over Annie's backside, using her weight as leverage. Annie continued to scream and carry on, her face rubbing in the dirt beneath her.

"I can't breathe, bitch."

"Maybe if you'd stop screaming you could," Tess snapped, knowing she wasn't sitting on the woman's chest in any way. "Cut this shit out and hold still." With one more grab for Annie's uncuffed hand, Tess finally captured it and closed the metal ring around her wrist.

"Annie Baldwin, you are under arrest for the murder of Jessica Slaydon. Anything you say can and will be used against you in a court of law." As Tess continued reciting

Annie her Miranda Rights, the woman rolled over and glared daggers at her.

Behind her, Denny and Malone approached, weapons drawn. When they saw that Tess had the suspect already handcuffed, they holstered their guns and radioed to the others.

"Get her out of my sight," Tess said, handing Annie over to Malone. She wiped her mouth with the back of her hand and when she pulled it back, it was covered in blood. She gently used her tongue to survey her teeth. They all seemed to be fine.

"Tell me I'm still pretty." Tess attempted to joke as Denny came over to her to make sure she was okay.

"You're always beautiful to me. Even if you do look like something from a horror movie." He grinned, looking down at her bloodstained shirt. She followed his gaze and let out a groan.

"It's bad, isn't it?"

"It's gonna bruise I'm sure, but your teeth look okay," Denny said, reaching out and gently pulling back her swollen lip to check her mouth. Taking the hem of his shirt, he gently wiped some of the blood off of her face.

"C'mon. Let's get her back to the station and get you cleaned up." He took Tess's hand and gently led her toward Malone and Annie as they made their way up the ravine.

Chapter Forty-One

Saturday, July 23rd, 3:15 p.m.

Denny and Tess opened the door to the sheriff's department seconds after Malone led Annie through it. As the four of them made their way across the freshly mopped floor of the lobby, Tess noticed someone sitting in the corner, near the coffeemaker and a small stack of outdated magazines. In the seconds it took for Tess to recognize Lydia Fontaine, all Hell broke loose.

With a feral scream, Lydia had sprung from her seat, coffee spilling on the floor, as she lunged herself at Annie. There was another scream, some scuffling. A grunt. Blood slowly oozed its way across the clean floors.

In a whirlwind, Tess found herself standing over Lydia Fontaine's prone form, as she clicked a pair of handcuffs into place. Beneath her, the older woman began to sob uncontrollably.

Next to them, Denny held his hand over a wound in Annie's neck as Malone called for an ambulance. Annie, it appeared, didn't seem to be mortally wounded as she was still wriggling in her cuffs and glaring at everyone she made eye contact with, all levels of profanity pouring from her mouth.

Sunday, July 23rd, 4:02 p.m.

Once the ambulance hauled Annie away to the hospital for assessment, Tess, aided by Denny and Malone, hauled a sniveling Lydia Fontaine to Interview One and placed her unceremoniously into a chair. Her handcuffs scraped the table in front of her as she reached out to steady herself.

"Do I really have to have these?" she asked, holding up her arms. Tess gave her a look of disdain.

"You ought to be glad we moved them to the front of you for comfort considering you just stabbed someone with...what was that? Bird scissors?" Tess questioned incredulously.

"They are gold stork embroidery scissors. I keep them in my purse," Lydia snapped, her tear-streaked face red and swollen from crying.

"So, what the hell just happened out there? Why are you even here?" Tess demanded, taking a seat opposite Jessica Slaydon's mother. She could feel Denny and Sheriff Malone's eyes on her through the two-way glass wall. "I told you we'd call you when we knew anything."

"You obviously knew something," huffed Lydia, casting a glare at Tess. "You arrested Annie. The fucking bitch."

"Wait," Tess said, holding up her hand and leaning back in her seat, confusion and surprise etched across her face. "How do you know Annie?"

"I don't *know her* know her," Lydia clarified. "But she's Jessica's sister." A stunned silence filled the room.

"Okay ...." Tess made a face. "Explain."

"Well, Jessica is my daughter. Not my biological daughter, but my daughter just the same. My husband Brad and I adopted her the day she was born. Her biological mother was young and wasn't fit to raise children. CPS was waiting in the wing for the baby to be born. Whisked her away as soon as they could. Apparently, Jessica wasn't the woman's first baby. And unfortunately, she wouldn't be the last." Lydia paused, staring off into the corner of the room as though there was someone there. She eventually turned and looked back at Tess.

"Anyway, we took the baby home, named her Jessica. The first few weeks were rough. The doctors said she was having drug withdrawals, crying all the time. Eventually though, she started to thrive. Put on weight, acting like a normal baby. As she grew into a toddler, she was a happy kiddo. Smiling and laughing all the time. Oh, that giggle!" Lydia smiled fondly at the memory and then her face saddened again. "Jessica was four when my husband was killed in a car accident. It was raining, late at night.

Teenager wasn't paying attention ...." Lydia folded her cuffed hands on her lap and hung her head for a moment. "It was a dark time for Jessica and I. We were suddenly a family of two. I was a single mother, trying to figure out kindergarten pickup, packing lunches, setting up play dates and therapy sessions, all while also dealing with my own grief and emotions, trying to maintain employment and a home. It was horrible." Lydia sighed then, and stood, pacing around the small room while deep in thought. "We were finally finding our way in the world, the two of us. Finding our groove. Jessica had just turned five when CPS called me. Apparently the mother had given birth to another baby, a girl called Annie. The CPS worker wanted me to take Annie in an effort to keep the siblings together. I told her I understood her point but that I couldn't do it. I told her about the loss of my husband, and that Jessica was doing well. I didn't want to rock the boat so to speak. I felt bad about it, but I was just one woman, raising a young daughter alone. I couldn't take on another. I told her no."

"So, what happened to Annie?" Tess asked, feeling bad for the young children in Lydia's tale, if it did prove to be true. It did not, however, excuse the slaughter of Jessica or the brutal attack on Annie.

"As far as I know, she grew up in the system. Being moved from one foster home to another." Lydia stopped her pacing and let out a sob, her shoulder shaking. "I feel horrible but how can I be responsible for another woman popping out babies every few years when she can't take care of them or herself? How is that my problem?" Large tears slid down her cheeks again as she stood in the corner of the room. Leaning up against the wall, she rolled her head to look at Tess. "I never told Jessica. Never told her she had a sister. Is that horrible of me?"

"You didn't want to upset her. No one can fault you that," Tess commiserated, "You were in a tough situation." She paused, tapping her fingers on the cool metal of the table in front of her as questions rolled through her head. "How did you know that the woman we brought into the station today was Annie?"

"Because she showed up at my house a couple of years ago, looking for Jessica," Lydia explained with a frown. "I asked her to leave. Told her there was nothing there for her. That her sister knew nothing of her. She didn't seem to like that much. Annie got mad at me, shoved me up against the doorway of my own house and went on about how dismal her life had been growing up in foster care, as though it were *my* fault. She was very angry and at one point I thought she was about to hit me. Just then, one of my neighbors happened to bring his trash out to put in the bin. He paused and asked if everything was alright. I nodded and told him my friend was just leaving. Annie left quickly after that in a huff. I only saw her one other time after that. At Walmart. We made eye contact over the apples in the produce section, and she stormed off. Fine by me. She is not my concern."

"Did you ever end up telling Jessica about her? Give her a heads up that she had a sister looking for her?"

"No," Lydia sighed, swallowing audibly. "Seeing how things have turned out, I wish I would have. Did she kill Jess?"

"According to Neil, yes." Tess offered, deep in thought. "We haven't had a chance to question her yet because she was attacked ...." She let the words hang in the air.

Lydia looked at her feet in shame, squirming under Tess's disapproving gaze.

"Do you think that Neil knew who Annie really was? Or did she just cozy up to him to get to Jessica?" Tess wondered aloud, watching Lydia for any kind of tell.

A look of surprise crossed Lydia's face as Tess's words seemed to roll around in her thoughts.

"Oh, dear God .... You think Annie had this planned from the beginning? To destroy Jessica's charmed life?" A low wail emanated from Lydia Fontaine's chest. "I should have told Jessica the truth. I should have just been open with her and told her everything. Then maybe Annie wouldn't have tracked her down, destroyed her marriage, and then killed her out of jealousy." And with that, the older woman collapsed onto the cool tiled floor of the interrogation room and sobbed.

Chapter Forty-Two

Later that evening, Annie was behind bars, lamenting that she was being played by Slaydon and that she had never even met Jessica, much less killed her. It wasn't until she was faced with the evidence that her tough-girl facade began to crumble.

Sitting across from her in an interrogation room at the county jail, Tess lightly tapped her fingertips rhythmically on the table.

Annie Baldwin, neck bandaged and a scowl on her face, sat quietly, glaring back at Tess.

"I like the new duds," Tess commented, pointing to Annie's worn khaki jail-issued scrubs. Annie's scowl deepened but she said nothing.

"Joking aside, how is your neck?" Tess asked, genuinely interested. She was rewarded with an eye roll.

"I was stabbed in the neck with fucking scissors! How do you think I feel?" Annie snapped, reaching up to gently touch the edges of her bandage, her handcuffed wrists making the movement look awkward. "Do I really need to wear these in here? It's not like I can go anywhere." She rattled the cuff chains for emphasis.

"Sorry, it's not up to me," Tess said, not willing to placate the woman. "Once we are done talking, you may have them removed."

"Then let's get this over with," Annie sighed. She leaned back in her chair with a huff, waiting impatiently for Tess to continue.

"Why? Do you have a date? Neil's in lock up. Men's ward," Tess stated, watching Annie for any reaction to Neil's name. And there it was: an eyebrow twitch. Almost imperceptible.

"Neil?" Annie asked, her attempt for innocence falling short. "You mean my brother?" Just moments ago, the woman had claimed to not even know Neil despite Tess speaking to them together at Neil's house. Tess resisted rolling her eyes at the drama.

"Come now, Annie. We all know that Neil Slaydon is not your brother. In fact, he doesn't have any siblings. However, our victim, Jessica Slaydon, does." Tess watched the color drain from Annie's face.

"I don't know what you're talking about. I never met Jessica."

"Stop lying to me, Annie," Tess warned. "Lydia Fontaine told me a little story about Jessica and of course, being the cop I am, I had to do a deep dive, research facts, make sure everything adds up. And you know what I found?"

Annie swallowed audibly, her face pale. When she said nothing, Tess continued.

"According to CPS records, Jessica Elizabeth Baldwin, was adopted at just three days old and her last name changed to Fontaine. After she married Neil Slaydon six years ago, she became Jessica Slaydon. Following?"

Annie nodded, not making eye contact with Tess, so she continued.

"Four years after Jessica was born, the same woman, Erica Baldwin, gave birth to another baby girl. This one was named Annie Marie Baldwin. Due to extenuating circumstances involving drug usage and CPS violations, the baby was immediately removed from the mother's care and sent to foster care. That baby was you."

Annie remained still, but her dark blue rage filled eyes turned to glare at Tess. A muscle in her jaw twitched as she crushed her molars together, her mouth in a tight line.

"Why did you kill your sister, Annie? Was it because she was adopted and raised in a loving, safe household and you were cast to the side like an unwanted pup?" Tess asked, baiting her, willing her to break, so that she would finally talk. "What that must have felt like. Knowing you had a sister out there that got everything she wanted. And you? Constantly getting shoved from one house to the next with all of your earthly belongings in a garbage bag. I'd be upset too."

"You have no idea what it was like!" snapped Annie, her lips trembling. "Yes, I knew I had a sister. And yes, eventually I hated her."

"When did you find out about her?"

"I don't remember specifically. I was maybe ... seven? eight? I overheard the social worker talking to one of the foster moms. I had ... I had gotten into some trouble—stolen something—and the family was trying to send me to a different home. I heard them asking if I had anyone else who would want me and the social worker mentioned I had a sister, but the adoptive family didn't want me, either."

"When in reality, it wasn't that the Fontaines didn't *want* you. They just couldn't take you. There were things going on in their lives at the time that were out of their control," Tess explained, "Had the social worker known that you'd overheard any of that, then maybe they could have explained it to you better."

Annie just shrugged, "It doesn't matter now. After years of getting abused, neglected, shoved from home to home, I finally aged out of the system. I only have to look out for myself now. I don't need CPS or Lydia Fontaine to fucking tell me I was unwanted. I could figure out that all by myself."

"So, why did you decide to track your sister down?" Tess asked, "How did you go about it?" Inside, she felt sorry for Annie as a child, but Adult Annie was a whole other issue.

"Once I was eighteen, I was given all of my paperwork. Social security card, birth certificate, stuff like that. There was even a picture of my mom in there," Annie sighed, her face crumbling even further. "I looked her up on the internet, did some sleuthing of my own. It took me a few years to track down names and addresses but I found both my mom and Lydia. Never did find out who my dad was," she shrugged. "My mom died from an overdose a couple of years ago. Luckily, Jessica and I were her last children. Apparently there was a boy before Jessica, but I could never find any information about him."

Annie stood then, pacing the small interrogation room, her handcuffed arms in front of her. "I found Lydia Fontaine first. I just wanted to get to know them. I meant them no harm. Really I didn't. I ... I just wanted a family. But Lydia wouldn't have it. She told me that Jessica was happy the way things were, that she didn't even know about me, and that I should just stay away. Lydia even offered me some money to disappear."

"Did you take it?"

"No," Annie shook her head, "I just wanted a family. I wasn't looking for a handout." Tess wasn't sure she believed her..

"Then what happened?"

"I told Lydia I was leaving but I didn't really. I kept digging around, asking questions. I finally tracked Jessica down." Annie continued to pace a circuit around the room. "I wasn't expecting what I found."

"And what did you find?"

"Jessica had everything. A hot husband, a nice house, newer cars, great job. And she was beautiful. She had everything I didn't." She paused for a moment, thinking. "I didn't approach her at first. I got most of my information from Facebook. She had everything set to 'public', so it was easy to spy. Their house was on the market, and she was posting pictures of the new one they had just put an offer in for. That's how I found the address."

"So, you waited in the bushes for her to be home alone and then shot her?" Tess tried to reign in her sarcasm but fell short. Annie just scowled at her in response.

"No. As I said before, I didn't set out to hurt her. I tried to talk to her one day. Her husband, Neil, had already gone to work for the day. I had seen him leave, so I decided to go knock on the door and introduce myself. It didn't go well. At first, Jessica was kind but then she seemed to get confused and agitated. She said I was lying, and that she didn't have any sisters. She wouldn't let me into the house to talk and before I could explain further, she'd shut the door in my face." Tess agreed with Jessica's decision: she wouldn't have let a stranger in her house either.

"So how did you meet Neil then?"

"It was by accident, actually." Annie slowed her pacing. "I was sitting in the coffee shop in town when he walked in. The place was hopping, line almost out the door, but I was lucky enough to have a table to myself. When I saw him enter, I knew exactly who he was, but he didn't know me. We made eye contact a couple of times while he waited in line and then when he got his coffee, he looked around for a seat. I offered him one at my table. I wasn't using the whole thing, so why not?" she shrugged. "At first, I just wanted to make small talk, maybe get him to open up a little about his life. I just wanted to learn things about my sister. I never did tell him that I am Jessica's sister."

"He still doesn't know?" Tess asked incredulously, "He never figured it out? Even after everything?"

"Nope, I don't think so. At least, not that he's expressed to me."

"Okay, so you're sitting at the coffee shop, making small talk with your brother-in-law, even though he didn't know that. Then what happened?"

"We just kinda hit it off. He told me about his job, about how he thought his wife was cheating on him again. Apparently, she's done it before." Judgment dripped from Annie's voice. "We sat there for hours, well after the crowd died down. Eventually, when we finally parted for the evening, we exchanged numbers. I told him to give me a call if he ever wanted to talk or hang out again. At that point, I was starting to dislike Jessica. I mean, Neil seemed like such a nice guy and here she was, cheating on him. Using him. Throwing it all away. And for what? A quick roll in the sheets with a man that wasn't her husband."

"Neil told me himself that they have an open relationship. That they have since they lost their son to stillbirth a few years ago," Tess pointed out. "He's not as righteous and perfect as you've made him out to be either. They both agreed to explore sexual relationships outside of their marriage vows. Don't try to pin this all on Jessica."

"I'm not, but what you call an open marriage, I call cheating," Annie huffed, holding her shackled hands up to wave Tess off before dropping them again. "It's just ... Jessica had everything. Everything except Neil. He had noticed them moving apart and felt the distance. He told me it started after losing their son, like you said. He told me that Jessica started cheating on him, multiple times, and that he'd just started giving up." She paused her pacing to sit back down on the metal folding chair near the desk. "He ... started flirting with me. Wanting me. Of course I wasn't going to say no to that. I decided maybe I could have Neil to myself and show my spoiled sister what she was taking for granted. It all started out innocently enough but before we knew it, we were madly in love, meeting multiple times a week to hook up. He'd cry about his life. I told him what he wanted to hear. We'd have sex." She shrugged, shaking her head. "I'm not going to lie. I was having fun. I was secretly ruining Jessica's chances at happiness while having steamy sex multiple times a week."

"What changed then?" Tess asked, leaning back in her chair and watching Annie avoid making eye contact with her.

"Neil told me Jessica was pregnant." Just saying the words caused Annie's nostrils to flare slightly and her jaw to clench. *Obviously a sign of distress*, Tess observed.

"And did he seem happy about it?"

"Yes," Annie said dully, shoulders drooping. "He was ecstatic. It was all he'd talk about for weeks. At first, I was shocked by the news. He'd made me believe that he and Jessica were barely talking but apparently they were doing more than that! We got into a fight over it. He said that they weren't really talking much, that they had just slept together once or twice a few weeks before and well ... there you go. Baby on the way." An angry tear slipped from her eye. Wiping at it, she turned and stared at Tess angrily. "He said he wanted to work on his marriage."

"I had a renewed drive to hurt Jessica, and by hurt I mean destroy. I didn't want her dead, I just wanted her to lose everything: the house, her job, her good reputation, and most of all ... her husband. I started spreading rumors about her around town. Nothing big or over the top, but just enough to get tongues wagging. And where Neil was concerned, I laid it on thick. I became everything he ever wanted. I was every fantasy personified," Annie sneered.

A wicked grin spread across her face and Tess knew then, without a doubt, that Annie Baldwin was indeed capable of cold-blooded murder.

"When Neil found that stupid rubber belly band, he came crying to me. Oh! It was hard to keep the look of shock off of my face then. Jessica had played him like a fiddle, trying to keep him close to home with that stunt. What she wasn't expecting was me. I was angry at her at first, for hurting him like that. I was in love with him, and she'd hurt him. But then Neil decided he wanted to talk to Jessica, get her side of things.

"I was angry. Deranged. I wanted Neil all to myself and his lying whore of a wife was trying to get him back. It all happened so fast. I remember shoving my gun in my purse like I always do, but this time I made sure it was loaded. Then I headed over to the Slaydon house to see if I could stop Neil from talking to her—if I could intervene somehow.

"It was Fourth of July, late. The main door to the garage was open so I went in that way, mostly so I could spy. I could hear their voices before I even made it halfway across the garage. They were in the kitchen, arguing."

"About what?"

"The rubber belly. How she was lying about being pregnant in the first place. He wanted her to pull her shirt up and show him the truth, but she wouldn't. It sounded like they were both crying," Annie paused, biting her lip.

"I quietly opened the door from the garage to the kitchen and peeked inside. They didn't even notice me. Looking back now, I should have looked for the dog first before going in. He really could have done some damage."

Or you could have just not gone over there at all, Tess thought grimly as she waited for Annie to continue.

"I saw Neil by the refrigerator, red faced and crying. Jessica was over by the sink, also crying. She was going on about how she was so sorry that she lied to him, but she wanted them to be happy the way they were when baby Adam was on the way. She started telling him how much she loved him and just wanted him home with her. That she knew he'd found someone new. And this is the kicker …."

"Yes?"

"He believed her!" Annie exclaimed, "He actually thought that Jessica wanted him back, that she deserved him back. I'm the one that deserved him! It was me who took care of him while she ran around doing whatever the hell it was she wanted. It was me who took care of him when she was just 'too sick' to get out of bed with 'morning sickness', when in reality all she wanted was attention! It wasn't enough to have the fancy new house on the cul-de-sac. It wasn't enough to have a well-paying job and college degree. It wasn't enough that she was raised in a loving home with a mother who cared for her every need. It wasn't enough that she was supported and encouraged to chase her dreams. It wasn't enough that she had all the latest fashions and a decent bank account. She just had to lie to manipulate her husband to stay with her when he clearly wanted me.

"It was then, in that moment, that I snapped," Annie shrugged, "I remember pulling out the gun and cocking it. They both turned to me when they heard the sound. There was a look of recognition in Jessica's eyes almost instantly and when she turned to the knife block to grab a knife, I shot her in the back of the head. She dropped like a sack of bricks. It made a much bigger mess than I thought it would, and frankly, it was kind of gross. There were chunks of brain and bone laying around, blood spatter everywhere." A disgusted look crossed her angry features.

"What did you do then?" Tess asked, more than a little concerned by Annie's lack of empathy.

"I went to Neil ... comforted him. He was in shock, but I helped him see the truth. Helped him see who Jessica really was: a lying, selfish bitch."

The two women sat in silence for a moment, Tess giving Annie time to speak without distraction. Finally, Annie continued.

"We needed to clean up the mess, of course, so I helped Neil wrap what was left of her head in a plastic bag. He carried her upstairs to the bathroom and laid her in the tub. The whole time, that damn dog was scratching at the back door making me think that somebody was coming.

Anyway, while I cleaned up the kitchen, Neil ran down to Piedmont's to get some trash bags and saw blades. Once he got back, we got to work. We cut up the body, stuck it in bags, and cleaned up the bathroom. We were both exhausted, but we got it done.

"I went back to my apartment to wait for a few days. Neil was supposed to slowly dispose of the body parts, drop that wretched dog off at the pound and then call you guys. You know, make it look like his wife was a missing person. Then you showed up unannounced that one day and caught me there so Neil told you I was his sister. Obviously, you found that to be a lie." Annie looked at Tess pointedly before continuing. "Needless to say, we were supposed to meet up and head to Canada together. Get away from all these accusations. But then you just had to find the body in the river." The look of accusation in Annie's eyes, as though Tess had done something horribly wrong, made the hair on Tess's neck stand up.

Tess knew one thing for sure: Annie Baldwin was greatly disturbed and dangerous. They had enough evidence against her and Neil to put them away for a long time, whether she had confessed or not. The evidence told a story of its own. They had a recently fired gun in the same caliber that shot Jessica Slaydon, covered in Annie's fingerprints. They had surveillance video showing Neil's late-night discount store shopping spree and daily jaunts around the block in a baby-less stroller. They had blood evidence in the house and on the stroller. They had the confessions of both suspects. And they had poor Jessica's dismembered body.

If only Jessica had told the truth about her apprehension to an open marriage. If only Neil would have remained faithful. If only Jessica hadn't faked a pregnancy. If only Lydia had told Jessica about her sister. If only Annie wouldn't have let envy take root. If only ....

Chapter Forty-Three

Three days later, Tess found herself lounging at home, taking a much-needed break. Her face was starting to heal, but an ugly mottled bruise still covered her top lip. She'd been checked out by a dentist after arresting Annie and was given the "all clear". She'd luckily dodged the bullet of having her teeth knocked out. Even though the dentist gave her the green light for normal activity, Tess found herself frequently checking her teeth with her tongue, looking for any looseness. So far so good.

She must have dozed off snuggled with Otter, Max at her feet, because when she woke again the sun was starting to set in the western sky. She sat up, quickly making her way to the restroom and then into the kitchen. Noticing her phone on the counter, she checked her messages. One from Malone, checking on her, and another from Denny. "How about dinner tonight? We can eat in if you don't want to go out. I can pick something up," it read. Tess smiled and quickly looked at the time stamp. Two hours ago! She hadn't meant to sleep that long!

Quickly dialing Denny's number to apologize for missing his text, she was interrupted by Otter giving an excited bark. Max immediately added to the fray, barking and running for the door. She turned and looked out her front door and there was Denny. He smiled at her through the glass and her heart melted. She felt butterflies in her stomach as she ran to open the door for him.

"I'm so sorry!" she exclaimed. "I fell asleep and didn't see your text until just now. I was just about to call you!" She grinned as she looked up at him.

"It's all good. I figured you were asleep," he said, stepping into the foyer. He had a takeout bag in his hands, which he set on the small table, next to her car keys. Max and Otter began sniffing the bag expectantly.

"Yes, I was exhausted," Tess agreed, gently pulling the two dogs away from the food.

"So, I see you still have Max," Denny commented. "Lydia isn't taking him back to Cleveland?"

"No, not immediately at least. After her little stunt with the scissors down at the station she's got some legal issues to figure out first. I told her I'd keep him until she's able to take him back home."

"That's nice of you, Tess." Denny gazed down at her, a smile playing on his lips as he reached for her hands. "Speaking of Cleveland though ...."

"What about it?" Tess asked, giving him a confused look. "I thought you closed the case up there?"

"I did," he sighed, his face suddenly looking serious, the smile gone from his eyes. "Come here. I need to talk to you." He gently led her to the couch and motioned for her to have a seat.

"What's going on, Denny? Is Natalie okay?" Tess asked, an edge of panic in her voice. It wasn't like him to be so serious when they weren't working. Something was troubling him and she was worried she wouldn't like it.

"Yes, baby, Natalie is fine," Denny answered, taking a seat next to her, the warm leather of the couch creaking under his weight. A sad smile crossed his face and he seemed to be having difficulty meeting Tess's eyes.

"Then what is it? You're worrying me. It better not be that you're leaving me for Lindsey because I swear—"

A low chuckle filled the air. "No, Tess, I'm not leaving you for anyone. I love you. Don't you know that yet?" He smiled then, so big it reached his eyes.

Her heart skipped a beat. He'd finally said the words, finally expressed his true feelings to her. She felt herself smile, despite the lingering feeling of unease surrounding them.

"I love you too, Denny," she breathed, leaning in to press her lips to his. His reaction was instant, as he wrapped his arms around her and drew her close to him. Deepening the kiss, he pulled her onto his lap, her legs straddling his hips.

Tess let out a sigh as she felt his strong hands caressing down her back to cup her backside. Her arms snaked up to encircle his neck and pull him closer, as he continued kissing her.

"Tess ..." he finally said, pulling away enough to see her, yet close enough that their foreheads were still touching. "I have to talk to you about something ... and I'm afraid you aren't going to like it much."

Tess pulled back from him, a worried look crossing her face as she watched him closely. She gently placed her hands on his chest. "What is it, Denny? What happened?"

"Well, you know how I've been working on that case in Cleveland?" he asked, watching her closely, his eyes never leaving hers.

"Yes ...." she mumbled, not liking where this was headed. Her brain was going a mile a minute, her thoughts all over the place.

"They've offered me a transfer to the Cleveland office," Denny blurted out in a rush. He sighed, running his fingers through his dark hair. He pulled his gaze from hers, too worried to see the hurt and fear in her eyes. "It would actually be a promotion with a hefty pay increase."

Tess's mind was reeling. Transferring to Cleveland? After they'd only just gotten together? No, this couldn't be happening. She must have heard him wrong.

"You mean, you're moving? To Cleveland?" her voice broke as tears threatened to fall. He'd be living over three hours away! This couldn't be happening. Tess suddenly felt like she might be sick and pushed off of his lap. He resisted letting her go for a second, but then did, a pained expression on his face.

"How long have you known about this?" she asked as she paced the living room trying to wrangle her thoughts. When he said nothing, she cast a look over at him and repeated, "How long, Denny?"

"A few days," his whispered reply was quiet as he leaned forward on the couch and hung his head.

"A few days?" Tess asked incredulously. "Like before or after you came here and poured your heart out and told me about your life after Cassie? Before or after I brought you into my bed? Did you know then?" Anger suddenly welled in her. She had feelings for Denny and had just admitted so. She'd given herself to him, body and soul, only to have him tell her that he'd known about a job transfer to Cleveland for a few days? Surely he hadn't been playing her, he wasn't the type. Denny had always been honest and straightforward. Tess's emotions were playing havoc on her. She loved this man. Trusted him with her life. And now, in the course of mere seconds, felt like he had betrayed her. But had he?

"Tess, it wasn't like that," Denny's head snapped up at her accusations. "That night I came over for dinner and my boss kept texting me? Remember that?"

"Yes."

"He was hinting at it then, and I told him no thanks. That my life was here. That *you* were here." He paused when Tess finally stopped her pacing to focus on him. "But since then, as in earlier today, I found out that I may not have a choice in the matter."

"Can they do that? Make you uproot your family on their whims and just ... move?" Tess asked, a mix of frustration and horror filling her voice.

"That's how my boss seemed to say it at least," Denny shrugged. "When I first told him no thanks, he kept pestering me about it, saying it was a good move for my career. As the days have gone by though, he seems to have gotten more aggressive about it." He sighed, leaning back on the couch and rubbing his hands over his face. "On my way over here, while I was waiting for the food to be ready, I got an email from the Cleveland office. I'm required to report for an interview a week from this Friday."

"This can't be happening," Tess cried, the tears that had been threatening to fall finally sliding down her cheeks. "What can we do?" She took a deep breath and stopped sniffling. Her heart breaking with each step, she walked back over to the couch. Sitting down beside him, she took his hands in hers and looked into his deep blue eyes.

"What do you want, Denny? If I wasn't around, would you want to move to Cleveland?"

He said nothing for a moment, seeming to mull the idea around in his head. He finally looked up at her. "I don't know, Tess," he admitted honestly. "I think that Natalie and I could be happy anywhere, but if you weren't there then what's the point? This is our home. Her friends are here, her cousins are here ... you are here."

"Have you told her yet?"

"No. I wanted to get all of the information before saying anything to stress her out." He looked Tess in the eyes again, "But back to you. Would I want to live in a city where you are not? No. I love you, Tess. Natalie loves you."

"I don't want you to go," Tess cried, "I've only just made detective, and I most definitely can't leave my dad here. I have to live in Swain County while I work at the department. Maybe ... maybe we can alternate weekends and visit each other?" She hated the words even as they came out of her mouth. Anxiety churned in her stomach.

"I've thought of that. But you know what? It's not what I want. At the end of the day, this is just a job. I can walk away from it if I need to. I don't want to. I love being in law enforcement, but my family comes first. I could always get on at the county level somewhere close."

"So, what will you do?"

"I don't know yet. I still have to think, weigh the pros and cons. And, since the interview is mandatory, I guess I'll go to that just to see what the deal is."

"Denny, I won't ask you to change your career because of me. I—" she cried. He leaned forward and wrapped his arms around her again and pulled her back onto his lap.

She sat straddling him as she had before he'd told her the news, but this time, she had tears in her eyes.

"Baby, don't cry. Please don't cry. I'll talk to the director in Cleveland, let him know I don't want the position. If they won't listen, then I'll find something else, okay?" He pulled her head down to rest on his chest as he planted a kiss in her dark hair.

"I don't want you guys to leave. If anything, I'd love it if you lived closer. Then I could help more with Natalie, and we could do more things together." Tess didn't add that she'd daydreamed about living together or maybe even getting married to Denny one day. It was too much to think about. She had to stay strong. She knew this was a hard decision for him, but she also didn't want him to lose out on a promotion at work on her account.

"Tess, trust me. I love you. I'm not ready to lose you for a job," Denny's voice whispered in her ear and before she could respond, she felt his lips leaving a trail of kisses down her neck and across her collarbone.

She moaned and pulled away from him so she could see his face. His eyes smoldered as they drank her in. She'd seen that look before.

She leaned in, gently pressing her lips to his, her arms wrapping around his neck. Tightening his arms around her, he pulled her closer to his body. She could feel his hardness pressing against her and deepened the kiss.

"Oh, Tess," murmured Denny, his hands sliding down to cup her rear end. "If you only knew what you do to me. Knew all the things I want to do to you."

"You can show me …." she said, her voice husky and low. It was all he needed to hear. She didn't know if their time was now limited so she was going to take every minute that she could.

Chapter Forty-Four

Tuesday, August 16th, 11:34 a.m.

Tess sat in a grimy chair, waiting for Neil Slaydon to be brought to her. All around her voices hummed, chairs scraped the tiled floor, and Tess began to think that maybe she should have just come to the jail officially and requested a quiet room to speak to Slaydon. But no, here she was, eyeing the black phone receiver hanging next to her. Trying to ignore the used ball of chewing gum stuck to the bottom of the plexiglass barrier, she tapped her foot impatiently.

Finally, the interior door opened, and a guard walked through leading a gaunt and pale Neil Slaydon. If not for the fact that he'd cut his wife up into fish bait, Tess would have almost felt sorry for him.

A look of surprise crossed his face when he saw that it was Tess who had come to visit him. As the guard led him over to the empty chair on the other side of the plexiglass barrier from Tess, Slaydon didn't take his eyes off of her.

The guard stepped back, finding a place along the cinder block wall some feet away to wait. Slaydon just sat there, staring back at Tess, not moving, his shackled hands laying in his lap.

Tess, trying not to think about the germs and other substances on the phone, picked up the receiver and held it close to her ear. Unsure if he was going to even talk to her, she waited.

After a moment, Slaydon sighed and picked up his receiver.

"Hello, Detective," he greeted, his voice low and hoarse. He was not the same arrogant man she'd met before.

"Hello, Neil. How are you holding up?"

"How do you think? I'm in fucking jail, awaiting trial. My wife is dead, my life is over." He hung his head, sitting quietly for a few moments before looking back at Tess. "What do you need, Detective?"

"I came by to let you know that we have Annie in custody," Tess began. Neil looked slightly relieved as Tess continued. "She has told us her side of things. How she embedded herself into your life to get closer to Jessica, how she tried to destroy—"

"Wait, what?" Neil interjected, confusion etched across his face. "She was trying to get to Jess? What are you talking about?"

"Annie and Jessica were sisters," Tess explained, "I thought you knew. That you'd figured it out, or she'd told you."

A stunned silence passed between them as Neil processed what Tess had just relayed. *Sisters? And Lydia had never mentioned it?*

"No, Annie never said a word. She told me she was new to the area, had just gotten out of an abusive relationship, and was going back to school for nursing. I even gave her some money once. She said she needed some protection because she was taking some night classes on campus."

"Well, she played you, Neil. In reality, she and Jessica were sisters. Lydia adopted Jessica at birth but when Annie was born, she couldn't take her, too. Annie told me that she used you to get to Jessica. She'd tried talking to Jessica, explaining who she was but your wife didn't believe her and sent her away. When you walked into the coffee shop that day, Annie knew exactly who you were. She'd been stalking you and your wife for months."

"What? This can't be true," Neil said, his eyes closing as his mind ran wild. "You're not shitting me?"

"Of course not, Neil," Tess empathized, "Annie used you. She seduced you, which was easy because of your open marriage. She became everything you wanted in a woman to get you to fall in love with her and leave your wife. You see, Annie grew up in the foster system, being shoved from one home to the next. Jessica, on the other hand, lived a charmed life filled with love and encouragement, and Annie hated her for it. When Jessica sent Annie away it was yet another blow. Annie decided then to destroy Jessica's perfect life. That's when she decided to seduce you, break up your marriage, and spread lies about Jessica throughout town. Annie thought that if she could make Jessica go away, she could have you and the life she so desperately wanted. That she could replace Jessica."

"But did she have to kill Jessica?" Neil breathed, a sob escaping his throat. His eyes reddened as tears threatened to fall.

"I think that when Jessica faked the pregnancy, Annie snapped. The night that you went to confront Jessica for lying about the pregnancy, Annie followed you. She came in through the garage door and listened as you and Jessica fought over the lies. That's when she came into the kitchen."

Neil Slaydon began sobbing in earnest then, bending at the waist and laying his head on the table ledge in front of him. The inmates next to him cast weary glances and scooted away to resume their conversations. Tess felt sorry for not getting a conference room for privacy, but she'd honestly thought that he'd known that Annie was actually his sister-in-law.

"This isn't all your fault, Neil." Tess attempted to calm him, "There were things you didn't know, lies that were circulating."

"But this *is* all my fault. No matter how you play this, I am exactly where I should be."

"Why do you say that?" Tess inquired, leaning closer to the scratched plexiglass.

"Because I guess I *did* kill my wife. After all, it was my money that bought the gun for Annie."

About the Author

A.L. Hatcher holds bachelor's degrees in both forensic investigation and forensic pathology as well as an associate degree in veterinary technology. Because of her love of animals, she's been a registered veterinary technician for over 20 years. However, her passion for writing began in childhood when she would write her own short stories and picture books.

Today, she spends her time caring for animals, reading, listening to true crime podcasts, and writing fiction about crime, suspense, and all things dark. She lives in the Midwest with her family, some chickens, and a menagerie of pets.

We'd love to hear from you!

If you enjoyed this book, please consider leaving a review on Amazon, Goodreads, or wherever you review books. Reviews help other readers find books that may interest them and also help provide author feedback.

Please feel free to follow the author on Facebook, Instagram, and TikTok @alhatcherauthor or sign up for her newsletter at http://www.alhatcherauthor.com

Email: alhatcherauthor@gmail.com

A.L. Hatcher is currently hard at work on the next Tess Dane Thriller.